Gospel

Choir

Murder

MARIETTA HARRIS

This is a work of fiction. The characters, places, and events in this book are the products of the author's imagination and are fictitious. Any resemblance or similarity to real people, living or dead, companies, institutions, organizations or incidents is entirely coincidental and not intended by the author.

Copyright © 2014 by Marietta Harris

ISBN: 13: 978-0-692-39439-7
        10:0692394397

Book cover by Julie Trombley (ajulietrombley@gmail.com)

Other Books
The Other Side of Alzheimer's, a caregiver's story

Coming Soon
THOU SHALT KILL
MURDER BY PRAYER
THE RED HEAD GIRL

RBMB Publishing
2181 N. Tracy Blvd.208
Tracy CA 95376
(209 487-0658)
RBMB1263@yahoo.com

Printed in the United States of America

FROM THE AUTHOR

Hi. I am Marietta Harris, the author. I get a shiver of delight whenever I say that. Ever since I was a child, I've been fascinated with the idea that a story can be manifested in an imagination, put into an order, written down, and published to impact thousands of people.

I'm a native San Franciscan who has traveled as a vocalist and musician; I lived briefly in Europe, but now reside in the San Francisco Bay Area. Years ago, after retiring I starting a new life, I finished my first book, *The Other Side of Alzheimer's, a Caregiver's Story,* based on my own experience caring for my mother.

After self-publishing *The Other Side of Alzheimer's,* I was invited by various groups to speak to their members who are now experiencing life as caregivers for the first time. I toured in Germany and Italy and was interviewed for a TV show in Pasadena, CA. I continue to do motivational speaking.

My favorite books have always been mysteries, though, and I have finished my first mystery called "The Gospel Choir." There will be many more.

Thank you for purchasing my book!

I hope you read a book to a child so that writing will grow in their spirit.

Marietta Harris

Contact me at:
Website: mariettaharris.com
Email: mariettaharris@yahoo.com

The Gospel Choir Murder

Acknowledgments

Thanks to a special friend Carol Fairweather, for the endless hours you spent reading and editing this manuscript. Also for the great suggestions and all the other efforts, you did to make this book possible. Carol words can't express my appreciation enough for your help. Without your input and direction, this book would not have been written.

To a wonderful lady Edith Gladstone my deepest thanks for devoting your precious time and energy editing my words. I can't express how much I appreciate you assisting me in getting this book finished.

A true friend, Janice Buxton who believes in me and without your continued encouragement helps me realize my written voice is worth sharing. Words can't express how much you mean to me.

To Julie Trombley the best book designer ever. You are a wonderful and gifted lady. Thanks for helping my vision come to reality. I wish you continued blessings and can't wait to work with you in the future.

Special thanks to San Joaquin Sheriff Department. Lieutenant James Hood, Deputy Sheriff Carlos Prieto, and Deputy Sheriff Ian Lenzi.

Any mistakes with police procedures are mine.

The Gospel Choir Murder

On a typically hot day, the housekeeper knocked at Room 1205. No one answered. This was her last floor and she was anxious to finish. Using the master key, she opened the door, calling out as she went in, "Housekeeping."

She flicked on the light as she entered the dimly lit room. In the bathroom, she glanced at a stack of used towels under the sink. As she continued around the curve into the bed area, she called out once again, "Housekeeping."

She shook her head at a large red spot on the carpet thinking how difficult it was going to be to clean up the wine.

"Señor?" "Señorita?" She assumed the lump she saw was a pile of pillows and headed over to make the bed. Flinging back the covers, she stepped back. There was a nude body in the bed with a knife protruding from the neck, and more blood. Looking around wildly, she screamed, "Asesinato, asesinato," as she ran out into the hallway.

Chapter 1

At the ungodly hour of 6 a.m. on Saturday the phone rang. Evelyn opened an eye. My God, that can't be the phone. I just fell into bed three hours ago. Whoever it is will not be glad I answered this phone.

Turning over, she flicked on the light, propped herself up on one elbow, and jerked the phone off the cradle. Just as she was about to yell "WHO is it?" she heard, "Sister Jenkins."

It was someone from church. Softly she responded, "Yes, this is Sister Jenkins."

"Good morning. This is Sister Watson; I hope it's not too early to call."

Evelyn heard herself say pleasantly, "Good morning Sister Watson, it's not too early at all." You had to lie to the Pastor's wife. No matter how angry you were, when she called, you had to be pleasant; that's what we church people do.

"Is anything wrong?" This better be good.

"I just received some bad news. My father is ill and I won't be able to go on tour with the choir as planned."

Evelyn smiled, "I'm sorry to hear about your father; is there anything I can do to help?"

Sister Watson sighed. "Pastor and I will be fine but please keep my father in your prayers. Would you tell Brother McDaniel? I'm sorry for calling you so early. I'll be praying for the choir."

"You will be missed. We'll keep your father in our prayers. You have a blessed day."

Lying back down, Evelyn softly prayed, "Thank you, Lord." Everybody in the church knows Sister Watson is tone deaf. In fact, she couldn't carry a tune if you stapled it to her chest. But since she was the Pastor's wife, no one dared tell her. Now, since she's not going on tour with the choir, everybody can relax.

Sister Watson was liked well enough, but no one was really close to her. There is always a mystique about the Pastor's wife. She had to have a room by herself. None of the woman in church would ever dare have the Pastor's wife as a roommate; it just wasn't going to happen. She didn't want anyone to know about her private moments and nobody wanted to share theirs.

Everybody walks on eggs when she's around, being careful to keep their conversation on a church level. The music in the van always has to be religious. Even the driver drives slowly, fearing he'd have an accident with the Pastor's wife on board. Now, since she's not going, the women in the choir could wear pants and be comfortable.

Evelyn knew she'd have to change the sleeping arrangements, and update Jessie, the choir director, but it was worth it.

Five years earlier, Evelyn had attended Gabriel Missionary Baptist Church worship service and sat in the back of the church as a visitor. Six months later, she joined. The church had a membership of over a thousand people. Three months later, she joined the choir. Evelyn's voice was that of an average background singer, so she never led any songs. But she became an instant hit when her fellow parishioners learned she was a travel agent.

Evelyn loved to travel and had worked as an assistant to a travel agent for several years but had always wanted to be her own boss. After taking college classes and receiving her certification, she opened her own travel agency. She'd even recently hired an assistant to manage the office while she was away.

Evelyn liked the church. Pastor Watson was an intelligent visionary. It didn't hurt that he was really good looking. She was delighted when he asked her to handle his travel arrangements for a convention. When he returned, he spoke in church about how smoothly the trip had gone and urged parishioners to use Evelyn's company for their own travel needs.

Everyone from church going on vacation started coming to her looking for a discount. Members referred members and her business grew. At twenty-eight, she was a successful business woman.

She really wasn't looking forward to telling Jessie McDaniel about Mrs. Watson's change of plans. He was the best director the choir ever had, but he was fragile and sometimes harsh.

Jessie had grown up in Gabriel. Everyone remembered him as the talented little boy who was the lead singer on almost every song. When Jessie sang, the choir was electrifying. They sang a little louder, swayed a little more, and clapped with more feeling. The Holy Ghost would take over and folks would be shouting and praising the Lord. When he got older, he became the choir director.

Under his leadership, the Gospel Choir of Gabriel Missionary Baptist Church of Oakland, California was one of the best choirs in the Bay Area. Jessie was indispensable and he knew it.

Chapter 2

Evelyn rubbed her hand across her head and felt the tight and curly roots of her hair. There was no way she was going to miss her hair appointment today.

Since it was still only a little after six, she decided to sleep a few more hours before calling Jessie. She reset the alarm for 9:30, turned her back to the phone, pulled the covers up around her neck, and felt the soft pillow's embrace.

At 8 o'clock, the phone rang.

"Oh, hell!"

Jerking the sheets off, she moved toward the end of the bed with her gown wrapped around her body. This time she decided to let the answering machine pick up the call. After the beep, she heard Jessie talking frantically.

When he realized he was talking to a machine he hurriedly identified himself. "I just heard Sister Watson isn't going on tour. This is a matter of life and death. Call me!"

Evelyn smiled. Anytime Jessie was in a panic, he talked fast and proclaimed the problem to be a life or death matter. She put off calling him back.

Instead, Evelyn started her regular routine of showering without getting her hair wet, conditioning her hair, putting lotion on her body, and applying makeup. Dressed in a light blue suit with matching hat and shoes, she was almost ready to leave the house.

Time to call Jessie. He must be shedding his skin by now. Sitting at the kitchen table, she dialed. He answered immediately.

"Jessie, this is Sister Jenkins."

"Evelyn," he interrupted, "I just don't know what to do. If Sister Watson is not going, we need a replacement. God knows I'm kind of glad; you know the woman can't hold a note. Anyway, we need another alto. I've been calling around to our choir members. I can't find anyone else who can go on tour. Some can't afford it and others can't take off work."

Evelyn still couldn't get used to young people calling her by her first name. She knew it was a sacrifice to go on tour. Some members who were out of work had agreed to go because it would give them the opportunity to look for jobs during the day at a various stops. Others would be on summer vacation.

"Jessie, can you find a singer who is not a member of our church?"

"Good idea. I'll make some phone calls."

"I'll keep the room reservation but only until ten tonight so we don't lose the deposit if you don't find someone."

En route to the hairdresser, Evelyn called her assistant, Deborah, to check in.

"Evelyn, there's a problem. Randy Sullivan hasn't called in yet with his credit card number."

"Call and tell him if he doesn't pay by five he won't be able to go."

They discussed the changed reservation for Mrs. Watson and other reservations in progress.

As she ended the call, Evelyn parked and walked over to the hair salon. As always, it was crowded. The owner was a church member, so many of them had become her clients. At the reception desk, Evelyn learned that her stylist was running late. Susan was always running late. As frustrating as waiting was, finding another good hairdresser would be too much of a challenge.

She took a seat in the waiting area. A strong odor of burning hair and nail solution permeated the air. KBLX radio's rhythm and blues distracted Evelyn for a while, but thirty minutes later, a fuming mad Evelyn was ushered to the hair washing station, and prepped.

When Susan finally started styling her hair, she had lots to say. Susan knew everything about everybody at church and she wasn't afraid to talk about them.

"Sister Jenkins, I'm praying you will have a successful tour but I have my doubts. I don't like to talk about the sisters but you know Gwen Harrison and Diana Miller are troublemakers. Not many people in the church like them."

"Why not?"

"Gwen always wants things done her way. Diana is just a follower of Gwen. Wherever they work in the church there's always a conflict. They don't comply with rules and regulations. When they joined the Usher Board, they shortened the length of the uniform. You know Pastor Watson won't let the ushers dress like strippers. He went off and suggested they join the choir. They can't cut the length of the choir robes. You've seen them. They still refuse to stop wearing them short dresses two sizes too small."

Two and a half hours later, Susan was finished. Looking in the mirror, Evelyn sighed. As usual, she'd go home and roll her hair in the style she liked.

She sat down at the laptop with her Crab Shack takeout and checked her emails. Randy had finally paid for his trip (good!).

Evelyn was getting excited about the tour. It would be her first as part of a professional-sounding choir.

Pastor Watson had scheduled concerts in Los Angeles, Las Vegas, Phoenix, and San Diego. She had contacted each pastor and made the arrangements. She was also coordinating vans, accommodations, flyers, and food. If this worked out, she would be adding touring to her company's specialties.

The third stop on tour would be Phoenix, Evelyn's home town. She and her brother, Charles, were PK kids (Preacher's Kids). Her dad was a minister, her mother a retired schoolteacher. Charles became a police officer over their father's objections. It had been years since she'd seen her family. It was time to visit.

Nine choir members, two deacons, two musicians and Jessie, the choir director, would leave on Monday in two fifteen-passenger rented vans. The deacons would do the driving.

Rev. Osborn, pastor of Power House Missionary Baptist Church in Los Angeles, had scheduled them for a concert at his church on Tuesday night. And members of his congregation agreed to house members of the choir in their homes to defray hotel costs. Being a preacher's kid, she was used to this practice in Afro-American Baptist communities.

Evelyn finished putting together travel packages for the choir members with departure times for each stop, cell phone numbers of the choir members, info on the homes assigned and the concert churches. A personal thank-you letter from Pastor Watson rounded out the package.

Chapter 3

As she was completing the last folder, she called Jessie.

"Evelyn girl, I've been so busy today I forgot to call you. I found an alto to replace Sister Watson. Her name is Valarie Houston. She's twenty-three years old and a dedicated young lady. The girl can sing and she knows all the songs. She can't pay for the trip until Monday. Is that a problem? Also, can she share a room with another choir member?"

"I'll have her share a room with Monique Gilmore and Carol White. They are all the same age."

"You know Gwen and Diana are going to pitch a fit. Especially since Valarie's not a member of our church. I swear they think they own the choir." They both laughed.

Gwen and Diana grew up in Gabriel MBC and felt entitled to criticize anything and everyone.

"Why is it that some older church members feel the need to treat new members so mean? Members like that can turn a church upside down."

Evelyn agreed, "Yeah, it's going to be a challenge. I'll tell Pastor Watson about Valarie so he can give Gwen and Diana a talking to. You know they'll do anything for him."

"Yeah, he knows how to calm them B's down."

"JESSIE, that's no way to talk about them."

"Girl, you know if Pastor Watson wasn't married them heifers would have dropped it 'cause it's hot' a long time ago.

You see how they dress; all they need is a corner. They've been like that since they were teenagers, straight from the streets. Over the years they've calmed down some. You should have seen how they acted years ago. They were a terror."

"NO! Are they really that bad?"

"Girl, you're out of touch. Both of 'em been after Pastor Watson every since he walked in the door. Watch their faces when he walks in church. We have got to talk more often. The stuff I know will curl your hair. 'Cause girl, everything that happens in church ain't always about church. You'd be amazed at what I see from where I sit."

Evelyn snickered, "We'd better talk later. Are we having rehearsal before we go?"

"No," Jessie said, "I'm going to have the choir sing two of the songs tomorrow at the eleven a.m. service. I asked Valarie to come so she can find a robe to fit her. It'll give her a chance to meet the other members and sing with the choir. Please talk to Pastor Watson 'cause I don't want to go off on nobody tomorrow."

She agreed and they ended the call.

By the time Evelyn had made a folder for Valarie, showered, laid out her Sunday clothes, and rolled her hair, it was midnight. She set the alarm and put a post-it on the phone reminding her to call Pastor Watson. Sunday was going to be busy.

Chapter 4

When her business became successful, Evelyn had bought her Oakland condo from an elderly couple moving to Florida. The price was right and the area was perfect, bustling with shops and restaurants. Sunday morning she woke up to a very warm room. Putting on her robe, she headed downstairs and turned on the coffee maker.

While waiting, she turned the TV to Pastor Jakes of *The Potter's House.* She loved watching him preach the word. How wonderful it would be if the choir was invited to sing at his church. Rev. Jakes was really getting into the message so she knew he was nearing the end of the program. It was almost seven-thirty. The rich smell of coffee filled the room. She poured herself a cup and sat on a stool at the kitchen island looking out the big bay window to the Bay Bridge.

It was time to call Pastor Watson. After several rings, he answered. "Pastor Watson, I hope it's not too early to call"

"No, Sister Jenkins. I've been up for hours working on today's sermon."

"How is Sister Watson's dad?"

"He's doing much better. Seems he didn't have a heart attack after all. He's just been working too hard and needs to slow down"

"I'm glad to hear that."

She took a deep breath; there was silence for a moment. "Well, Pastor Watson, I have a little problem and need your help." She explained about Valarie and asked if he would make a comment during church service to welcome her.

"Certainly, I know this can put a strain on the others, especially since she's not a member. I know some choir members can be malicious. I'll try and calm them down."

Evelyn was thankful for his insight. She knew that, like most pastors, he knew his flock and without her naming names, he knew who she was talking about.

"I'll make sure Deacon Jackson gives you the church's funds for the tour," he added. "Is there anything else you need me to help you with?"

"No everything else is under control."

Pastor Watson encouraged her to call him if she needed any assistance during the tour. "I asked Deacon Jackson to assist with the offerings after each concert. He'll keep a record of the amounts but give you the money. Sister Jenkins, you will be in charge of all the money. Use it for gas, meals, and any emergencies. I know some of the members may have money issues, so if you need to help them feel free to do so.

"I understand," she said

Evelyn thanked him for allowing the choir to go on this adventure and added, "I asked Jessie to bring some of our old concert tapes to sell after each concert."

"Good; you can also use those funds to help with the expenses. I asked Deacons Woods to assist with selling the cd's after each concert. He'll keep a record of the sales. Sister Jenkins," he said, "as we discussed when I agreed to let the choir go on tour, you will be in charge. The Deacons are there to assist you."

"I understand," she said.

He added, "I'll be praying for the success of the tour."

As they hung up, Evelyn looked at the clock. She would need to rush to be at the church early enough to meet Valarie.

Even before she arrived at the church, Evelyn knew what would be happening there, since it was the same every Sunday. The large sanctuary would be bright from the sun shining through the stained glass windows. The ushers would be sitting in the last two rows, ready to pass out fans, bulletins, and Bibles. Many of them liked to serve in the choir area because it was less work. Deacons, who sat on the front row, were deciding who was going to read the scripture or pray.

A huge flower arrangement would decorate the front of the pulpit. Children would be running up and down the aisles. Choir members are expected to be robed and ready for early morning worship by 7:45 and 10:45 for morning worship. They line up soprano, alto, tenor, and bass. At exactly 8:00 or 11:00, Eric the organist starts playing. The choir marches in singing, "We come to praise Him, we come to praise Him, we come to praise Him and lift His Holy name."

14

This Sunday, Evelyn decided she was only attending the 11 o'clock service.

The parking attendant directed Evelyn toward the rear wall. As she retrieved her robe from the backseat, Gwen parked and starting walking behind her. Evelyn walked more briskly toward the church. Then she heard Gwen's voice, "Good morning."

Evelyn cringed before responding in a light and airy tone. She really didn't want to hear Gwen's complaints today.

Gwen was 5' 5", but with four-inch heels, she appeared taller. She was trying to catch up with Evelyn, who glanced back and thought Gwen could be mistaken for a hooker. Today she was wearing a tight blue dress with a V neck top that looked a size too small. Her long blond wavy weaved hair was flowing down her face and back. Her makeup was always just a little over the top. She loved colored eye shadow, which she changed to match every outfit she wore. Her friend Diana wore her hair the same way, but it was red.

She was talking loud. "Sister Jenkins, I heard Sister Watson's not going on the trip. Did Jessie really find a singer who's not a member of our church to take her place?"

Evelyn took a deep breath and said, "Yes, yes he did. I hear she's a wonderful singer and will fit right in with the choir."

"Well I don't know how you feel but this is just crazy. I'm sure he could have found somebody in the choir instead of her."

"We needed someone fast to replace Sister Watson. I think she'll be an asset for us.

"Um I don't know 'bout that," Gwen said. "We don't need any mess 'cause I can't deal with messy people."

"I know," Evelyn said, as she turned her head and smiled. (The only messy person in the choir was Gwen.) They walked into church together. As usual, it was noisy. Service hadn't started so the big double doors leading into the sanctuary were open. Some members stood in the foyer talking; others searched for a seat in the sanctuary. People who had attended early morning service were leaving. They both turned to the left and walked toward the choir room.

As the door opened, it was obvious that not all the choir members were there. There were chairs four rows deep around the grand piano in the middle of the room. It was big enough for the 45 members of the full choir. Along the walls were closets divided into sections for each voice part. Standing near the piano was a young woman about twenty years old who was being ignored by everyone. This must be Valarie.

She was a slim young lady with short natural hair, wearing a black skirt and white blouse. She was short even wearing heels. Holding her jacket in hand, she looked out of place. No one had introduced themselves, so Valarie must be feeling awkward, standing in the middle of the room.

Evelyn remembered how they treated her the same way when she first joined the choir. In fact, if it weren't for Pastor Watson, she would have quit the choir.

Why is it that some members who have been in a choir for a long time are so evil? They run in packs. They argue about the songs even though they can't play a note and the talented singers are shunned by them. Some of these women were looking for a husband and others were divorced and bitter. Yet when they sang it sounded heavenly. Go figure, she sighed.

Gwen walked past Valarie without saying a word and joined the women in a group off to the side putting on their choir robes. After placing her robe in the closet, Evelyn walked over to her.

"Hi, she said, "I'm Sister Jenkins. Are you Valarie?"

"Yes, I was looking for Jessie," Valarie replied in a soft voice.

"I don't think he's here yet. But on behalf of the choir I'd like to welcome you," Evelyn said. Valarie thanked her, seeming to relax a little.

"Are you the lady I'm supposed to give the money to?"

"Yes," Evelyn responded. "Please don't forget to bring it tomorrow. I prepared a folder for you. It will give you all the information you need regarding the tour."

"Thanks so much."

More choir members arrived. Those who had attended the early service already had their robes on. They took their seats around the piano.

Evelyn ushered Valarie to the closet to help her find one of the extra robes. Valarie put it on and sat next to Evelyn.

Sarah Johnson and her sister Mary sat in front of them. Evelyn tapped them on the shoulder and introduced Valarie. They welcomed her, and other choir members introduced themselves. While they were talking, Jessie walked into the room, looking sharp in a pin-striped burgundy suit and shoes with white shirt and matching tie.

Jessie was tall and thin but his clothes fit him perfectly. He wore a buzz cut, which looked good on him with his nice shaped head. His glasses were stylish. You could always count on Jessie to look stylish even when he dressed casually.

He came in with the organist, Eric Parker, Jr., a twenty-one-year-old college graduate. Unlike Jessie, Eric looked like a man's man. He was somewhat muscular, tall, with somewhat tighter pants with straight legs, the business-casual look. He was a very attractive young man. Like Jessie, Eric has been a member of Gabriel since he was a little boy. His mother had been the senior usher for over twenty years. Unlike Jessie, Eric, Amos Tucker the drummer, and Nathaniel Hendricks the pianist, didn't have any formal musical training but you couldn't tell it when they played. Jessie insisted they dress appropriately for church, so they all wore suits. Nathaniel wasn't going on tour because he had a prior commitment.

As in most black churches, Gabriel Missionary Baptist gave children the opportunity to learn how to play instruments during church service. Children who wanted to play sat and watched before trying to play an instrument. Most of them wanted to play the drums or organ. When they played well enough, they were allowed to play for the offering or after church. Eventually, they joined the children's choir. Once they played really well, they were allowed to play for one of the choirs. Most churches have at least fours choirs, free music for church services.

Eric had played the organ for over eight years and was very gifted. Even without benefit of lessons, his playing sounded professional. He took pride in his appearance and was well mannered. Evelyn was looking forward to having him tour with the choir.

Jessie went over to the piano. As soon as he did, the choir members stood up ready to sing the devotional song. Before starting, he looked around the room and spotted Valarie.

"Valarie, would you please come to the piano?" Timidly, she walked over to the piano. The whole choir followed her with their eyes.

Jessie said, "Good morning, everyone." We all responded, "Good morning."

"Some of you may have heard that Sister Watson's father is ill and she won't be going on tour. Since no one was available to go from our choir, I asked my good friend Valarie to take her place. She graciously accepted my invitation. Valarie is a wonderful young woman and has a beautiful voice. I hope you will all welcome her."

Voices murmured assent. Gwen's voice rang out, "Brother McDonald, we're so glad to have her. Does she know all the songs?"

Jessie looked at her for a minute; you could see the angry swelling up in his face. "Of course she knows the songs, Gwen. I hope YOU remember all the words as well."

There was a hush over the room. Gwen sat down in silence. Jessie turned, "Valarie, don't forget to take that robe with you after church. Those of you leaving tomorrow for the tour, please meet in this room after service. Everyone else, we ask you to pray for our success."

Gwen should have known to keep her mouth closed, thought Evelyn. Everyone knew Jessie didn't pull any punches with her. They had history long before Evelyn joined the church. He knew how messy Gwen was. He was always telling her off.

When Jessie sat down and started playing a devotional song, "Jesus, Keep Me near the Cross," the choir joined in. Young Brother Amos Tucker, the drummer, prayed. After prayer, everyone lined up to march into the sanctuary. Nobody said a word; it was like the air had been sucked out of the room.

Jessie announced, "Today we're singing 'His Mercy Endureth Forever' and 'Praise Him in Advance.'"

Carol invited Valarie to stand in line with her and the other altos. Evelyn and Gwen were up front with the sopranos far away from Valarie.

The music started. Forty choir members stood in line ready to march through the double doors into the sanctuary.

Chapter 5

Medium loud and joyous, the organ, piano, and drums filled the church. This was how Gabriel Missionary Baptist Church started morning service every Sunday. Seating capacity was 1,200 people. Today almost every seat was filled. Four aisles led to the pulpit. The choir would march down the two inside aisles. Ushers stood in front of the outer doors to stop anyone from coming in during the choir processional.

The congregation stood facing the aisles that the choir used. The air was thick with the aroma of flowers and perfume. Some members of the congregation swayed and clapped. Others sang with the music.

We, the choir members, know what is expected of us. March down the aisle, turn left or right, depending on what side you're on. After four steps, make a half turn and continue to the choir stand.

On the pulpit level were the ministers' chairs. One very large chair in the middle faced the very large podium. To the right side near the pulpit were two rows of chairs for the ministers' wives. In the choir stand directly behind the pulpit on a custom-made four foot platform stood Jessie, This gave him additional height directly behind the Pastor's chair.

There was silence. All eyes were on Jessie. He waited just long enough for the congregation to feel apprehensive. He turned to the musicians and nodded his head. Immediately the organ, piano, synthesizer, and drums started playing louder. You could feel the explosion in your bones vibrating with every beat. Jessie held his right arm up in the air.

He was in charge. Everyone was spellbound. You could feel the tension, anticipation, and joy. Then just as it became intolerable, he lowered his arm.

That was our cue to start marching. We always started with the left foot. No singing yet. We just marched like drones, left, right, left, right down the aisles. We stayed exactly two steps apart from each other facing forward, looking at Jessie. The congregation clapped. Sopranos and altos were on the left side; tenors and basses on the right. Everyone wore red and white robes with black shoes. It was mesmerizing. Everyone waited to hear the choir sing that first note. Jessie made them wait and wait, and wait. When the first two choir members reached the first step, Jessie lowered his arm.

The choir sang. "We come to praise him." The sound was harmonious and astonishing. Immediately he put his arm back up. The choir stopped singing but kept marching. The musicians kept playing. The audience was in an uproar. "Sing," somebody shouted. The congregation went wild. They knew the song and they wanted us to sing but Jessie kept his arm up.

He turned to the organist and pianist; they stopped playing. Now it was just the drums and nothing else. The congregation really wanted the choir to sing. The drummer kept playing. Finally, Jessie motioned to the other musicians; they loudly joined in. It was more powerful than the beginning. The sound of the music hit the walls and reverberated across the building. It's a show and we were all part of it.

Then Jessie lowered his arm and we sang as loudly as we could, "We come to praise Him." The audience was really clapping. Most of the choir was now in the choir stand, facing one another. Jessie directed us to turn and face him. Somebody shouted, "SING!" Somebody else shouted "Hallelujah." Jessie signaled the choir to sway with the music. Forty bodies swaying in unison, Jessie clapped his hands; the choir clapped too.

Jessie raised his arms: SING!

With a thunderous noise, the choir sang "We come to praise Him, we come to praise Him, we come to praise Him and lift his Holy Name."

The entire congregation exploded, clapping, moving, and singing with us. We swayed from left to right and they did the same. The whole church was in sync, clapping and singing at the same time. Just when people thought they couldn't take it anymore, the left door of the pulpit opened, and there stood Dr. Edward W. Watson, Pastor.

He wore the same color robe as the choir but his robe was velvet with black doctoral bars across the arms. He was tall and slender with broad shoulders. His face was perfectly structured and surrounded by a full head of black, wavy hair. He was clean shaven with well manicured eyebrows, and beautiful skin with full lips. He was every woman's dream.

The audience was stunned, especially those visiting for the first time. Their eyes followed him from the door to the big chair in the middle of the pulpit. Jessie stood tall behind him and the associate pastors sat behind him in their robes. It was like they were invisible. Everyone was focused on Pastor Watson. Once he reached his seat and laid his Bible on the chair, he turned to Jessie and nodded.

The choir sang "Make a joyful noise."

It was too much. An overpowering spirit of the Lord engulfed the entire church. Some people started shouting. Some cried. Others sat down from exhaustion.

The more we sang, the stronger everyone felt the Power of the Holy Ghost. When the singing suddenly stopped, the Spirit of the Lord took over and people shouted.

Ushers ran around trying to comfort people. Many people just sat and cried. Ushers fanned members. Visitors looked around, not knowing what to focus on. Some succumbed to the Spirit of the Lord by lying on the floor. There was an anointing in the house.

Dr. Watson was standing with his arms open, tears rolling down his face. The spirit had now reached the deacons. Two were standing; one bent over with his head in his hand.

Gabriel was not a traditional Baptist Church. There were printed programs but Pastor Watson let the spirit of the Lord lead the service. This was one of those Sundays.

Tears ran down Evelyn's face. The more she thought of how good the Lord has been to her, the more she cried. Others did the same. A few members had to be taken out.

Pastor Watson stood at the pulpit, "Hallelujah."

Evelyn and others began to dry their eyes. She looked down the row of sopranos to find Valarie. Someone was handing her a tissue. Evelyn hoped Jessie had prepared her for their type of service. It was an overpowering experience.

Most people hadn't noticed Sister Watson sitting in her special chair. She had led the ministers' wives into the sanctuary when Dr. Watson entered. She looked like a pastor's wife: tall with a beautiful figure, she wore a tailored yellow suit, a matching hat, and rhinestone shoes. Her large matching handkerchief covered her knees. She looked elegant. The wives sitting behind her were dressed in different colors but everything matched from hats to shoes.

Sister Watson was overcome with emotion. Ushers attended to her and some of the other wives. Jessie directed the choir to sit down. He enjoyed watching the congregation's reaction but he never lost his composure in public.

It was only noon, but it felt like they'd been in church for hours. That's how service began every Sunday.

Pastor Watson called out "Isn't God good?" and everyone responded, "All the time." He took the pulpit. Evelyn and the other members who were going on tour joined him at the altar. Deacons Jackson and Woods, the drivers, also stood with them. Evelyn found herself standing next to Valarie.

Pastor Watson asked everyone to welcome Valarie. In unison the congregation responded, "Welcome." They would be representing Gabriel Missionary Baptist Church and its Pastor. He encouraged anyone who needed prayer to come to the altar. The remaining congregation was asked to stand and point their right hands toward them. They prayed for the success of the tour.

As Rev. Watson neared the end of his powerful sermon, the organist played to emphasize his words. There was shouting and praising God. Some were crying, standing on their feet, holding their hands in the air. Others were saying "Amen," "Say that!" and "Hallelujah," all at the same time. With Pastor Watson's benediction, the service ended.

Church members hovered around talking to each other while choir members headed for the choir room. Pastor and Sister Watson shook hands with members and visitors. Everyone smiled. Little did they guess know that not everybody would return.

Chapter 6

Within fifteen minutes, all that remained in the choir room were the touring choir members, Eric the organist, Amos the drummer, and two deacons who were driving the vans. Everyone had disrobed and was sitting around the piano. A smiling Valarie sat down next to Evelyn. "Sister Jenkins, I have never been in church service like this."

"It's like this every Sunday. Perhaps you'll consider joining once we get back?"

"I sure am thinking about it; this is the best church service I have every attended."

Pastor Watson and Sister Watson walked in.

"I expect you all to treat each other like Christians. I'm depending on Sister Jenkins to ensure you all have a place to sleep (everyone laughed). Sister Jenkins, if you have any problems please tell the deacons. They know how to contact me day or night."

Evelyn stood and asked if she could say a few words. Pastor Watson agreed. She passed their itinerary and reminded everyone the vans would be leaving promptly at 10:00 a.m.

Evelyn looked across the room at Gwen and Diana, sitting behind the Pastor, frowning. They were going to be a real challenge.

Valarie, Jessie, and Carol White walked off. Carol had a two-year-old-son she had been raising alone since her husband died in Afghanistan. Now she was unemployed and going on the tour to look for a job. She scheduled a job interview close to her family in Las Vegas.

Deacons Jackson and Woods joined them. "Can we pick-up the vans today?" Evelyn nodded. "That will be great. We can check them out before we leave. We don't want any problems on the road."

She gave the deacons a copy of the contract agreement and asked them to call her if there were any problems. The building was now quiet. She placed her shoes and robe in the garment bag. Deacon Jackson walked Evelyn to her car.

Chapter 7

When Evelyn got home, she changed clothes, warmed some food, and sat down for her Sunday meal, thinking about all the things she needed to get done before leaving tomorrow. First she'd pack first: casual clothes to wear in the van pant suits for during the day, exercise clothes, and church dresses for the concerts. It was August and it should be warm for the entire trip. If anything was missed she'd enjoy shopping for it.

Next, she checked her e-mails and organized all her documents for the trip. Just as she was finishing, the phone rang.

"Sister Jenkins, this is Deacon Jackson. I just wanted to let you know we have the vans gassed up."

"That's wonderful."

"Deacon Woods and I will drive them home and be at the church parking lot at 10:00 a.m. Since you don't live far from the church, would you like me to pick you up?"

"Yes, that would be so nice. Have a blessed evening, good-bye." She was glad she didn't have to leave her car in the church parking lot.

With the money Evelyn had in hand and the offerings they expected to collect, there should be more than enough for the tour. She was pleased with how things were progressing. In Los Angeles, She and the deacons would be staying at the

Holiday Inn Express Suites. As a perk for driving, the deacons each had their own room.

Just when she thought life was without problems, the phone rang. "Hello Sister Jenkins, this is Gwen."

Evelyn knew this wasn't going to be good.

"I called because I wanted to make sure Diana and me are staying together."

"Yes, I have you, Diana, and Sarah sharing a room.

Gwen said, "Thanks, we're going to party in L.A. I know Sarah's engaged but she ain't married yet."

Evelyn signed, "Well I'm sure you ladies know how to act."

"Yes we do," Gwen said. "Diana and I are still looking for our Mr. Right. Please don't have us with Valarie. We don't know her and really don't want to."

Evelyn could hear loud talking and laughing, with hip hop music blasting in the background. She didn't want to argue. "Gwen, she's a nice young lady and I hope you give her a chance."

"I'll try but I'm just saying what I feel. I'm looking forward to the trip. Well, that's all I wanted to tell you, see you tomorrow, bye."

Evelyn's "Good-bye" went unheard. Gwen had already hung up.

Evelyn placed Valarie with Carol and Monique. Monique had been in the choir for several years and they were all around the same age. They should get along well.

Evelyn sat down and poured herself a glass of wine. She realized how angry she was. This is not going to be a good trip. Gwen and I are heading for a showdown and I hope I don't lose my cool. Just then, the phone rang again.

"Evelyn, my God how are you?" Jessie sounded drunk but she didn't want to believe it.

"Hello Jessie, how are you?"

He laughed. "Girl I'm fine." There was loud music in the background and it sounded like he was in a club.

"Sounds like you're having fun."

"Yes I am. I'm trying to enjoy myself before tomorrow 'cause I know I'm going to have to rip Gwen a new one if she keeps acting like a bitch."

Evelyn felt offended because she didn't know this side of him and she really didn't want to. Before she could say anything, he said, "I'm sorry I shouldn't have said that, you don't know me that well, but girl, you're going to have to get with it. This ain't going to be no picnic."

"I accept your apology."

He continued, "She just gets me so angry. Valarie told me how she acted in the choir room. I could pull that weaved hair off her head. Let me stop before you think ill of me."

"Well, I do understand your frustration; I'm annoyed with her too. Has Gwen always been so unpleasant?"

"Yes, she grew up in the projects. You can't take her anywhere without her causing trouble. I was sorry they agreed to go on this tour. Gwen is nothing but a troublemaker. When she and Diana get together, it's double trouble. Pastor Watson knows all about them. I called to tell you I talked to Valarie and explained how they act. It would help if you can keep them apart as much as possible."

Evelyn didn't tell him about Gwen's call. "I'll do my best, Jessie."

Someone in the background was shouting, "Come on Jessie."

"I have to go. I'll see you tomorrow. Don't forget to bring your brass knuckles." He was laughing as he hung up the phone.

Evelyn sat back stunned. What other surprises would there be? The only thing she knew about Gwen was that she was single and worked as a hairdresser.

She thought about calling her mother to ask her advice but instead decided to go to bed early. This, she thought as she felt herself drifting to sleep, is going to be a strange tour.

Chapter 8

It was 7:30 when Evelyn opened her eyes. Birds chirped outside her window. The sun was shining and her bedroom was already really warm. She styled her hair, put on a lightweight pair of pants and a tank top with sandals and headed downstairs to cook breakfast.

Next she watered the plants, locked all the windows, and cleared the messages on the answering machine. She checked to make sure the condo was completely secure and checked in with her assistant, Deborah.

When the doorbell rang, Evelyn was ready. In his early forties, Deacon Jackson was a nice looking man. He was six feet tall with a dark complexion and neat little mustache. He spoke in a strong baritone voice, "Good morning. It's a beautiful day for a drive. Are you ready for this wonderful experience?"

"I'm starting to feel a little excited."

"So am I. This is my first concert tour but I'm sure we are going to have a great time in the Lord." He gathered her luggage and turned to take it to the van. She grabbed her briefcase and tote bag, locked the front door, and activated the alarm system. He escorted her to the van and opened the passenger door.

"We should be In L.A. by five o'clock barring any problems with traffic."

They were still several blocks away from the church when Deacon Jackson said, "I hope you don't mind but I agreed to pick up Monique Gilmore. She is a college student. She's one of those nice quiet shy withdrawn young ladies who never cause any problems." He turned the corner on 41st street.

"That's not a problem. I'm praying this will be a blessed trip"

He parked in front of an apartment building and walked inside. Evelyn felt uncomfortable sitting in the van alone. This wasn't the safest part of town. She checked to make sure the doors were locked. Within a few minutes Monique and Deacon Jackson appeared, laughing as they walked walking toward the van.

Evelyn was stunned when she saw Monique. At church, she wore loose fitting clothes on her thin 5 foot 9 frame, with her hair in a bun, and flat shoes. She appeared to be a shy young woman.

Today Monique was wearing a very revealing outfit. Her well-proportioned body was squeezed into tight shorts and her pony-tailed hair was topped with a straw fedora. She wore sandals with heels and carried a large purse. That was very expensive luggage for a college student. Evelyn was shocked. "Wow! I never would have known you."

Deacon Jackson gazed at Monique with a smile as she got into the van. "Doesn't she look wonderful? Now we know who to get for our fashion show extravaganza in September."

"Thank you," Monique said, looking embarrassed. "I am a model but I guess you wouldn't know that by the way I dress at

The Gospel Choir Murder

church. I have been modeling during the week for almost a year. I'm traveling to Europe soon."

"Well I'm truly impressed. You look amazing."

When they arrived at the church, Deacon Woods, who drove the other van, parked next to them. Three other cars parked next to the vans. Brother and Sister Williams got out of their Mercedes with Cory Williams, their son.

They all walked toward Evelyn and Monique. "Wow" said Deacon Woods, "Monique, is that you?" Everyone laughed.

Deacon Woods was the same height and almost the same size as Deacon Jackson, but he was little thinner and clean shaven. Wearing a football hat with a black shirt and pants, he didn't look much like a deacon. They were the youngest of all the deacons and you could tell by their interaction they were really good friends.

"Good morning everyone," said Brother Williams. Everybody knew that Brother and Sister Williams had money. He was a broker at his own real estate company. Sister Williams was a stay-at-home mom. Cory was an only child but didn't act like a spoiled brat. He was a tenor with an angelic voice.

Everyone treated him like a younger brother. Evelyn assured his parents she would take good care of him. Just then, the other tenors, Alex and Randy, arrived. Randy's wife got out of the car, waved, and said hello to everyone.

With his slim build and short dreadlocks, Randy looked younger than 23 in his white shirt with jeans. He'd been unemployed and was looking to find a job in Los Angeles while on the tour. His wife was a cute Caucasian with long dark hair and blue eyes, dressed in a T-shirt, thin black pants, and high heels. Occasionally she came to church with him. Even though they usually attended different churches, it didn't seem to interfere with their relationship. They made a cute couple and everyone liked them.

Alex Garcia was also a very handsome young man. Women in church were always flirting with him but he didn't seem to let it go to his head. He wore his hair long and most of the time it was in a pony tail. Alex was a school teacher. His mother offered Spanish classes during the week at the church. Since they were both near the same age, Evelyn had Alex and Randy room together.

Deacon Jackson and Deacon Woods finished loading the luggage into the vans. Cory was getting last-minute instructions from his parents.

Alex came over to Evelyn. "Sister Jenkins, you look very nice today." As Evelyn said, "Thank you," he turned to Monique and said, "WOW. Monique, you look amazing." She smiled and said, "Thanks Alex. You just haven't seen me without my church clothes."

"No, I haven't and I must remedy that during this tour," he said and walked away.

Gwen drove in with Diana and Carol and parked near the vans. As soon as they got out of the car Gwen called a loud greeting "Good morning everyone." Deacon Jackson loaded their luggage into in a van. Gwen and Diana each wore their hair in a ponytail with eye shadow matching their green and blue outfits. Carol wore a sundress with a large belt. Valarie had on a T-shirt and jeans.

Gwen's loud voice rang out. "Monique is that you? Girl you look so different. What have you done to yourself? I didn't even recognize you." Diana added, "Wow, girl you look good." Evelyn spoke up. "I think we need to get started."

Deacon Jackson asked everyone to meet in front of the altar inside the church for prayer. To their surprise, Pastor Watson was standing in the pulpit in a casual suit.

"Good morning everyone." They all responded but were somewhat uncomfortable in their attire gathered around the altar. Everyone knelt. He prayed, asking God to protect them and keep them. When Pastor Watson finished he walked out with them. He spoke privately with the deacons as everyone got in the vans.

At last, everyone was installed in the two fifteen-passenger vans, the luggage was loaded, and it was time to start the journey to Los Angeles. Evelyn, Monique, Valarie, Randy, Alex, Carol, and Jessie were in the first van with Deacon Jackson. The others rode with Deacon Woods.

While traveling, the conversation ranged from church activities to personnel problems and concerns. They switched the music from religious to R&B. Evelyn was surprised to learn that Valarie was from South Carolina and studying to be a schoolteacher. Sarah was getting married in six months to her boyfriend, Gary.

As they neared Fresno, Deacon Jackson suggested they stop for gas and a rest break.

Deacon Woods drove up to a gas pump and everyone got out. As the doors opened, Gwen and Diana talked loud about how they needed to go to the restroom. Evelyn suggested everyone get snacks and continue. Others wanted to stop at a restaurant. The majority agreed to go on. Back in the vans, the atmosphere changed. In the van Deacon Woods was driving Gwen and Diana bickered and complained. The van that Evelyn was in remained pleasant and cheerful. They had no idea what was happening in the other van.

As they neared Los Angeles, Evelyn called Pastor Osborne to let him know where they were. He said he would contact his members and have them meet the vans at his church.

Plans were announced for the next day. Monique, Valarie, and Sarah were setting up a trip to the fashion row and were trying to convince Evelyn to go with them. Randy was scheduled for a job interview. Deacon Jackson was going to stay in and get some rest. Jessie and Eric said they were going to music stores to see what was new. Carol was planning on visiting museums and maybe shopping.

Traffic was heavy as they neared the church. It took 45 minutes to reach the Power House Missionary Baptist Church.

As they drove into the church parking lot, there was complete silence. The church was large and magnificent, as was its parking lot. No one expected it to be this large.

Evelyn felt something like a pit in her stomach. Everyone was a little nervous; you could see it on their faces. Jessie broke the silence when he said, "Oh, we ARE having a rehearsal tomorrow." Everyone laughed nervously.

Just as they parked the vans, one of the church doors opened. A tall man came out wearing a white dashiki with white pants and white shoes and wearing a gold cross. He walked over and introduced himself.

"Welcome, welcome. I'm Pastor Osborne. I'm so glad to see you." By now, everyone was out of the vans. Even Gwen and Diana were quiet.

Evelyn broke the silence, "Pastor Osborne we are so thankful that you allowed us to be here. You have a beautiful church."

"We are certainly happy you decided to come to Power House. Let's go in so I can introduce you to the members of the congregation." Everyone walked toward the church door. It opened onto an amazing sight.

Entering the sanctuary was like going into an arena. It was awesome, quiet, and reverent. Everyone stood in awe. Pastor Osborne ushered them down the aisle in the sanctuary to the front. There sat members of the congregation who had volunteered to host the choir. Pastor Osborne introduced them. They were sharing their homes with the choir. They all proceeded to the dining room where there was a repast. Everyone was friendly. Based on the cars in the parking lot, it was evident these people had money. The food was a feast. There were appetizers, finger sandwiches, fried chicken, sushi, fruits of all kind, coffee, tea, sodas, and four different kinds of salads, dinner rolls, cakes, and pies. Some of the choir members packed food to go. After an hour, they broke off in groups with their sponsors.

After prayer, Jessie asked Pastor Osborne if the members could meet at the church for rehearsal the next day at 6:00 p.m. He agreed.

Choir members left with their assigned sponsors and Evelyn made the final arrangements with Pastor Osborne. She and the Deacons drove the vans to the Holiday Inn. While walking to the lobby they discussed how impressed they were with the church décor. They agreed Pastor Watson had never told them how large the church was. Deacon Jackson helped Evelyn unload her luggage. Deacon Woods told them how argumentative the ride was after the Fresno stop. Evelyn said she would have a talk with Gwen and Diana. After checking in, they went to their rooms.

Evelyn was tired. She showered and ordered dinner in her room. She couldn't help thinking about the day. For choir members they were a strange bunch. Being with them for just this short time had already revealed how different they were when not in church. Diana and Gwen were inseparable and disruptive. Monique was a model and not the shy young lady she seemed in church. Jessie and Eric were closer than she'd thought. Randy and Alex acted as they appeared to be at church. Cory and Amos were the youngest but appeared to be very mature for their age. Sarah, who said she getting married, didn't seem to be very happy. She hoped that outsider Valarie would be able to adjust to all these personalities.

Chapter 9

On Tuesday morning, Evelyn woke up rested. She called Deborah to see if there were any urgent concerns at the office, but all was fine.

"Are you enjoying the trip?"

"So far it's going well. I tell you I have found out more about these people in one day than I knew in the year."

"Is it good or bad?"

"Remember when I was trying to explain who everyone was and I told you Monique was this shy young lady. Well, we picked her up and she's dressed in this hot sexy outfit and tells everyone she is a model. I tell you we were blown away."

"How are they getting along with Valarie?"

"So far so good, but I don't expect that to last. I'm keeping my fingers crossed. I'll call you every day and let you know how it's going."

"Well if anybody can handle them I know you can."

Evelyn was starting to feel optimistic. This tour was going to be a real success. Perhaps other churches would use her services to schedule their tours.

She decided to go shopping and sightseeing. She'd have an early dinner before rehearsal, and then check for tour attractions that could be used in a brochure. Calling the hotel operator, she was transferred to Deacon Jackson's room. After four rings, he answered. His voice sounded almost slurred. Evelyn was ready to apologize for waking him too early.

"Good morning, Deacon Jackson," Evelyn responded with an apologetic voice. "I'm sorry if I woke you."

Deacon Jackson said, with a firmer voice, "Oh, Sister Jenkins, that's all right. I'm going to visit with some family members who live here in L.A. I told them I'd be there by 11:00 a.m., so I really need to get up."

"How was your evening? Did you go out and enjoy Los Angeles?"

He laughed. "Sister Jenkins, I'm too old to be out late at night; my nightlife days are over. I stayed in the room, ordered dinner, and slept like a baby." They both laughed. "How was your evening? I know you young people have energy to burn."

Evelyn laughed. "Brother Jackson, I'm almost 30 and I really have never been a nightlife person. I too decided to eat in and went to bed early."

"Well it sounds like you have a good head on your shoulders. Nightlife can be hard on you. When you get older it will catch up with you."

Evelyn smiled. "That is so true, so true," she said. "Well I'm going down for breakfast; perhaps I'll see you there. Have you talked to Deacon Woods this morning?"

"No I haven't talked to Ken," he said. "I'll call him and if he's up, we'll meet you downstairs, say in 20 minutes?"

She agreed and they ended the call. She decided to call Jessie and see how things were going.

After two rings, Jessie answered. "Hey Sister Jenkins, how are you doing?"

"I'm rested. It sounds like you are up and ready to go." Jessie was laughing,

"We're having a great time. Mrs. Hudson's sons, Adam and Abdullah, play for this band so we went to see them last night. It was awesome. This house is off the hook. I think we're in Beverly Hills. I tell you, I love L.A. We got in late but what a blast. The guys are getting dressed and we're off to check out some record stores and do some sightseeing. Adam has a class, so he's letting us use his truck for the day. I'm really glad we stayed with Mrs. Hudson. She's cool. By the way, Sister Hudson has a meeting at the church at 5:00 p.m. so we can have rehearsal then. She called Pastor Osborne and he said it was all right with him. I'll call the others and make sure they know to be there at 5. Did you see that church? We better be real good." As usual, Jessie was talking fast and dictating the conversation. She just waited until he took a breath.

"Yes I think that will be all right as long as the Pastor agrees. Jessie, make sure you tell everyone about the time change. I'll tell Deacon Jackson and Woods." She could barely get a word in before Jessie continued.

"That's great," he said. "I'm really praying we sound good. Eric, Amos, and I will get there early, maybe 4:30, so we can hear how the instruments sound. You know most churches don't take care of their instruments. And we really need to rehearse with the microphones. Can you call Pastor Osborne and see if someone will be there for a sound check?" Finally, Jessie stopped talking so she could answer.

"Yes," Evelyn said. "I'll call him to see if someone can meet you there early for sound check. I'll ask the Deacons to be available just in case anybody needs a ride. Maybe the choir can have dinner together?"

Jessie sounded disappointed and said, "I don't know. The guys and I were invited to this concert at Adam's church and it starts at 7 o'clock. You know we see our choir members all the time. If we have to, maybe we can eat together after the concert tomorrow night?"

Evelyn didn't want to cause any friction and it really wasn't that important to her. "That sounds like a great idea, if the others agree we can certainly consider having dinner after the concert. Besides, it will give us a chance to firm up our plans to leave the following day for Las Vegas." They said good-bye.

Riding down the elevator, she thought she saw Gwen and Diana leaving the hotel, but by the time the elevator reached the lobby, there was no sign of them. She must have been mistaken. They were staying at a sponsor's home, not at the hotel. She quickly dismissed the idea.

As soon as Evelyn got her plate, she saw Deacons Jackson and Woods coming down the elevator. She found an empty table large enough for the three of them. The Deacons looked rested, wearing Hawaiian shirts and black pants. Deacon Woods was wearing a straw fedora.

Deacon Woods spoke first, "Good morning, Sister Jenkins. Looks like a great day doesn't it?"

"It's a beautiful day, how was your evening?" she asked.

"Very restful," he said. "I spoke with the family when I got in, just to let them know we made it safe. The room was nice and comfortable. I fell asleep by 10."

"It sounds like we all did the same thing. Deacon Woods, what are your plans for the day?"

"My wife is sending me on a mission. I'm supposed to go to fashion district downtown and buy myself a new suit. She says I need to update my wardrobe. I haven't bought a new suit for a long time."

Grinning, Deacon Jackson joined in. "Man, you mean Vanessa lets you buy your clothes? Joann doesn't trust me at all. The last time I bought something she said I was out of touch." They laughed.

"Sister Jenkins," continued Deacon Jackson, "You might know Ken and I have been friends for years. We grew up together and moved from Los Angeles to Oakland around the same time."

"That's wonderful. It's good to be able to travel with your best friend. It sounds like we'll all have a busy day. I talked to Jessie and he's hoping to have rehearsal at 5 o'clock instead of

6. Pastor Osborne gave them permission. I hate to have them at the church without one of you. They want to do a sound check at 4:30.

Deacon Woods said, "I'm going shopping but I'll be back here by 4:00 p.m."

"Well, I'll try and get back by 3:30," said Deacon Jackson.

Deacon Woods interrupted, "You know, if you want, you can meet us at the church? I'll be back before then and Sister Jenkins and I can meet you at the church. Besides, if any of the choir needs a ride I'll be here and I can pick them up."

Is that all right with you, Sister Jenkins?" Deacon Woods asked.

"Yes, that would be great."

"You know I didn't want to mention this with the others around, but riding down here I heard Sarah talking on the phone with her fiancé, Gary. They were arguing and from what I heard, he's threatening to come to Los Angeles. Needless to say, when Gwen heard that she went off. She started telling her it wasn't that kind of trip and if she did it, everybody could do it. It was a mess."

"Sarah is a nice girl," he added, "I really don't want us to have any trouble so I just needed to alert you." They all agreed to keep an eye on the situation. Saying good-bye, Evelyn picked up a cup of coffee to take back to her room.

She turned on the television and pulled out her cell phone. After speaking with Pastor Osborne, Evelyn felt more comfortable with the time change.

Because hotel prices are so low in Las Vegas, Evelyn had been able to get eight hotel rooms at Circus Circus for the entire group. Evelyn called the hotel to confirm the reservations. Then she called Pastor Mason of Witness Center Church of God in Christ in Las Vegas to make sure the details for the concert scheduled Friday were completed. "Witness Center, this is Sister Dee Cummings, the church secretary, may I help you?"

"Sister Cummings," Evelyn said, "This is Sister Jenkins. How are you today?"

"I'm very well thank you, how are you?"

"I'm doing very well. I was calling to make sure all the arrangements have been completed for the concert on Friday night."

"Oh Sister Jenkins, we are so looking forward to hearing your choir. Yes, all the arrangements have been made. We put out flyers and announced it on our broadcast. Pastor Mason has been telling everyone how wonderful your choir sounds. In fact, he's going to videotape it and sell DVDs after the concert. I'm sure that will help with your finances. Now as I understand it, you will be here on Thursday, is that correct?"

"WOW we didn't expect all that. Yes, that's the plan. Do you have my cell number?"

"Oh yes, if I need to reach you I'll call you. We scheduled the church to be available for the choir on Friday for rehearsal if you need it. Let me know what time you'd like to be there. I'll have one of the Deacons meet you."

"Thank you for everything."

"God bless you too," Evelyn said. "Good-bye."

Everything was falling into place. That was enough work. She was going to check out L.A. She called for a cab and went to a shopping center near the hotel. It was a wonderful day. Evelyn shopped until 2:00 and then went back to the hotel, to rest and eat before rehearsal.

Meanwhile, Gwen, Sarah, and Diana found Fashion Alley, where the three of them enjoyed themselves. They ate Mexican food before taking a cab back to the house where they were staying.

Deacon Woods also found Fashion Alley. He parked the van and went shopping for his new suit. By 2:30, he was back at the hotel admiring his buys. He called for room service and then he called Evelyn. They agreed to meet in the lobby at 4:30. Despite the traffic, they were at the church by 5:00.

Deacon Jackson and the other members arrived a few minutes late. Everyone was in a good mood. A deacon from the church opened the door and the choir proceeded to the choir stand.

Jessie and the other musicians were already there, impressed with the musical instruments. He placed each choir member in the order they were to sing. After vocals, the whole choir rehearsed the songs in the same order as the program. They sounded good and after the last song it was evident they were in good form.

Randy asked to say a few words and announced that he got the job and would start in three weeks. He thanked everyone for their prayers and said that after the San Diego concert he was returning to Los Angeles to find a place for his family. At 6:30 pm, they had prayer and were dismissed.

As they were leaving, there was a loud commotion in the women's bathroom. Evelyn rushed to see what was happening and found Gwen and Monique having a serious argument. Gwen was cursing and Monique was defending herself. As soon as Evelyn opened the door, both stopped talking. Evelyn asked, "What's going on?"

Although they continued to look at each other with hatred in their eyes, Gwen said, "Nothing is wrong, Sister Jenkins." She hurried passed her and left the room. Monique started primping, putting on lipstick, before gathering her purse and walking out, leaving Evelyn standing alone.

Evelyn thanked the church deacon before leaving; hoping he hadn't heard what was going on in the bathroom.

Shaking her head, she headed for the parking lot. Everyone else was already there. It was unusually quiet. Jessie, Amos, Cory, and Eric left to go to the concert. Gwen, Diana and

Sarah were in a van with Deacon Jackson. Monique, Valarie, Carol, Alex, and Randy rode with Evelyn and Deacon Woods.

During the ride back, Carol said she hoped she'd find a job in Las Vegas, too. She needed to get a job to help support her son. Her husband's family lived in Las Vegas and agreed to help. Since her husband was killed in Afghanistan, his family was eager to have her and her son close by. Everyone said they would pray for her.

The deacons dropped everyone back to the homes where they were staying and returned to the hotel. No one mentioned the confrontation. Once they reached the hotel, Evelyn said good-bye and went to her room. What was going on, what she was missing? Who were these people?

There was a message from Deborah when she got in, so she e-mailed her the information she wanted. Pastor Watson called and asked how everything was going. Not wanting to upset him, she told him everything was fine. After watching TV for a few hours, she finally went to sleep.

Chapter 10

Wednesday was the day of the L.A. concert. She awoke early, had breakfast in her room, and decided to visit a museum and enjoy the day. The hotel phone rang. Cory Williams asked if she'd heard from Jessie or Eric. They hadn't returned to the house where they were staying and he was concerned.

Evelyn's voice started quivering, "Oh my God. Did you call Jessie on his cell phone?"

"Sister Jenkins, I don't know the number and I didn't want to tell Sister Hudson."

She had him hold on as she looked for her cell phone and dialed Jessie's number. He picked up.

"Jessie, where in the hell are you? Why didn't you return to Sister Hudson's house? Cory just called and is worried sick."

"Oh Sister Jenkins," Jessie said, "Girl, we forgot to call Cory, I'm sorry. Cory went back to Mrs. Hudson's early. Adam, her son, invited us to stay at his house. We called Sister Hudson last night but I guess she thought Cory knew. I'll call him so he won't worry. The concert was awesome."

"I'm glad to hear you had a good time, but please talk with Cory. I don't want any problems." She told Cory, who thanked her and apologized for worrying her.

Evelyn sat back in the chair, taking a deep breath to calm down. She was relieved there was no crisis but realized these choir members were not as mature as she had thought. She would have a talk with them before the concert.

She enjoyed the museum and returned to the hotel by mid-afternoon. She met Deacon Jackson in the lobby at four. They picked up Carol, Monique, and Valarie. Deacon Woods left early to get Gwen, Sarah, Diana. Everyone else would be brought to the church at five by their sponsors.

The audio team of the church had the microphones set up. After Jessie had the group practice marching in, they did a final sound check, and then assembled in the choir room to change into their robes. Evelyn pulled Sarah aside to discuss the problem of having her boyfriend on tour. Sarah said they had a fight and she didn't invite him on the tour. He said he wanted to attend the concert. Sarah apologized; it wasn't her intention to cause any trouble. Evelyn felt she was being honest. She realized she couldn't stop him from attending the concert as long as it didn't interfere with the choir. With that, Evelyn was satisfied.

By 6:30, the church started filling up. There was excitement in the air as people greeted each other. Deacon Woods volunteered to sell their CD's in the front of the church before and after the concert. Deacon Jackson was tending to the needs of the choir, getting water and anything else they needed.

As in most black churches, the service didn't start on time. The musicians of Power House Church played while waiting for the praise team to arrive. Finally, at 6:45 they walked in, took their respective microphones, and lined up in front of the pulpit. The young men had on white shirts and black pants. The young ladies wore black and white dresses.

Jessie and the choir were still in the choir room. By the time the praise team finished, the church was almost full. Jessie and the choir were ushered around to the front entrance of the church. They lined up outside the front doors in the foyer.

Older parishioners wore church suits with hats to match. Pastor Osborne and wife wore matching colors. He had a gray suit with gray shoes and tie to match. His shirt was purple. Sister Osborne had a gray suit with purple shoes and blouse. Her hat was a mixture of both colors. She was stunning.

After the praise team finished, Pastor Osborne stood up and shouted, "Isn't God good?" The congregation responded, "All the time," which ignited the congregation. Everyone began clapping and calling "Hallelujah." The musicians began to play upbeat praise tempo. Now everyone was in a celebratory mood. Members were clapping, standing and worshipping. Finally, the music slowed down. Everyone was standing with their hands raised to the sky and singing Hallelujah, Hallelujah. Finally, Pastor Osborne encouraged them to take their seats. He welcomed them to Power House Baptist Church. While everyone was praising God, Eric and Amos exchanged places with the church musicians. Eric sat at the organ. Amos sat at the drums and used his own sticks. Jessie waited at the side entrance to the pulpit.

Pastor Osborne introduced Jessie, the director of the choir. Jessie walked to the pulpit wearing a burgundy suit, white shirt, and tie. With microphone in hand he shouted, "Praise the Lord." Everyone responded "Praise the Lord." He thanked the pastor for allowing them to come and lift up the name of Jesus. He encouraged everyone to buy a CD that would be available for sale after the concert.

He shouted, "Are you ready to give God praise? In unison, the congregation shouted back "Yes." He turned around, raised his hand, and the music began. The lights dimmed and the doors in the back of the church opened. The congregation looked back over their shoulders. Evelyn and the choir members were ready. But for the music, there was no other sound in the building. Jessie lowered his arm and they began marching in. The entire congregation stood up. The music was getting louder. As they neared the pulpit, each one took a microphone. On tour, Jessie led the group the same way Kirk Franklin leads his singers. His energy excited the congregation. "Are you here to praise the Lord?" The audience responded in unison, "Yes!" He turned to Eric, Amos and the church musicians who had agreed to play with them and nodded. Immediately, they played louder: "Worship the Lord, and Praise His Holy Name." The congregation recognized the tune and started clapping.

Evelyn and the choir stood still, mikes in hand, waiting to sing. Jessie kept his back to the audience and the music continued. The audience wanted to hear the choir sing. As always, Jessie made them wait. Jessie turned back around. "Are you sure you came to praise the name of the Lord?" Oh, it was on now. They responded loudly, "Yes!" He turned back around and pointed to the choir. They started singing. Now members were standing up shouting, clapping and moving from side to side.

Cory led the next song with a slower tempo in his clear melodious tones. By the time he finished, some members were shouting and some were crying.

It's customary to take a break and allow the Pastor to have an offering period. After the fourth song, Jessie led the choir back to the choir room.

Pastor Osborne took over the pulpit. "Let's show this choir our appreciation with our offering." Afterwards, he offered prayer and reintroduced Jessie and the choir for the second half of the concert.

They walked behind Jessie and took their places in front of the microphone, singing five more songs. Jessie gave his usual show-stopping performance. The spirit of the Lord was high. The congregation stood, shouting and dancing in the aisles. By the time it was over, everyone was exhausted. Members of the congregation greeted each member of the choir to express their thanks. Deacon Woods sold CD's. Deacon Jackson met with the finance committee to collect the money from the offering.

It took half an hour for everyone to pack up. They assembled in the parking lot and decided to eat at the famous Chicken and Waffle restaurant. As they walked to the vans, a strange man was near. Sarah stopped in her tracks. She ran to his arms. After he kissed her passionately, she turned around, a little embarrassed, "Everyone, this is my fiancé, Gary Stevens."

He was a tall, handsome young Afro-American man in an expensive suit, with diamond studs in both ears, and a tattoo on his left hand. Even standing beside a new Mercedes, he looked out of his environment.

The choir members greeted him. He smiled and complimented them on how well they sang. He said he'd never been to a religious concert before. He then turned to Sarah and whispered something in her ear. Sarah turned to Evelyn and said she was going with Gary and would see them later.

Gwen murmured, "Well I'll be." Diana added, "Well ain't that nothing." Everyone ignored them. Evelyn decided this was not the time to say anything.

In the van, there was a mixture of excitement. They were all pleased with the concert. Deacon Woods told them they sold over 20 CD's and made $300. Gwen was angry. To her, Gary looked like a well-dressed thug. The others ignored her. Eric, the organist, was quiet. When asked, he said he wasn't feeling well.

Jessie said, "I was afraid they were going to just sit and watch, but thank God I was wrong. Man, was I wrong." Everyone laughed.

After an hour and a half enjoying chicken and waffles, they left the restaurant and the deacons took them to their respective homes. They agreed to be ready to leave for Las Vegas at 10:00 in the morning.

Chapter 11

When Evelyn and the two deacons got back at the hotel, they stopped in the lobby. All three agreed it was inappropriate that Sarah had her fiancé drive down to Los Angeles. Deacon Jackson said he was really surprised she would even date that kind of guy. Evelyn was upset because Gary's being there could cause tension among the group. Gwen and Diana had already commented that they would have had their boyfriends join the tour if they had known it was going to be that kind of tour. Evelyn agreed to speak with Sarah the next day.

Eric returned to the house with Jessie and Cory, still complaining that he wasn't feeling well. Thirty minutes later, after everyone else went to bed he walked to the Walgreen's a few blocks away. After buying Tylenol, he was attacked on his way back. He fought as best he could and stumbled back to Sister Hudson's house, his face covered with bruises and with a deep cut on his left arm. Mrs. Hudson called the police while her son Abdullah and Jessie took Eric to the emergency room. The police met him there and took his statement. He was treated for cuts and bruises and released. The police asked him to come to the station the next day to look at mug shots. Eric assured them he didn't see their faces and couldn't recognize them but agreed to come to the police station the next day. Later, Sister Hudson called Evelyn.

Evelyn was sound asleep when the phone rang at two-thirty in the morning. She opened her eyes, looked at the clock and cursed. "What in the hell is going on?" She answered the phone sharply, "Hello!"

"Sister Jenkins, this is Sister Hudson." She sounded upset. Immediately Evelyn switched her tone. "Sister Hudson, What's wrong? "

"I'm afraid we've had a little incident with Eric." She explained to Evelyn what had happened. Eric was OK, barring the stitches.

All the while she was talking Evelyn could feel herself getting angry. "What was he thinking going out at that time of night by himself?" She apologized to Sister Hudson for shouting and for the trouble Eric had caused.

"Sister Jenkins, the main thing is that he's okay. He's at my son's house now with Jessie. The hospital gave him some medication. The police want him to go to the police station in the morning to look at mug shots.

"Sister Hudson, thank you for all your help. We'll be by to pick him up at 8:30. I'm glad you were able to help him. Please tell your son thank you for all his help."

"It's no problem. I've raised two boys so I'm used to emergencies. I didn't even know he left the house until he came back all beat up. Lord knows I'm just glad he didn't get killed."

"Thank God he's all right." They both hung up.

Evelyn dialed Jessie. Eric was all right. "Sister Jenkins, I have never been so scared in my life. He had to have stitches. He says his body hurts but he's alive. I really appreciate Sister Hudson helping. The police took a report and photographs. He said he didn't see their faces. The police took Eric's clothes. They want him to come in to look at pictures."

What did they take? She asked.

"They took his money, the wallet with his debit card and cell phone. He's going to call the bank and my cell phone carrier to let them know what happened. The police said if there is any activity on either one it will help track these guys."

"Oh my goodness," Evelyn said, "Make sure he makes that call. How are you?"

"I'm all right. This is so crazy. I guess we have to wait until Eric is finished at the police station before we leave."

"I'll work this out. Call me if anything else happens. I'll tell the deacons in the morning. We'll pick you up at 8:30."

"O.K. Eric called his parents and told them what happened. They were upset but Eric convinced them he wanted to stay with the tour. They're sending him some money. I just can't believe he would go to the store without telling anyone, as late as it was. Sometimes the boy just don't think right. We'll see you tomorrow. Good night Sister Jenkins."

Evelyn sat back on the bed, took a deep breath, and shook her head. Oh my Lord, this is unbelievable, she thought. Who are these people? She decided to let Deacon Jackson know what happened. Reluctantly, she called his room, knowing it was 3:00 am, but there was no answer. Feeling somewhat relieved because she really didn't want to tell him on the phone, she left a message.

Turning off the light and sliding back under the covers, she tried to relax her mind. How in the world are they going to leave for Las Vegas tomorrow?

Chapter 12

At 6:45 a.m., Evelyn's phone rang again. "Sister Jenkins, this is Pastor Watson. I'm sorry to call you so early." Having slept on and off since talking with Sister Hudson, she was still half asleep. She tried to sound wide awake.

"Good Morning Pastor, How are you?

"Well I'm blessed. Before we go any further, I want to let you know I have Deacon Jackson on the other end with us."

Deacon Jackson said, "Hello." Evelyn was stunned.

Pastor Watson continued, "I received a call from Brother and Sister Parker telling me Eric was mugged."

"I talked to Jessie last night. Eric was asleep."

Deacon Jackson said, "Yes I know," which stunned Evelyn. She didn't know he knew anything about last night since she hadn't told him in her message.

"I wanted to talk to you both and get your opinions. After what has happened, should the group continue with the tour?"

"Pastor, I think if the others agree we should continue" said Deacon Jackson. "I spoke with Eric this morning and he wants to stay. I'll take him to the police station. If he's physically able, I think we should continue. It takes six hours to drive to Las Vegas. We should be there before nightfall. He can rest all day tomorrow."

"Do you agree, Sister Jenkins?"

"Yes, If Eric feels well enough I think we can continue with the tour. We're all staying at the same hotel so we can keep a close eye on him."

"I'm praying for you all. How are the others?"

"As far as I know, Pastor, they're doing really well. The concert was awesome."

"I heard," said Pastor Watson, "Pastor Osborne called me and told me how exceptional the choir sounded. He said you were truly a blessing. I'm sorry this happened and I really need you both to really keep a close eye on the choir. Sister Jenkins, how are the finances?"

"Pastor they are really good. We made $300 in sales alone for the CD's. I so glad you suggested selling them."

"I'm praying we won't have any other problems." Pastor Watson prayed and ended the call.

Evelyn immediately received a call from Deacon Jackson, who apologized for not answering the phone when she called earlier. Jessie had called and told him what happened. Deacon Woods agreed to drive the choir members to Las Vegas. The luggage and garment bags would be placed in Deacon Jackson's van and he would drive Jessie and Eric to the police station. Evelyn said she'd ride with Brother Jackson too.

The rest of the choir was shocked when they heard about Eric.

Gwen, Diana, and Sarah were the last members to be picked up. They were all exceptionally quiet, especially Sarah.

She was wearing large sunglasses and avoiding eye contact. Sarah never said a word about her evening or her fiancé. Evelyn had wanted to pull her aside but she didn't want to make a scene. Evelyn hoped Gwen hadn't caused any problems.

Choir members rode with Deacon Woods. At 10:30, the choir left for Las Vegas.

Meantime, Evelyn, Eric, Jessie, and Deacon Jackson drove to the police station. The police hadn't received the surveillance tape from Walgreen's but they completed the paperwork. Eric insisted he couldn't identify the criminals; he didn't see their faces. They were finished by noon.

During the drive to Las Vegas, Eric revealed to them he was gay. Evelyn told him that it really didn't matter to her or anybody else, but privately she wondered if Jessie might be involved with him.

By 7:30, they had arrived in Las Vegas. The other choir members met them in the lobby to get their luggage. Gary Stevens appeared in the lobby too. Unbeknownst to them, he had followed Deacon Woods' van to Las Vegas. Sarah was shocked to see him. Gary wasn't supposed to be on this tour. He hadn't asked their permission to tag along. His presence was awkward and disrespectful.

Evelyn pulled Sarah aside and asked her why Gary was in Las Vegas. She apologized. She said she asked him not to come but he insisted. Both Deacon Jackson and Deacon Woods pulled Gary aside to ask why he was following them. Gary said he wanted to attend the concert in Las Vegas and wouldn't be any trouble. They knew he had a right to do what he wanted but they didn't want any trouble. Gary assured them he made a reservation on his own and would not be disruptive. Gwen commented again that if she knew this was going to be that kind of tour she would have asked her boyfriend to come too. Sarah apologized to everyone and told them she was keeping the room arrangements as planned. Gary said he was only staying until after the concert. Gwen, Diana, and Sarah proceeded to their room. Deacon Woods pulled the young men aside and told them to take care not to get in any dangerous situations.

Everyone went to their respective rooms. Just as Evelyn was unpacking, Jessie called. "Hello Sister Jenkins." Evelyn sat on the bed prepared to have a long conversation. "Hello Jessie. What's happening?"

"I know you're mad as hell. You know I've known Sarah for a while. I just can't believe she picked that jerk to marry. You know he don't go to church and I think he's into drugs."

"Really?"

"Maybe he enjoyed the concert so much he'll want to be saved; it wouldn't be the first time. You know we haven't had time to talk.

"Jessie, I know this is my first concert but you were amazing. I've always been impressed at how you are at our church but you are awesome. I didn't know you could move the service like that. You are a very talented young man."

"Thanks Sister Jenkins, from you that means a lot. What's going on with Monique and Gwen? You know everybody heard them arguing after rehearsal. I hate that Gwen is always causing problems.

"I don't know what happened. I didn't realize everyone heard them. I may have to intervene if it affects the choir.

"Girl, I told you she's been like that for years. Can you believe Monique's transformation? I didn't want to make a big deal about it but she looks hot. I think Gwen is jealous. By the way, if you haven't noticed, I think Alex is really attracted to Monique so don't be surprised if you see them going out together."

"Really? I could see them together."

"Yes, but I don't want no hanky panky on this tour. It's bad enough Sarah's boyfriend is here. How is Eric doing?"

"He's going to stay in and sleep."

"Well, I'm going to take a hot shower and go to bed."

"I'm hitting the streets, Girl; you know we're in Las Vegas. I got to get my grove on. Have a good evening."

"You too, Jessie. Please be safe."

Since it wasn't too late, she decided to call Deborah at home. She answered on the second ring. Evelyn took a breath, and told her everything that had happened. It was good to talk to someone who wasn't in the church.

Deborah answered with, "Are you kidding me? What was he thinking? This is the guy that plays the organ right?"

"Yes, and I thought he was mature. Then for some reason he tells me he's gay which didn't make any sense to me at all. Maybe they beat him up because he's gay."

"Well, you be careful. "

"I'm going to bed. I'll call you tomorrow."

"O.K. boss lady. Take care."

Chapter 13

Evelyn woke up Friday morning still tired. These people were exhausting. The phone rang. She turned over to answer.

It was Valarie speaking in a whisper. In a soft voice she said, "Sister Jenkins, I really need to talk to you privately."

"Is something wrong?"

"I really would like to talk with you in private, if you don't mind."

"Certainly, let's get together after breakfast. We can talk in my room."

Valarie agreed and hung up.

Evelyn lay back on the pillow. Now what? Thinking back over the last few days, she realized that Valarie had been very quiet. I hope Gwen hasn't been acting her usual ugly self.

I'm really starting to get tired of this tour, she thought. They act like children.

Evelyn made up her mind that at breakfast she was going to have a serious talk with the choir. This tour was not hard. All they needed to do was act like Christian adults. If they didn't get it together, she was going to suggest the tour end in Las Vegas. Her phone rang again.

"Sister Jenkins, this is Sarah. I know it's early but I really need to talk to you. Can I come to your room? I'll bring coffee." Evelyn was annoyed but curious, so she agreed.

Evelyn put a robe on, brushed her teeth, and combed her hair. She was trying to straighten the room as best she could when she hear a soft knock.

Opening the door, Evelyn was aware Sarah was still wearing the clothes she had on last night. She had dark glasses on. Her face looked swollen. Sarah hurried into the room carrying a purse and coffee, as if someone was following her. Evelyn closed the door and locked it.

Evelyn smiled, trying to calm Sarah. "Please sit down."

Sarah handed her a coffee and took a deep breath. "Sister Jenkins, I really hate to bother you but I feel I can talk to you. I'm having problems with my boyfriend."

So—Sarah had downgraded the relationship from fiancé to boyfriend.

"Thank you for the coffee." Evelyn sat on the end of the bed. Sarah slowly sank into the chair.

"I'm sorry to hear that. What kind of problem are you having?" The room was silent and slowly Sarah took a deep breath, put her hands on the sunglasses, and took them off.

Evelyn gasped. Sarah's left eye was bruised and bloody. Her right eye was blackened and swollen. Before she could compose herself, Evelyn stood up and shouted, "What the hell?" Flinching, Sarah started to cry. Realizing she probably scared the girl; Evelyn went to her and put her arms around her to comfort her.

Evelyn said, "I'm so sorry I didn't mean to react like that but who did this?"

Sarah was crying so hard it took her a few minutes to compose herself. Finally she said, "Sister Jenkins, my boyfriend and I had a terrible fight. He didn't want me to go on this tour in the first place. When he showed up after the L.A. concert, we got in his rental car and went out to eat. Gary's really jealous. He started accusing me of flirting. We got into an argument and I told him I couldn't take it anymore. So, I was shocked to see him last night here in Las Vegas. After we went to dinner last night, he started punching me. I got out the car in the middle of the street and ran. I couldn't go to my room so I wondered around all night in the casinos so he couldn't find me. I'm so scared." She lifted her shirt. There were bruises on her arm and stomach.

Evelyn was shaking with rage. "Where is he now?"

Sarah was trembling said "I don't know if he's in the hotel or not. I really don't want Gwen and Diana to see me like this. I even stayed in the women's bathroom. Diana called me on my cell and said he kept calling the room asking for me."

"I think you need medical attention." Sarah hastily said she'd rather not. Evelyn gave her Tylenol and convinced her to let her take pictures of the injuries. Evelyn suggested she shower and get cleaned up. She needed time to think. Her first thought was to call the police. Instead, she decided to discuss this with Deacon Jackson. This was way beyond her control.

Hearing the shower, she took her cell phone and walked out of the room. Standing in the hall, she called Deacon Jackson. She explained the problem with Sarah.

"Sister Jenkins," he said, "what the hell is going on?" He too was shocked. It took him a while to speak finally he said, "I'll call Pastor Watson and let him know. Is her boyfriend still here?" Evelyn said she didn't know. "If she was my daughter I'd find him and beat the hell out of him. Oh Lord," he said. "We just dealt with the police in Los Angeles and now Las Vegas. I think we just need to go back to Oakland 'cause this is just crazy."

Evelyn agreed. Deacon Jackson said he would call Pastor Watson and let him know what was happening.

Evelyn was back in her room before Sarah came out of the bathroom. She was sitting on the unmade bed when the bathroom door opened. Sarah was still crying. Evelyn took more pictures of her bruises and tried to comfort her. She asked her to call and have Diana bring her a change of clothes but not to tell her why. Fifteen minutes later Diana knocked on the door.

Opening the door a few inches, Evelyn said, "Hi Diana. I'll take those," as she reached for the luggage bag.

"What's going on?" Diana stretched her neck trying to get a peek inside. Evelyn continued to block the door.

"Sarah had a little accident, but she'll be fine."

"You know she didn't come back to the room last night so Gwen and I were wondering if she stayed in the room with her boyfriend.

"She's here with me. Thank you again and I'll see you downstairs for breakfast."

Reluctantly, Diana handed the bag to Evelyn, turned, and left.

Evelyn ordered breakfast. She let Sarah take a nap on the second bed. It would give her a few hours' sleep before meeting the others. She knew this incident should be reported to the police.

Deacon Jackson called to say he'd left a message for Pastor Watson. He asked Evelyn if he should take Sarah to the hospital but she told him no.

Chapter 15

Fifteen minutes before the housekeeper discovered a body, the choir members were standing outside enjoying the warm weather, talking, and laughing. Evelyn and the others had been waiting there at least twenty minutes. Sarah had put enough makeup on to cover the bruises. She still had on her sunglasses. They all agreed to go out to lunch together, but someone was missing.

Evelyn volunteered to go upstairs and see what was holding up the last person. She took the first elevator up and pushed the button for the twelfth floor. By the time, Evelyn reached it; the terrified housekeeper had already taken the elevator down to the lobby. A few guests were talking in the hallway. Several were standing in front of the maid's cart. Evelyn hurried toward Room 1205, expecting to walk past them.

The door of room 1205 was open. No one told her what was wrong but someone said she shouldn't go in the room. Disregarding what she heard, she walked around the cart past two of the guests who looked at her in disbelief. Evelyn walked in anyway. The drapes were still drawn. As she passed the bathroom, she called out, "Deacon Woods?" Evelyn was angry so she rushed into the room still puzzled as to why people were standing outside the door. She stopped in her tracks when she saw the gruesome scene. Lying on the bed was Deacon Woods' nude body. The bedcovers were thrown back halfway across the body. Dried blood was splattered on the wall, the ceiling, headboard and the carpet nearby.

Evelyn screamed. She couldn't move. She just stood there and screamed. A knife was sticking out of the back of his neck. His head was turned to the side. His eyes were open. The mattress was soaked with blood. Blood had run down his left arm over his watch. There was a pool of dried blood on the carpet under the arm. On the floor was a pile of clothes.

One of the guests from the hallway came in to comfort her. Guests from adjacent rooms were coming out into the hall to see what was happening. Evelyn ran out of the room into the arms of another male guest. She leaned on his shoulders, sobbing uncontrollably. She was shaking. She'd seen dead bodies before but not like this. Evelyn started moaning, "Oh my God, oh my God." The man asked her if she knew the person and she replied, "Yes."

"The police are on their way," said the women from the room across from Room 1205.

Evelyn was still weeping and shaking. "Deacon Woods' been murdered" she shouted. "Murdered, call the police!" They assured her the police had been called.

Other guests standing in the hall gasped when they heard the word "murder." They moved away from the door and started congregating down the hall sharing what they had heard. The man that had ushered her out of the room walked out behind her.

His wife put her arms around Evelyn. "I'm so sorry your friend is dead."

Evelyn was shaking; her legs were getting weak. "Why don't you sit down in our room to wait? I'm sure the police will be here soon." She gently nudged Evelyn toward their room. Dazed, Evelyn sat down.

"Would you like a glass of water?"

Evelyn moved her head up and down responding with a "Yes." So many thoughts were running through her head. "Oh God! Oh God!" "Who could have killed him?" The woman handed her a glass of water.

Evelyn didn't realize she was still crying until she looked down and saw her chest was wet from tears. There she was in a hotel room with strangers watching her and waiting for the police to lock her up.

"Who would do this?" she spoke aloud.

"We just checked in."

Evelyn sat thinking. A stranger must have killed Deacon Woods. She surmised this was a robbery or an attempted one.

Evelyn was starting to compose herself. She saw that the doors of both hotel rooms were still open. The couple was now standing in a corner of the room looking at her suspiciously. Evelyn decided to wait outside in the hall for the police. They could be the killers.

Evelyn thanked them for their help and headed for the door.

She turned to them and said "I'll wait for the police in the hall." With frightened looks on their faces, they agreed. They both had started thinking that Evelyn could be the killer and were relieved when she volunteered to leave the room. As soon as the door closed, they locked it immediately. Several people were standing in the hall but nobody wanted to talk to her. They were standing far away from Room 1205. She stood alone.

Fumbling through her purse, she found her cell phone. She called Deacon Jackson but his phone went to voicemail. She called Pastor Watson but no one answered. She left a message on both phones asking them to return her call immediately. The initial shock was starting to wear off.

This was murder. She'd been a strong woman all her life. She took a deep breath and noticed that none of the other guests were near her. Her legs were trembling. She knew more than the police about Deacon Woods. If anyone could solve this crime, she decided it was her. Evelyn knew a little about procedures and what to expect. She had helped her brother Charles study for his police exams. Maybe some of that stuff could help her figure out who killed Deacon Woods. Staying outside of the room was the best she could do for now. She hadn't touched anything in the room. The door was already open.

But if she was going to solve this crime, she would have to go back in the room. She needed to really see what was in there. As scared as she was, Evelyn decided to go back in the room to get a mental picture of what it looked like. First, she fumbled through her purse and found a notebook and pen. She didn't trust her memory.

No one was near her so she took a deep breath and walked back into the room. She took a good look around. With cell phone in hand, she realized she could take pictures, so she did.

She could smell a foul odor of liquor and decomposition. That had to be because the room was hot. The body was face down. It was a vicious attack. Dried blood was on the ceiling, headboard, and the nightstand all over the top part of the bed. Looking around, she noticed something on the night stand, a wallet, keys, and a half-opened bottle of scotch. Oh my, she thought, I didn't know Deacon Woods drank. She took a picture. She had seen dead bodies before, but nothing like this. Looking at the clothes on the floor, she saw a shirt and a pair of pants. The bulge in the pants' back pocket looked like another wallet. Why would he have two wallets? This couldn't be a robbery. She had the tour money. Maybe he used one for personal use and one for church money.

She walked out of the room, automatically turning the light off. Instantly she realized her fingerprints would be found on the light switch. Evelyn hastily found a Kleenex, wiped the light switch and put it back in her purse. Evelyn didn't know what to look for but she started taking notes of what she had seen.

The choir is going to freak out, she thought. Of all the times, nobody calls me back. This is unbelievable. His wife will be out of her mind when she hears of this. Who did this? Should she go down to the lobby or wait here for the police. We just got here, why would anybody kill Deacon Woods? This must be a case of mistaken identity.

Her mind raced. Could one of the choir members have done this? After all, she really didn't know any of them well. If she could remember everything that happened in the last few days, maybe she could at least exclude some of them as killers. No one had shown any hostility toward each other that could culminate in murder. She had to look at this tour from a police perspective.

What confused her was the liquor. Maybe the killer brought it? It certainly couldn't be Deacon Woods. She just couldn't imagine choir members drinking but maybe they do. Somebody must have followed him back to the hotel and killed him.

Down in the lobby, Gwen was complaining loudly. "What is going on? Where are Sister Jenkins and Deacon Woods? I'm tired of waiting." Quietly, the others were also getting annoyed too. Then the real commotion started.

Chapter 16

Still yelling, the housekeeper sped past her cart to the elevator with her arms in the air. Guests peered out of their rooms into the hall. As she passed them, most ran back inside and locked the doors.

People started calling the hotel operator. "Talk slowly," she said. But most of them were incoherent. It was something about a maid who was running screaming down the hall of the twelfth floor. The operator transferred the calls to the police dispatcher. After all, they could be talking about a bomb and she wasn't taking any chances.

A 911 operator received a call from a guest who said a maid was screaming down the hall of her hotel and no one knew what she was saying. Another 911 operator took a call from the same hotel, saying a maid had found a dead body in a room. A front desk clerk received still another 911 call. All of these calls were transferred to the police dispatcher. He issued an all-points bulletin directing officers, a SWAT team, and emergency vehicles to proceed to the hotel immediately. It was clear something devastating had occurred and he wasn't taking any chances, especially not after 9/11.

Hysterically pressing the down button of the elevator, the maid looked back to see if anyone was following her. It took only seconds for the elevator to come, but it seemed liked hours. She ran inside and pushed the button several times for the ground floor, her fingers shaking. She had never seen a dead body, never.

The elevator opened into the lobby and the still screaming housekeeper ran toward the front desk. Everybody in the lobby turned to see what was happening. The only person who seemed to know what she was saying was a desk clerk who spoke Spanish. Her eyes went wild when she saw the housekeeper running toward her. She dropped the papers she was holding and responded in Spanish, "What are you talking about?" "Asesinato, asesinato en sala 1205."

"Murder, murder in room 1205," the clerk turned to the manager and whispered what she had heard. He froze then told another clerk to call 911. Some of the people around them overheard and looked around. "What happened?" "What's going on?" "What's she talking about?" No one answered. The trembling housekeeper was murmuring to herself in Spanish and making the sign of the cross over and over. The desk clerk walked around the counter and put her arms around her trying to comfort her. She led the maid around the counter and escorted her to the back room. In the background, approaching police sirens screamed. People started to panic and headed out of the lobby. Some grabbed their luggage and headed for the front door. Others were crowding into elevators or rushing into the casino. No one wanted to get involved.

Those that remained in the lobby were murmuring and trying to determine what was happening. Some of the guests who had heard that the 911 operator was called started sharing the story about the maid.

Jessie and the others were still standing outside. Choir members were starting to get worried. Evelyn still hadn't come back down. Jessie called Evelyn's cell phone but it went to voice mail. He walked inside to a row of hotel phones and dialed 1205 but there was no answer. He told the others, "This don't make sense, where could they be?"

Suddenly police vehicles were storming the hotel. It felt like an invasion. SWAT police ran from a truck toward them with guns drawn. More were now stationed at hotel exits. Some choir members rushed back inside. Others were stopped and ushered back inside by uniformed officers. No one was permitted to leave.

The choir members were dumbfounded. Yellow tape was going up around the pillars. The police directed them to stand in an area near the lobby door. They looked at each other in horror. No one was permitted to leave. Every officer was on high alert not knowing what to expect.

Chapter 17

As soon as the police entered the hotel, the manager raced toward them explaining what had happened. He escorted the captain to the back room where the housekeeper was sitting, rocking her body back and forth. She told them what she had seen.

The captain left the office and directed his men to keep the exits blocked until further notice. He and several other officers along with the SWAT team members got on the elevators and went up to the twelfth floor. The other elevators were shut down and returned to the lobby. Some officers took the stairs and were told to bring anyone they found down to the lobby.

On the twelfth floor, some hotel guests stood waiting by the elevators. When an elevator opened and they saw the police, guns drawn, some started telling them about the maid. Without stopping, police directed them to go back to their rooms and remain inside.

Now the only person standing in the hall was Evelyn. Seeing them scared her. She couldn't move a muscle. She was standing in front of room 1205, the crime scene and knew that didn't look good. They rushed toward her with guns drawn. Several voices shouted to her, "Put your hands up." Afraid she would be shot; Evelyn dropped her purse and put her hands in the air as ordered. The first officer grabbed her arms, forced them behind her body, shoved her face first against the wall, and handcuffed her. She could hear running and heard men's voices. Her heart was beating fast. She started sweating. She was surrounded by men with guns.

As they patted her down, somebody yelled at her, "Who are you?"

"Evelyn Jenkins," she said. An officer entered the room and yelled, "There's a body in here, Captain." He immediately looked at Evelyn. She was the number one suspect. Too scared to say anything she waited for the police to speak.

"What are you doing here?" Evelyn explained she was the tour coordinator and that she knew the deceased. Evelyn said she found the body, but the police knew the maid had reported the murder. After searching her purse, the captain had her taken, in handcuffs, down to the lobby. He stationed an officer at the door of 1205 and two on either end of the hall, and then called his superior.

The captain reported that there was a murder and that a suspect was in custody. He was told to keep the hotel secure. Homicide detectives were in route. Evelyn was rushed to the elevator by six gun-toting officers followed by the police captain. They proceeded down to the lobby.

By now, Evelyn was shaking uncontrollably. No one said a word. She was seriously regretting her decision to wait for the police in front of the room. Oh, God! What had she been thinking?

Homicide Detective Washington took the call. He was told about the multiple 911 calls and the possibility of a murdered guest at the Circus Circus Hotel. Details were sketchy. His boss, Lieutenant Dan Sayers, made Washington the primary investigator. Sayers, a tall stocky 60-year-old, walked with a slight limp from a gunshot wound he had sustained when he was a detective. He was a hard guy to please but, for some reason, he and Washington got along. Both were short tempered but committed to solving crimes. Detective Washington's partner, Hamilton, on the other hand, was more of a people person. He could get a guy to confess just by acting like he was his friend. Together they made a great team. Sayers knew if anybody could solve this case, they could. Washington and Hamilton headed for the hotel.

Washington, a 45-year-old tall, thin Caucasian with short auburn hair and a mustache, had been on the job for over 20 years. He was dressed neatly in a suit. His partner, 30 year old Henry Hamilton, was a tall Afro-American, with an upper body sculpted by extensive exercise. In the office he was known as "GQ man" because he always sported a fine tailored suit. Hamilton had transferred to Homicide 7 years earlier. Together, they looked more like businessmen than police officers. They took turns being the primary investigator. They were so close they could almost tell what the other one was thinking.

Chapter 18

When detectives Washington and Hamilton arrived at the hotel, it was still on lockdown. As they walked into the lobby, the elevators were headed back down to the lobby with a suspect.

The manager was frantically trying to calm the guests but they weren't having it. Anger was erupting, including among the choir members.

Washington spoke loudly to get their attention. "Ladies and gentlemen, we apologize for the inconvenience but there has been an incident in the hotel and we need your cooperation."

People were still murmuring. Somebody yelled, "What's going on? Are we in danger?"

"Not at this time. Please continue to be patient and we will have you on your way real soon."

That really didn't help but he asked two officers to line the guests up and get their ID information, including names, addresses, phone numbers and driver's license. He also told them to get the hotel room that they stayed in. As he turned to speak with his partner, one of the elevator doors opened and there stood police with Evelyn in handcuffs.

Choir members were still huddled together trying to determine what was going on. Some were facing the window looking at the officers with guns blocking the entrance. Others were facing the elevators. Gwen noticed the bruising and black eye on Sarah. She asked her,

"Sarah, what the hell happened to you? You look like somebody beat the hell out of you." Embarrassed, Sarah started to answer, but just then the elevator doors opened. There was Evelyn in handcuffs surrounded by police officers. Jessie shouted, "Evelyn, oh my God, what's going on?" He wanted to run toward her but decided not to.

She tried to shrug her shoulders but the police were holding her too tight. They blocked her view of the rest of the choir.

Hamilton heard the shout, turned, and walked toward the group. These must be the choir members Evelyn had told the captain about. He knew they might have some information pertinent to resolving this murder.

Now almost everyone in the lobby was staring at the choir. Valarie, Monique, and Sarah started crying. Randy and Alex were trying to comfort them. Deacon Jackson started toward Evelyn but was stopped by Hamilton.

By now, the captain had come downstairs and was talking to Washington. Once their conversation was finished, Washington walked toward Evelyn.

As the police officer suddenly moved aside, there stood a tall man in a suit and tie facing her with a stern look on his face. "Ms. Jenkins, my name is Detective Washington. Why were you standing in from of Room 1205?

Evelyn was really worried and knew she'd better start talking fast. She took a deep breath, cleared her throat and said, "I was waiting for the police. Me and the other choir members had been waiting down here for over 20 minutes. The victim is a Deacon at my church. He was late coming down for breakfast. After waiting and he didn't call, I decided to go up to his room and that's when I found other people standing in the hall. The door was open and Deacon Woods was dead."

Washington wrote down something in his notebook then looked down at her and asked, "What friends are you talking about?" Evelyn couldn't point with her hands behind her so she nodded toward where the choir was standing. He turned around and looked toward where a group of Afro-Americans were standing. "When did you go upstairs?"

"It was about 15 maybe 20 minutes ago. Please, please, I didn't kill anyone; please take these handcuffs off?" After he finished writing he put his hand up and said "Give me a minute."

When Detective Hamilton approached the choir members, they all started talking at the same time. Gwen said, "What the hell is going on?" Deacon Jackson asked, "Why do you have Evelyn in handcuffs?"

Hamilton interrupted and asked who they were. Deacon Jackson said, "We're a choir. We're on tour from Gabriel Missionary Baptist Church in Oakland."

Jessie said, "What's happening, we haven't did anything. Why are you treating Evelyn like a criminal? Why is she in handcuffs?"

No way was Hamilton going to tell them about the murder, so he said; "I assure you all your questions will be answered. For now we're trying to investigate what has happened." They didn't like the answer, but they realized there was nothing they could do about it. Hamilton asked each one for their ID and told them something very serious happened in the hotel. As an experienced police officer, he realized anyone of them could be a suspect. For their protection, he said, police needed to search their rooms. They didn't like the idea but when Deacon Jackson said yes before consulting with the others, it forced the others to agree or look suspicious. After all, he was in charge and didn't believe they had anything to hide.

Hamilton turned to the others and asked, "Do you all agree?" Scared to say no they nodded approval.

A police officer collected their room keys and told them to stay where they were. As Hamilton walked back toward his partner, Washington met him in the middle of the lobby, where they could speak alone. He updated Washington on what he had learned from the group. They spoke for a few minutes and agreed Evelyn was probably telling the truth, but they decided to take her to police headquarters to question her further. Washington walked back to Evelyn and told the police officers to take the handcuffs off. Hamilton walked back to the choir members.

"Ms. Jenkins," Washington said, "I apologize for the inconvenience. But, as you know, this is a serious matter so I'm asking you not to speak with the other members about the murder."

Her hands were freed, but Evelyn didn't like this at all. A black woman in handcuffs was not how she wanted people to remember her, even strangers. Now everyone in the lobby thought she was a criminal. She was totally embarrassed and angry but knew the most important thing was to find the killer so she agreed.

"We need a statement from you," he continued. "This police officer will escort you to the police station."

The same police officer who was strong-arming her now had a calmer look on his face as was handing her the purse. Evelyn took it and said, "I don't know anything. Can I please talk to my friends?"

Washington said, "I assure you I will let you talk to them but right now this is a police investigation and I need your cooperation so we can find out who murdered your friend." His voice was sympathetic but firm, which calmed her down. She agreed to do all she could to help with the investigation.

"Thank you, Ms. Jenkins," he said with a half smile. "I really appreciate your cooperation and I am truly sorry for the way you were treated. I'm also sorry for your loss."

Evelyn tried to give a slight smile at the choir to assure them she wasn't guilty of anything but stupidity. She thought to herself, I really should have stayed in the room with that couple. It was too late now as she turned and followed the two police officers.

Washington walked toward his partner and the choir members, trying to decide what he was going to say to them. Just as he reached them, Jessie walked past the others and asked, "Why did you arrest Sister Jenkins?"

Washington stayed quiet, watching. Hamilton tried to calm them down. He continued, "First, Ms. Jenkins is not under arrest. As I told you, we have a very serious problem and need your help. Ms. Jenkins has agreed to go to the police station and we would like you all to accompany her. I assure you this won't take long."

Deacon Jackson said, "I don't know what information you want. Do we all need to go?"

"Yes, I'm afraid so. You can see with all the police around here we have a serious matter to deal with. You may know something that will help us resolve this problem. Thank you for allowing us to search your rooms. Once we get to the station, I'll be able to explain everything. You ID's and room keys will be returned to you there. I know this is an unusual request but believe me this for your safety. You are not under arrest. We just need to talk to you."

Since he was an Afro-American, they felt a little more trust in what he was saying. "Again, I apologize," Hamilton added. "We thought Ms. Jenkins might be involved but I can assure you she's not under arrest. We just need a statement from her so she's volunteered to go to the police station and answer some questions."

He continued, "Now I understand you all were down here waiting on another member of the group?" Most of them nodded yes.

Deacon Jackson said, "Yes we're waiting on Deacon Woods."

"Is he the only member not present?"

"No. Eric Parker is in his room but he's not going with us. Carol White went on a job interview. Those are the only choir members missing. Can I leave a message for Deacon Woods, Carol, and Eric, so they'll know where we are?"

Not wanting to alarm them, Hamilton said, "We'll get in touch with them and let them know where you are."

Diana said, "Why are you so concerned about us?" "There are lots of people in this lobby, why are you focused on us? Is it because we're black?"

Detective Hamilton responded sharply. "No! That's not the reason. We believe you can help clear up this matter. That's all I can tell you right now but I assure you it won't take too long."

Once they were told where Evelyn went, they agreed to go. They didn't understand what was happening. They were convinced Deacon Woods just decided not to join them.

Evelyn was standing near the elevators waiting. Washington walked over to her. "Ms. Jenkins do you have a home phone number for Deacon Woods?" "Yes, I also have a phone number for our Pastor. I left a message with him earlier. Do you need the phone number of Carol? She had an interview this morning and won't know where we are." The numbers were given to Washington.

Evelyn was escorted to the garage and placed in the back of an unmarked police car with tinted windows. How humiliating. People had been looking at her like she was a criminal. When the door closed, she realized there were no handles on the inside of the doors. B bars separated the front seat from the backseat and it smelled bad, really bad. Never in her wildest dream could she have pictured herself in a police car, let alone a suspect in a murder. She found her cell phone in her purse and dialed Pastor Watson's number again. Again it went to voice mail. She wanted to call Deacon Jackson but decided against it.

The police officers went back inside. Police were everywhere. Luckily they had left the windows open a little bit. It was hot. She wanted to cry but all she could think about was who killed Deacon Woods? Her mind started racing back to

Monday, the day they left. She tried to think of the whole day. Did she miss any signs of disagreement that might point to this?

Suddenly she realized how stressed she was. Sweat was running down her arms. All the while her brain was trying to comprehend murder. How can this be happening? Murder, that's the word she couldn't get out of her brain. This can't be happening, she thought. Nobody gets murdered on a gospel tour. We're all Christians. Christians don't murder Christians.

Monday, she kept thinking about Monday. She had made the sleeping assignments. There wasn't any friction or arguments between the choir members. In fact, everyone seemed to enjoy their room assignments, even Gwen. She didn't want to believe a member of the choir might be a killer. A stranger must have killed him, a sick crazy stranger. After all this is Las Vegas, she thought.

This was a horrifying brutal and personal murder. She remembered her brother telling her some of the procedures police use when there's a crime. Divide and separate. Now she could understand why the police didn't want her to tell the choir about the murder. She had been relieved because she wouldn't know what to say. Maybe someone saw something but didn't realize it. Yes, that had to be it.

It seemed like an eternity before plainclothes officers opened the door and entered the car. They tried to sound friendly when they told her they were going to police headquarters. As the car drove up the incline from the garage, the sun burst in the car, blocking her view. A mob of media reporters and camera people ran toward the car. She held back a scream as the officers assured her she was safe. No one could see inside the car because of the tinted windows. .

As the car passed the lobby, she noticed the choir wasn't there anymore. Now she was really scared. The ride to the police station was in complete silence. The knot in her stomach hurt.

She decided to try and think like the police. Her thoughts drifted back to Tuesday. She had been troubled by what happened between Gwen and Monique. She made a note to find out what the argument was about. Suddenly the reality of her situation rushed back. Evelyn was angry. Angry that Pastor Watson hadn't returned her call. She felt absolutely alone. She wanted to call her mother but decided not to alarm her. She should be back at the hotel in a few hours.

Chapter 19

Having made arrangements for the choir to be taken to the police station in a hotel limo, the detectives were on their way to Room 1205 when Washington's cell phone rang. His "Why was the hotel still on lockdown," his boss yelled. He was getting heat from the mayor. Washington gave him a quick update. His boss strongly encouraged him to quickly find out what happened. A spokesperson from the Media Relations Department had been sent to the hotel to speak with the press.

The police had an advantage, since the choir hadn't been told about the murder. They could still interview the choir members separately. And for legal purposes, Hamilton had obtained signed permission slips from the choir to search their rooms.

The elevator opened onto the twelfth floor. Both detectives walked past the uniformed officers toward the housekeeper's cart and Room 1205.

Both put on protective boots and gloves. First, they examined the door lock. There was no sign of forced entry. The EMT's were leaving. They confirmed that the victim was dead on arrival and the body was still in rigor, meaning the guy had been dead less than twelve hours. The coroner and criminal investigative technicians were on their way.

Washington and Hamilton continued inside the room. They observed the dirty towels in the bathroom. Continuing into the room, they smelled liquor as well as decomposition. They stood at the end of the bed looking at the body. Both took notes. Hamilton went into the bathroom to see what evidence he could find. A bag with men's toiletries was on the counter. Nothing appeared out of the ordinary. Hamilton snapped some pictures and then rejoined Washington in the bedroom. Even though the forensics team took pictures, Washington and Hamilton always took their own. That way they wouldn't have to wait for the forensic pictures.

Silently, they stood at the end of the bed contemplating the crime. The knife sticking out of the nude victim's neck looked like a steak knife.

The partners liked to bounce ideas off each other to make sense of the crime. They were coming to the conclusion that this was a crime of passion. The killer could be a woman or man. This crime didn't appear to have anything to do with a terrorist plot. Walking out of the room, Washington called his boss and explained their finds. Washington also told him they didn't believe it was a robbery especially since the victim still had his watch on and there was a wallet on the night stand. They would wait until the coroner arrived along with the crime scene investigators to complete processing the room.

Washington called the captain in the lobby to make sure they questioned everyone and obtained ID information. He also needed to detain any guests who were on the twelfth floor and bring them to police headquarters. They needed to find a witness who may have seen something suspicious. If no one had any information, they were to be released but ID information was to be obtained.

The SWAT team was told to stand down and return to headquarters. Within 30 minutes only uniformed officers were left in the lobby, with no need for guns drawn.

All the choir members had been herded into the hotel limo, with doors locked. They were frightened, embarrassed, confused, and bewildered. A few were looking around for Deacon Woods. There was still no answer from his room, Jessie said. In the confusion, none of them had checked their cell phones for messages. Now they were sitting in a stretch limo with no indication why.

At first, there was complete silence. Everyone was in a daze. Valarie started crying. She just met these people and felt alienated, scared. Monique tried to console her. Alex was trying to console Monique, having begun to feel protective of her. Everyone started talking. They weren't just scared, they were terrified. Cory, one of the youngest of the group, announced he wanted to call his parents.

Sarah agreed. But Deacon Jackson interrupted her. They shouldn't alarm their families unless it was absolutely necessary. "I know we are all confused and scared but let's find out what's going on before panicking. After all,' he continued, "they said Sister Jenkins is not under arrest so maybe it's just a mistake. Perhaps we can provide information to them that will help with whatever they are trying to resolve." They started thinking about what Deacon Jackson said but they were still scared.

Gwen said, "I'm telling you Deacon Jackson, if we're not back there in a few hours, I'm going to cause all kinds of hell."

After a few minutes of deliberating, Cory said, "I really don't want to worry my parents, if there's nothing to be worried about. I'll wait until we find out what's going on before calling them."

The choir members held hands and prayed, asking God to quickly resolve this matter. Everyone felt renewed home that they'd be back on tour in a few hours.

Meanwhile in Room 1407, someone banged on the door. Eric was sleeping and jumped up, startled. He ran to open the door and found police staring at him.

Detective Hamilton asked, "Is your name Eric Parker?" He nodded. "Mr. Parker, how long have you been in your room?" Eric told them he hadn't left since checking in the night before.

"What's goin' on?" The police were moving toward him so he backed up. The silent uniformed officers stood blocking the door. Hamilton kept moving toward him and, intimidated, Eric kept backing up to the middle of the room. "I'm sharing the room with Cory Williams; he can tell you I was here."

"Why, what's going on?" Noticing bruises on his body, Detective Hamilton became suspicious. One side of the room was in an upheaval. He walked to the bathroom and saw that only one set of towels were used.

Walking back into the room he said, "Well there's been a serious incident in the hotel and we need you to come to the police station."

""Are you talking about the guys that mugged me?" he asked. Hamilton immediately became suspicious, "What mugging?"

"Listen, I'm on tour with my choir. We just got here. I haven't left this room since we got here yesterday."

"We're here about a situation that happened in this hotel. The other members of your group are on their way to police headquarters for questioning. Please get dressed and come with us."

Why would the police want the whole choir to go to the police station? The detectives left the room. Too scared to argue, he dressed as two uniformed officers waited. They used the freight elevator to escort him to the garage, where he was placed in a police car and driven to the police station. Eric was sweating profusely.

Chapter 20

Waiting for the coroner to arrive, Washington started questioning guests on the twelfth floor. Some weren't in their rooms. Apparently only three rooms were occupied. One guest reported that he and his wife had just arrived that morning. They were downstairs eating and hadn't heard the housekeeper. Two other guests said they had just checked in when they saw the housekeeping run past screaming. They didn't understand what she was saying, but her hysteria was scary. They called the hotel operator about her. Another guest had heard her and called 911 from his cell phone.

Hamilton got up to the twelfth floor and agreed to check with the front desk about any other occupied rooms.

The coroner met Washington in front of Room 1205. He put on protective boots, walked inside, and began his examination. He estimated the male victim had been dead between eight to ten hours. "It was only an estimate," the coroner reminded Washington.

His preliminary finding for cause of death was blunt force to the head followed by a knife plunged into his neck, severing his spine. There were no defensive wounds on his hands. Most likely the killer surprised him from behind, overpowered him by forcing him face down on the bed. It appeared the killer straddled the victim from behind.

As Hamilton returned with the forensics team, the coroner noted scratches on the victim's neck and a condom under the bed.

The CSI technicians started processing the room. They took samples of body fluids found on the bed and fingernail scrapings, along with samples of blood spatter from the wall, bed, floor, and headboard.

The coroner completed his exam and now the forensics team had charge of the room. The victim's hands were wrapped in plastic bags to preserve any evidence. After the team finished checking for fingerprints, Washington was handed the wallet from the night stand. The forensics team took pictures from all angles. Hair and fibers were collected.

Hamilton checked the bed closely to see if there was something that could give him a feel for the killer. The blood spatter on the headboard and the wall was dry. The headboard would be taken to the laboratory for further processing, to determine if all the blood was the victim's

The coroner had asked that the body be transported face down. He wanted to remove the knife in his lab.

Washington decided it was no longer necessary to close off the exits. But they would make sure to gather ID information before releasing each guest. He called his boss and gave him an update.

In the lobby, Washington and Hamilton compared the list of room occupancy with rooms where there was no response;

they coincided. The forensics team remained behind. The housekeeper's cart would be taken to the crime laboratory for processing. The room was sealed and crime tape placed across the door.

The investigation would continue at police headquarters, with interviews of the housekeeper, Mrs. Jenkins, and the other choir members.

Chapter 21

As Evelyn rode to the police headquarters, she started writing in her notebook. Everyone close to Deacon Woods, starting with his wife, should be investigated. She could have had someone kill him. Evelyn didn't know what type of relationship they had—the conversation at breakfast hadn't made it sound as if they were having any marital problems.

Busy trying to figure out who had killed the deacon, Evelyn wasn't scared anymore. In fact, now she was determined to find the killer of Deacon Woods. Knowing as much as she did about him, she should have an advantage over the police. Maybe her initial reaction of sheer terror meant only that she was human. She could solve the crime. She was an intelligent logical woman with a college degree. Taking notes was the first step. Then what? Why hadn't Pastor Watson or Deacon Jackson called her back?

The fight between Gwen and Monique still bothered her. She knew Gwen was a hairdresser at a beauty salon in Oakland. She'd been at the church for some time. All she did at the church was sing in the choir. Rarely did she participate in any of the auxiliaries. She couldn't remember ever seeing Gwen and Monique even talking together at church. They seemed to have friends in different circles. Monique was a Sunday school teacher for the teenage class, very plain looking at church. She kept to herself. Gwen and Diana were always together. All of them were near the same age, so maybe they had more history than Evelyn knew.

Since this trip started, Monique had been a totally different person. Did that have something to do with the heated conversation she had heard in the bathroom?

The car stopped. Evelyn looked up and realized she was in the parking garage of police headquarters. The officers opened the door and escorted her past the front desk and into an interview room. She took a seat at a small table as the door closed and locked. She started to get scared again. The room was small, cold, and gray. The furniture was old: three chairs, the small table, and a camera in the corner of the ceiling. She was told someone would be with her shortly. She had refused the soda one of the uniformed officers had offered. Her stomach was in knots. She started to pray.

After a while praying changed to trying to picture what over the last few days could have led to murder. Carol had left early that morning for a job interview, she remembered. Everyone loved Carol. She and her five-year-old son were very active in church. Carol probably wasn't involved.

Chapter 22

Back at the hotel, the detectives were just getting off the elevator in the lobby. Now, with the guests' ID information the officers gave them, it was time to open the hotel again. The exits were cleared. Guests were released.

Hamilton went to the limo and asked Deacon Jackson for the keys to the vans. Deacon Jackson gave him the key for the van he was driving, but said Deacon Woods had the other key. Hamilton did not want to tell the choir members yet that Deacon Woods had been killed, so he simply told Deacon Jackson that a police officer would drive his van to police headquarters.

The driver of the limo was told to follow the police car to police headquarters. Uniformed officers were instructed to separate the choir members once they arrived at police headquarters.

The van key found in the victim's jacket was retrieved from the evidence bag. Both vans were driven to the police garage.

The police exited the hotel's garage, to avoid the news media. When they arrived at headquarters, the choir members were told to turn off their cell phones. They were escorted out of the limo and placed into different areas of the building.

Gwen asked, "Are we under arrest?" and was told "No." She was placed in a chair outside an office. Gwen really wanted to make a call but had to wait. What the hell was happening?

God, what if they had found those dresses? Damn it, I should have called Deacon Woods.

Chapter 23

Hamilton asked the manager at the hotel for any video and a copy of room entrance logs for all the choir members. They divided the list up. Each taking a police officer along, they searched the rooms of the choir members. Then they drove to police headquarters.

They went to Lieutenant Sayers' office to update him. As expected, Sayers wasn't happy. He was getting orders from his boss to solve this case before it affected tourism. This case was their number one priority.

Setting up in a conference room to go over their notes and to discuss the case, the detectives requested a background check on everybody in the choir.

First, they wanted to know: who was Kenneth Woods? He had no outstanding warrants or citations. Born in St. Louis, Missouri. He moved to Los Angeles in the early sixties with his parents, who divorced within two years. His mother had sole custody of the children. In 1987, he was questioned by the L.A. police regarding a shooting but wasn't held. Shortly afterwards, he moved with his mother and sister to Oakland, California. He married Vanessa Woods. They had two children, ages nine and thirteen. He had no alias. Police had been called for domestic violence five years ago, but no charges were filed.

Detective Washington knew they needed to notify the family before the story leaked to the media. He called the

Oakland Police Department and explained the situation. They agreed to make the notification. He gave them the numbers of the wife and Pastor Watson and suggested they ask the pastor to meet them at the victim's house. He faxed a copy of the victim's driver's license as proof of identity.

Hamilton called the missing choir member, Carol White, on her cell phone. He told her there had been an incident at the hotel and they needed to speak to her. Sounding upset to hear from police she declined, but once she was told the other choir members were there, she agreed to meet after her job interview.

They decided to interview the maid first. A Spanish interpreter was asked to be present. They reviewed the information they had on Louisa Hernandez. She was 42, born in Tyler, Texas, married to Jose Hernandez, a schoolteacher, for ten years, with two children. She has worked at the hotel for eight years. No criminal record.

Washington would ask the questions. The interpreter would relay the question to the maid. Hamilton would observe.

Louisa had been at the police station for several hours by now. When they entered the interview room, she was shaking. The interpreter sat next to her. Having never seen a murdered person or been in a police station before, she was terrified. The detectives reintroduced themselves and thanked her for helping them with the investigation.

Louisa asked if she could call her husband and check on her children. Washington assured her she could but he needed to find out what happened first. She was not in any danger. They offered her a beverage and sat down. "Please tell us everything that happened today at the hotel. What time did you arrive?"

Louisa said she clocked in five minutes before her shift started at 8 a.m. The hotel's printout showed she clocked in at 7:55.

She cleaned floors ten and eleven with no problems, she reported. Washington asked if anyone was in the hallway when she arrived on the twelfth floor.

Louisa said when she arrived on the twelfth floor a white couple was entering Room 1212 with luggage. The description matched the guest list.

She told them how she entered room 1205 and found the air conditioner off and the room dark. Crying, she explained how she found the body and how frightened she was. She couldn't tell at first if someone was in the room. The only things she touched were the light switch and the comforter. There was blood everywhere. No, she didn't see anyone in the room. The coroner's preliminary time of death had ruled her out as a suspect.

After the interview, Louisa called her husband to come pick her up. Before she left, they asked her to keep the incident to herself for now. Washington told her the hotel was giving her the next day off with pay.

After Louisa left, the detectives turned their attention to Evelyn.

She'd been waiting for over two hours. She was still trying to figure out who could have killed Deacon Woods. Oh God, Deacon Jackson probably doesn't know he's dead. Being friends for so long means they probable knew a lot about each other. Deacon Jackson might have some idea who would kill him. They were like brothers.

More than an hour later a police officer told Evelyn the detectives would be with her shortly.

Chapter 24

Even though the police had asked her to turn off her phone while waiting for the police, it rang.

"Sister Jenkins this is Pastor."

"Pastor, I'm terrified. Did you hear about Deacon Woods?"

"Yes, Sister James ran into my office screaming that something happened at the hotel where the choir was staying. While trying to contact the hotel to determine if it involved the choir, I got a call from the Oakland Police Homicide unit."

Evelyn gasped. "What did they say?"

"They told me Deacon Woods had been murdered." His voice gave away his distress.

"Yes, Pastor. He was stabbed. It was gruesome."

"Oh my God," he said sounding like he only just believed. "Where are you? Where are the other choir members?"

"I'm at the police station. Most of the others were also brought here. I think Eric is in his room. Carol left early this morning to go on a job interview but I gave the police her cell number. I don't know where she is now."

"I checked my messages. One was a call from Deacon Jackson about Sarah. Did her boyfriend assault her? Why was he with the choir? What's been going on? Do the police think you're in danger?"

Evelyn explained about Sarah's boyfriend. "Pastor I think he may be a suspect. The police said they didn't believe we were in danger. They want to question everyone in the choir. I don't know if somebody targeted Deacon Woods or if it was a robbery gone horribly wrong. I know none of us could have been involved. Pastor it was horrendous. Someone stabbed poor Deacon Woods."

There was a pause. "Sister Jenkins I apologize for raising my voice. I can't imagine what you and the others have been through. If the police feel the choir is in danger I want you to request police protection."

Trying to compose himself, he went on, "Sister Watson and I are going to accompany the police to Sister Woods' house for them to make the notification. When you call, I will answer. I've asked Sister James to keep this information confidential for now. I need you to speak with the choir members as soon as you can arrange it. Please find out how they are."

"The police asked us not to use our cell phones, so I think they all turned them off. I'll do what you ask. I can't talk much longer. They told me not to use my phone. I'll call you as soon as I can."

After they hung up, Pastor Watson decided to call one of the members of the church who was a lawyer. He asked him to meet with him after the notification to determine how to proceed.

Chapter 25

Evelyn went back to making notes, trying to think of anything out of the ordinary during the trip which could give a clue as to why this happened.

Making a list of all the members with possibly relevant information was her first step. She started with Deacon Jackson. All she knew about him was that he was a deacon at the church. She remembered him saying that he and Deacon Woods were friends before joining the church. He must know Deacon Woods' wife. They both seemed close and good family men. The deacons said they worked together.

Thinking back on the trip she did notice Gwen and Diana always rode in the van with Deacon Jackson but that probably didn't mean anything. She wrote it down anyway. Were Gwen and Diana really in the hotel lobby Tuesday morning and, if so, why? One of them may have seen something last night that could help find the killer.

She put a question mark next to Eric's name. The Los Angeles issues had to be resolved.

Looking at her phone, she noticed a missed call from Jessie.

Chapter 26

After interviewing the housekeeper, Detectives Washington and Hamilton went back to the conference room to regroup. They reviewed the background reports. On their way to interview Evelyn, they received a message that the coroner wanted to see them.

They took the elevator down to the coroner's office in the basement. As they entered, they could see the body of Deacon Woods on the table. The coroner was dictating his findings. "The deceased is an Afro-American man in his mid-thirties. He was found nude with a knife protruding from the top of his spine. A five inch wound on the back of the neck was consistent with the hotel's steak knife which was still in the body when I arrived at the scene. There are three small scratches on the victim's back and two on the chest area. There are no defensive wounds on the hands. A large contusion on the back of the head was caused by an unidentified blunt object. Overall, the victim was in good physical condition." He stopped when he saw the detectives. "I'm glad you got my message. I have some information that might help."

The body was lying face down, and the knife had been removed from the gash in the neck. The coroner handed Washington the knife in an evidence bag. There was something he found along with the knife which was not visible at the hotel.

He pointed behind the victim's left ear. They both leaned forward and saw a love bite. It looked fresh.

The coroner said Deacon Woods had had sex the night of the assault. Swabs from the condom, the love bite, and the scratches had been sent to the lab for DNA results. "I also requested a tox screen to see if he drugged. Testing would take at least a week."

There were old bruises on the body. He couldn't provide a complete report until the autopsy was finished.

The detectives were elated. Hamilton took pictures with his cell phone to study later. So far, they had a man who was found murdered on a religious tour with a choir. The killer apparently didn't bring a weapon so it didn't appear to be premeditated. The victim had sex before he was killed. They needed to find out who he was with.

Chapter 27

Sarah was escorted to an empty desk to wait for the detectives. She was tired and sore. Not knowing where Gary was worried her.

A police officer offered her a drink. She asked for a glass of water to take Tylenol to help with the pain. She kept reliving the night before. Everything had seemed fine until Gary flipped out. For a year, she'd been trying to make the relationship work, but there was no way she'd marry him now.

She had feared he might get in her room. She didn't know where he was and she was glad the police wanted to search the choir members' rooms. Sarah had considered herself to be an intelligent woman. Now she was questioning why she didn't see this coming. Maybe she was too lovestruck. Now she was scared of him.

Not knowing why the police wanted to question her made Sarah even more nervous. What if Gary had done something really bad? She was debating whether to file a complaint now or not. Maybe if she kept her dark glasses on the police wouldn't notice the black eye. Sarah sat quietly hoping to leave soon. Every now and then she would softly cry.

Chapter 28

Armed with their new evidence, now the detectives had leverage. They could interview the choir more intensely than they'd originally planned. They would treat them like suspects and not just witnesses. They hadn't ruled out the fact that Woods could have picked up a hooker. Somebody had sex with this guy. If that person was not the killer then, maybe one of them knew who the killer was.

The background check on Evelyn Jenkins showed no criminal record and no outstanding warrants. She'd had a business for almost a year and seemed to be doing well. Her brother was a police officer in Phoenix, Arizona. It didn't appear she was guilty of anything except hanging around the crime scene. Killers don't normally wait for the police outside a crime scene. But they reserved their opinion until after the interview.

The detectives entered the room where Evelyn was waiting. Both sat down across from her. Detective Washington spoke first, "Ms. Jenkins, we're sorry to keep you waiting so long but you can imagine this is a very serious matter and we need to make sure to get it right."

Evelyn shifted in her chair. She didn't tell them about her phone call to Pastor Watson. She didn't know it but the room was mic'd for sound and video. The conversation would turn up during the review of her interview.

All during the interview Detective Hamilton just sat and observed Evelyn's reactions.

Washington continued, "Now as I understand it you are the tour coordinator for the choir, is that correct? "

"Yes."

"So what do you do?"

"I made the arrangements for the trip, booked the hotels, rented the vans, and manage any outside financial needs.

Looking down at his report he said, "Are you the owner of Jenkins Travel in Oakland?"

"Yes, I moved to Oakland a few years ago."

"How did you get involved with this choir?"

"I'm a member of the church, Gabriel Missionary Baptist Church in Oakland."

"When was the last time you saw Mr. Woods alive?"

"Last night we arrived from Los Angeles. Deacon Woods drove the choir members in one van. Deacon Jackson and I came later in the other van. We arrived around 7:30 last night, unloaded the luggage and everyone went to their room. Deacon Woods and Deacon Jackson and I all have separate rooms. The other choir members are sharing rooms. The last time I saw him, he and Deacon Jackson were going to their rooms just after we got here. I spoke to him on the phone around 9:00 last night and then went to bed."

"How is the relationship between choir members? Do they get along?

"Yes! Deacon Woods and I have never had a disagreement. He's a very nice person; I mean he was a very nice man. I haven't seen him disagree with anyone in the choir."

Washington continued, "You said the choir was on tour, when and where have you been before coming to Las Vegas?"

"We left Oakland on Monday and drove to Los Angeles for a concert Wednesday night. We left Los Angeles yesterday morning and got here last night. We have, I mean we had a concert scheduled tonight."

"Well, in light of what has happened, I would say there will be no concert. Until we clear the choir you will need to remain in Las Vegas."

"Yes, under the circumstances I know there won't be a concert tonight." Suddenly she remembered she had to call Rev. Osborne to cancel the concert.

"When did you leave your room?"

"I never left my room last night."

"How well did you know Mr. Woods?"

"Well I've only known him from church. We've been working together on the tour. He and Deacon Jackson collected the offerings. Deacon Woods sold the CD's after the concert in Los Angeles. He and Deacon Jackson are close friends as well as deacons in the church. They both are van drivers. They've been members of the church for many years; long before I joined."

"Do you know if he was holding a large sum of money for the group?"

"No, I have the money for the tour."

"Do you know his wife or family?"

"Not personally. I've seen them but I've never really met them."

"Can you think of any reason why someone would harm him?"

"No, I'm sure nobody in the choir is a killer. We are all Christians."

The detectives looked at each other without any saying a word. They obviously didn't believe her, which meant they were suspects.

"Detectives, I saw the media at the hotel. Is this on the news?"

"Yes," Hamilton said, "the story is on the news, but the details about you and the choir have not been released. This is a high profile case. We don't like guests murdered in our hotels.

"Do I need an attorney? Do any of us need an attorney?"

"You are certainly welcome to have one, but for now you are not a suspect. You're not under arrest. We just need to gather as much information as we can about the deceased."

Evelyn was relieved to hear that.

Washington continued, "If you think of anything that will help us find the person who killed your friend, please call me." He handed her his business card.

"Are we in danger?"

"I don't believe you are, but we will have a uniformed officer stationed at the hotel. Please don't try to speak to any of the other members until we have questioned them. We are sorry for your loss."

They all stood up. Washington left the room and came back with a police officer to take her back to the hotel. Evelyn felt drained. Slinging her purse over her shoulder, she walked past the detectives and out of the room. She saw Deacon Jackson sitting in a chair looking like he had it together. Remembering what she was told; Evelyn avoided eye contact and walked straight ahead. She felt guilty knowing she was the only one that knew Deacon Woods was dead.

She was placed in an unmarked car and driven back to the hotel.

Chapter 29

Deacon Jackson tried to make eye contact with Evelyn, but stopped when he realized she was ignoring him. The detectives looked over, nodded and he stood up and walked with them into the interview room. Evelyn kept walking. As he sat down opposite the two, he had rarely felt as nervous in his thirty-five years.

"I'm Detective Washington and this is my partner, Detective Hamilton. We asked you here because we are investigating a murder."

Deacon Jackson's body tensed. "What murder?"

The detectives watched him closely to see his reaction to the news. "Kenneth Woods."

Before he realized it, he was standing up and the chair fell backwards. He shouted, "KEN'S BEEN MURDERED?" The detectives weren't expecting that type of reaction and they instantly stood up too.

Hamilton asked Deacon Jackson to sit down. They could see his shoulders begin to slump forward. Washington walked toward him. He picked up the fallen chair and set it upright. He placed his hand on Deacon Jackson's shoulders and felt him shaking. "Mr. Jackson," he said softly, "we're sorry to be the ones to have to tell you this. Please sit down."

Hamilton continued watching his facial reaction. Tears rolling down his face, Deacon Jackson slumped in the chair. He put his face in his hands and began weeping. Both detectives sat back down and waited. A tissue box was moved toward him.

They allowed him time to compose himself, and then asked if he wanted some water. He accepted. Washington went for the water. Hamilton continued, "I'm sorry for your loss. How long have you known Mr. Woods?" Wiping his eyes, the deacon took a tissue from the box and blew his nose.

"I've known Kenneth for over twenty years. We worked together at US Postal Service for years. How did he die? Is that why you had Evelyn in handcuffs?"

"He was murdered in his room. Is it safe to say that you and Mr. Woods were good friends?"

"Yes. We grew up together. Our families moved to Oakland when we were in our teens. His family and my family attend the same church. How was he killed?"

Washington returned with the water.

"By a knife in his neck." Both men watched for Jackson's reaction.

"Oh my God! Who could have done such a horrible thing? Why would anyone want to murder Ken? Was it a robbery?"

"That's what we're going to find out. When was the last time you saw Mr. Woods?"

"Last night. We got to the hotel from Los Angeles around 7:30. Ken, I mean Deacon Woods, and the others met us in the lobby to get their luggage."

"Why didn't you all come together?"

"One of our members was mugged and had to file a police report. The other choir members drove here in one of the vans. We had the luggage in our van. After finishing with the police we drove here and arrived last night. The choir members came down to the lobby to retrieve their luggage. That's when I saw Deacon Woods. Afterwards we went to our rooms. Deacon Woods called me and suggested we have dinner. I met him in the lobby and we went to eat at the Circus Buffet. When we finished, I went back to my room and went to bed."

Washington asked, "Did Mr. Woods go to his room?

"He said he wasn't tired and was going to check out the strip. That's the last time I saw him."

"Can you think of anyone in the group that would have a reason to harm him?"

Deacon Jackson had a shocked look on his face and immediately responded, "Nobody in the choir would kill him or anybody. We may have our little disagreements but we don't get angry enough to kill. Do the others know? Lord help us, I need to call Pastor Watson."

"He's already aware of the situation," said Hamilton. Shock and panic show on Deacon Jackson's face.

"Think, Mr. Jackson. Do you know of anyone in the church that might have a grudge or a reason to have him killed?"

"No! He and I volunteered to drive the vans for the tour because we both had vacation time. We wanted to help and it gives us time away from our wives. There is absolutely no one that I know of who wanted Ken dead. I've known him for years. Besides, he would have told me if he was having any trouble. Believe me we were that close. He is, I mean, he was a good man and friendly with everyone. Everybody loved him. This is just crazy. Somebody must have followed him back to the hotel."

Washington asked, "Did Mr. Woods drink alcohol?"

"No, Ken doesn't drink. I have never seen him drink liquor or smelled liquor on his breath. Gentlemen, we're talking about a church deacon. We have rules to live by because we represent our church."

"Are you saying he wouldn't have had an extramarital affair or perhaps met somebody for sex?"

"No, Ken wouldn't do that, he's married."

"This is Las Vegas and I've been a cop for years. We meet most married men here because they get robbed by a hooker."

"Believe me, detective, that's not Ken."

Detective Hamilton said, "Are you sure you don't have anything else to tell us about Mr. Woods?"

Washington got up and left the room. He called Bert in the garage to find out if the crime technicians were done processing the vans.

"Ken didn't carry a lot of money. He gave Sister Jenkins the proceeds from the concert last night so it can't be a robbery.

I can't believe this. I don't know how the others are going to take this."

"We would prefer telling them ourselves. If you can think of any information that might be helpful," as Hamilton handed him his business card, "please call me. We need you to remain in town. I'll let you know if and when you can leave."

Deacon Jackson stood up and realized his knees were weak. He sat back down to steady himself. "Are we under arrest?"

"No. We may contact you with some more questions. I'll have a police officer take you back to the hotel."

Just as he said that, Washington walked back in the room and announced one of the vans had been processed and he could drive it back to the hotel. He would need to pick up the keys from the officer in the garage.

"I understand." Deacon Jackson stood up and shook hands with the detectives as they walked out of the interrogation room.

Chapter 30

The detectives could tell this was going to be a long day as they walked back to their office. A call came in from an Oakland detective, Ben Davis. Washington put it on speaker so Hamilton could hear too. He said he, his partner, and Pastor Watson were at the Woods residence with Deacon Woods' wife, Vanessa, and her sister. They told her there was an incident at a Las Vegas hotel. They had a detective on the speakerphone who needed to ask her some questions.

Detective Washington spoke. "Mrs. Woods, this is Detective Washington from the Las Vegas Police. Is Ken Woods your husband?"

"Yes, what's this all about?"

"We just need to ask you a few questions. When was the last time you spoke with your husband?"

"Ken called me last night around 11:00. Is he all right?"

"When you spoke with him how did he sound?

"He sounded fine. He was telling me about the suit I had him buy and how good the concert was in Los Angeles. Listen, what's going on?"

Ignoring her request, Washington continued, "Are you and Mr. Woods having any marital problems?"

"My husband and I have a great marriage. Why? Did something happen to Ken?"

"We're doing an investigation. How well does your husband get along with the members of the choir? Any disputes?"

"No, Ken gets along with everybody." She turned to Pastor Watson. "Pastor Watson, What's this all about?" He remained silent.

"Does your husband know anyone in Las Vegas besides the choir?"

"No."

"Are you having any money problems?"

"Money problems? Hell no! I'm sorry, Pastor Watson." Pastor Watson nodded realizing she was getting upset.

"Does he have any enemies that you're aware of?"

"NO!" Her voice was loud and angry. At that point, Vanessa went off. "Look, I'm not answering any more questions until somebody tells me what is going on. He's a Christian man, family man. I know you think Afro-American men don't take care of their family but you're dead wrong. I'm not answering anything else until you tell me what is going on." There was a long silence.

Finally, Detective Washington said, "Mrs. Woods, I'm sorry to have to tell you this, but Mr. Woods is dead." Her wailing was loud and anguished and heart-piercing. They heard the sound of her knees buckling as she fell on the floor, a familiar sound but painful to hear. The Pastor was trying to comfort her.

131

Vanessa was not able to talk, so her sister asked how he died. Reluctantly, Detective Hamilton explained the circumstances of his death at which time he was told Vanessa had fainted and collapsed. They tried to assure Vanessa's sister they were conducting a thorough investigation and that they would find the killer. They promised to speak with them the following day. The call ended abruptly.

Homicide Detective Davis called Detective Washington back on his cell phone. He had left the house and was in his car with his partner. He relayed his observations as to how the wife took the news. He was convinced it was a real reaction. The wife was truly surprised.

Hamilton asked Ben Davis to check with other family members to find out if they know of anyone who would cause Mr. Woods harm. Davis said he'd call with an update.

After hanging up the phone, Washington and Hamilton sat silently for a moment. Notifications were always hard but this one was especially difficult.

Randy Sullivan was next on their list.

Chapter 31

Deacon Jackson got off at the ninth floor and opened the door to his hotel room. His possessions were tossed all over the room. Drawers were open. The police had asked for his room key. He expected them to check out his room, but not to ransack it.

But he understood why. The police had to rule out the choir. He just wished they would have told him. Was anything missing? There were messages on the hotel phone. That's when he noticed his phone was in the drawer of the nightstand. He thought, Evelyn must have been mad as hell as he looked down at the missed messages.

He picked up the clothes off the floor and smoothed down the bed before sitting down. That's when it hit him. Before he knew it, he was crying. It took him fifteen minutes to compose himself.

He dialed his home phone number. His wife picked up right away. "Joe, where are you? I've been calling you all day. What's going on?"

They talked for over an hour. It took that long for her to calm down. She wanted him to come home. He promised to call her every four hours. His wife would call Vanessa to see how she was dealing with this. He promised to call Pastor Watson and Evelyn to find out if they knew what he should do.

Chapter 32

Evelyn was also back at the hotel in her room. A few guests in the lobby had looked at her funny, but others didn't pay attention to her at all.

As she opened the door, she realized the police had been in her room and gone through her things. Evelyn realized now they weren't just questioning her; she was a suspect. She closed the door and immediately locked it. After all, suppose the killer is planning to kill other members of the group. Of course, they would check her room for evidence that could lead to the killer. Realizing she was a suspect made her even more determined to identify the killer.

Evelyn called her mother in Phoenix. When her mother heard her out, she demanded that Evelyn leave Las Vegas. Evelyn explained that she couldn't.

"Evelyn, please call Charles. Your brother can tell you what to do. After all he's a Phoenix police officer."

Evelyn agreed. She promised to call her parents every eight hours. She was alright, she assured them. As promised, she called Charles to see if he could help.

"Hello EV, what you doing, girl? I hear you're in Las Vegas."

"Charles, you won't believe what's happened." She told him the whole story."

"Maybe it was a robbery?"

"I don't think so. There was money in his wallet there on the nightstand. I mean, it looked thick like there was money in it. He gave me the money from the concert so it must have belonged to him."

"Do you think somebody in the choir killed him?"

"I really don't know these people that well so I'm going to keep an eye on them. I started taking notes of things I see and hear."

"EV, leave the investigating to the police. Do you need me to come get you?"

"No, Charles, besides I can't leave."

"Girl what the hell have you gotten yourself into? I'm going to tell you again, follow the directions of the detectives. I'm not going to ask why you decided to wait outside the crime scene but I do know you. Did the police say you were in danger?"

"No, but they have a police officer stationed in the lobby, I guess for our protection."

"That's what it sounds like. They're in the investigation stage so they won't take any chances, especially since it's a hotel. I don't think you need an attorney now, but if they ask you back for questioning you might want to consider getting one. I'll call a friend in Las Vegas and see what she can do."

He knew his sister was stubborn. Evelyn was never one to back down from a fight. He just didn't want her to become the next victim.

"Since you can't leave I'm going to tell you what to do. If you need me you better call. I don't want to have to come there and shoot somebody." Laughing, they ended the call.

She felt a little calmer. Despite what he said, Evelyn had already made up her mind; she would help find the killer.

She straightened up her room and decided to call her assistant.

"Deborah you won't believe what's been going on." She told her everything from the Los Angeles incident until she returned to the hotel, punctuated by Deborah's "What?" or "Oh my God." Evelyn was exhausted when she finished. She realized just how scary it was after saying everything out loud.

"What are you going to do? Are you coming home?"

"No, I think I can find out who killed Deacon Woods,"

"Girl, you must be crazy. Suppose whoever killed Deacon Woods is out to kill the members of the choir, including you? You need to get out of there fast. Listen, I like this job and I need to have a boss to pay me."

Evelyn smiled. "Think about it, I know these people, all but one and that's Valarie. There's no way she would kill Deacon Woods, she didn't even know him. I don't think any of the choir members killed him either. This had to be somebody he didn't know."

"You better be very careful. If whoever is the killer thinks you suspect them, you could be in danger. Whatever you do, do it on the down low."

"I will. I'll call you later and let you know what's going on."

Evelyn took a shower and ordered dinner. While waiting she continued making notes of things she had observed and focused on the questions the police had asked. Now that she was alone she decided to look at the pictures of the crime scene. She hoped they wouldn't be as shocking as remembered. She was wrong. They were pictures of a man she knew, a murdered man. Somberly she sat back on the bed.

Clearly, the detectives were trying to gather information to help solve this crime. Evelyn wasn't sure what Deacon Jackson had told the detectives but she did observe him leaving with Deacon Woods after they arrived in Las Vegas. She didn't know when they returned. One thing she did find odd was that Deacon Jackson always has his cell phone with him, but today he couldn't be reached.

Just then, Evelyn's phone rang. The caller cleared his throat, "Sister Jenkins, this is Pastor Watson."

"Hello Pastor."

There was silence as they both tried to think of what to say.

"Sister Jenkins, I've had a very emotional and exhausting day. Sister Woods is under a doctor's care. The shock was just too much for her so they had to sedate her. From what the police say, Deacon Woods was found in bed with a knife plunged in the back of his neck. Apparently, sometime last night or early morning he was murdered. Is that what happened? Have you talked with the others yet?"

"Pastor, I don't think they all know about it yet. We were taken to the police station and separated. They're being interviewed now. I don't know how they're going to take this."

"I've had the news on since I returned to my room and there's no mention of the murder yet. But I called Pastor Osborne and told him to cancel the concert. All he knows is that something happened to one of the choir members. He's going to contact you in case you need some help. I was told the choir will have to stay there for a few days. When they return, try and get them together tomorrow or whenever you can. I'm sure they will be devastated. I'm meeting with their family members in a few minutes."

"Pastor, the last time I saw all of them they were in the lobby but I believe they are still waiting to be interviewed by the police. When I left they were going to interview Deacon Jackson."

"My real concern is when the media starts to report on what happened and releases the name of Deacon Woods. His wife is having a hard time. Thank God the police have been able to contain the information but I'm sure it's just a matter of time before someone finds out what happened.

"And Sister Jenkins, I need you to keep the choir as close to you as possible. I don't know how they're going to react when they find out about this. Try and get a conference room in the hotel so we can have a conference call. Can I count on you?"

"Yes Pastor. I'll make sure to keep in contact with you. When I am able to, I will have Deacon Jackson call you."

"That will be a help. Some of the family members are starting to arrive and I need to talk to them. Please call me if you need anything."

"I will."

Chapter 33

Diana had been sitting in an empty office for almost two hours. She walked around the room trying to calm her nerves. She hated authority. Abandoned at birth in Oakland, she never knew her birth family. The Millers adopted her from foster care when she was nine, and she lived with them and their three kids. Mr. Miller was a disciplinarian and Diana fought back constantly. Living in the Oakland projects, she had to be tough. Fighting was her specialty.

In tenth grade she met Gwen Harrison, who became the only person she trusted. They understood each other. Together they could beat anybody. Neither one of them had an ambition to go to college after high school. They settled on getting a job and partying. Now she was seating in a police station wondering what the hell was going on. She longed to talk to Gwen. Gwen always made sense of things.

An officer came in and offered her something to drink. She asked for a soda and drank thirstily. Soon, Hamilton came in and asked her to follow him to the interview room. In her haste to leave the room, she left the soda on the table. A police officer picked it up and took it to the crime lab, as they had done with drinks left behind by the other choir members.

Detective Hamilton ushered her to a chair. Washington joined them. Hamilton opened his folder to review the background report. Diana tried to read it upside down. Two moving violations. A juvenile record showed she was adopted at the age of nine and was in and out of trouble. No arrests. Currently, her record was clean. She'd been a cashier for a supermarket chain for the last four years.

"Ms. Miller," Washington began, "I'm sorry you had to wait so long but we really appreciate your cooperation in this matter."

Diana folded her arms in defiance. "I don't know what you people want with us, but this is totally ridiculous. We've been treated like criminals for no reason."

"Ms. Miller I assure you we didn't call you down here for nothing. May I ask what did you do yesterday?"

"We didn't get to Las Vegas until around 1:30. After we got here all of us decided to do the tourist thing. You know, walk on the strip to check out the sights."

"As I understand it, you came in the van that Mr. Woods was driving, is that correct?"

"Yeah."

"When was the last time you saw Mr. Woods?" Diana's eyes opened wide. Both detectives noticed her hesitation.

"Deacon Woods? The last time I saw Deacon Woods was when we got our luggage from the other van."

"Are you sure that was the last time you saw him?"

"Yes", she said after a pause. "Why do you ask?"

"What did you do after getting your luggage?"

"Gwen and I went back to our room. We got dressed and went out on the town."

"When did you return to the hotel?"

"Late last night, I don't remember what time."

"So you never saw Mr. Woods again?"

"No! Why?"

"Mr. Woods was murdered last night"

"What do you mean he was murdered?" She said with a defiant voice.

It took a moment for the words to sink in. The detectives continued to stare at her. "Did you say he was **murdered**?" her voice rose. "Who murdered him? Where was he killed?"

Still observing her reaction, Hamilton answered, "He was murdered in his room last night."

"What? Who did it?" Her voice was cracking and her eyes were filling with tears.

"That's what we're trying to find out." Diana was crying, really crying. They offered her a tissue box and waited.

"How?" she sniffled and blew her nose.

"Someone stabbed him to death."

"Stabbed?" Diana was getting hysterical as she stood up and started pacing. "Is someone going to kill me?"

Detectives Hamilton touched her shoulder in an effort to calm her down. With a calm voice he said, "No, we don't believe you are in danger. Please sit down."

Diana was shaking as she slowly sat back down. "I want to go home!"

Ignoring her, they continued. "Ms. Miller, are you sure the last time you saw Deacon Woods was early last evening?" "Were you ever in his room?"

"No, No I have never been in his room. He was married. Gwen and I walked around the strip. We went to a night club, had drinks, not a lot. We went to eat. Played on the slot machines, then I went to my room. That's it."

"What time was that?" Diana didn't say anything. He repeated the question. "What time was that?" They could see her mind was working trying to think of an answer.

She cleared her throat and said, "We saw Deacon Woods when we were leaving."

"So you lied. You did see Mr. Woods?"

"No, I forgot. We were leaving around eleven last night and we saw him in the lobby."

"Did you speak to him?"

"Yes, he kind of was telling us we weren't dressed like Christian woman. Gwen and I got mad and left the hotel anyway. I didn't see him again. We knew if he saw us, he was going to say something. After all, he's a deacon and all."

"So you were angry that he said something about how you were dressed?"

"I guess. We weren't angry enough to kill him, if that's what you mean. I'm just like not all that Christian. I'm still young and I like to live my life."

Now Hamilton wasn't so friendly. "Do you lie all the time? I don't think you know how to tell the truth."

Her body stiffened. "No, I'm telling the truth. We saw him in the lobby then we went to dinner."

"What time did you get back?"

"I got back around one-thirty. I played on the slot machines then I went to my room."

"Where was Ms. Harrison?"

"We got separated. I don't know where she went."

"Was she in the room when you got there?"

"Yes, she was sleep."

"What time was that?"

"Around two-thirty."

"Did either you or Ms. Harrison leave the room?"

"No."

"Is there anyone you know who had a reason to hurt Mr. Woods?"

"No, Nobody in the choir would do that! Was he robbed?"

"No, we don't believe he was robbed."

"You sure we're safe?"

"We believe this was someone who targeted Mr. Woods. Ms. Miller, we found some items in your room with security tags on them. We also found a joint. Do you know anything about that?"

It took Diana a while to answer. No matter how bad Diana usually acted, she was scared now and started crying again. "I don't know about any dresses but the joint is mine. Am I going to jail?"

Detective Washington waited to respond. He wanted her to sweat. Finally, he said, "Lucky for you, it's not enough to charge you in Las Vegas, but we did confiscate it."

The detectives stood up and walked out without saying another word, leaving her there alone about five minutes before returning. She was still crying. After a few minutes Detective Washington said, "We're going to let you go back to the hotel but don't leave the city. If you think of anything that will help in this investigation, I need you to call me." He gave her his business card. Her hands were shaking.

"An officer will take you back to the hotel."

Slowly Diana stood up and weakly shook their hands.

"Thank you." She followed the police officer out of the room and looked around for other choir members. None were visible.

Back at the hotel, Diana didn't care that people were looking at her walking with a police officer. She insisted he walk her to her room. Once there she locked the door and cried.

When Diana wiped her eyes, she looked up and realized the room had been ransacked. Not that it was in perfect order when they left. The drawers were open. The clothes in the closet were taken out and put on the bed. She was rooming with Gwen and Sarah. They must still be at the police station. She started looking for her things. Separating her things from the others, she gathered them up in one corner. Everything was there. Her stomach gripped in a knot. Repeatedly, she checked to make sure the door was still locked. What if they were wrong and somebody was after her?

In all the chaos, Diana had forgotten to turn her phone back on. There were several missed messages. She jumped when the hotel phone rang. It was her mother.

"Diana, are you all right? Why didn't you answer your phone? "

"The police made me turn it off while I was waiting at the police station."

"The police station, what do you mean the police station? Why were you at the police station? Pastor Watson called and asked me to meet him here at the church. The other parents are here too. What the hell is going on?"

Diana told her mother everything. The police didn't want it known to the media yet but everyone will know soon. She tried to assure her mother she was safe. Diana didn't tell her how scared she was or about the drugs and shoplifting. Even though they didn't get along that well, her mother ordered her to come home immediately. She told her mother the police had asked them not to leave and promised to call her before she went to bed. She would keep her cell phone on all the time.

After talking to her mother, she felt a little better, but still scared. She packed her clothes in her luggage and took a shower. Thinking Evelyn was probably still at the police station she decided not to call her. Leaving the room was not an option so she ordered a hamburger, ate, and lay down on the bed.

Her mind was racing. If her mother found out about the drugs, she would kick her out the house. Now that scared her more than being murdered. She turned on the television to watch the news. In case she fell asleep, she put all the lights on in the room even though it was still light outside.

In times like these, she longed to have a man in her life. She was tired of being alone. Gwen was a good friend but she was getting older. That job at the supermarket was supposed to give her an opportunity meet men. Problem was most of them weren't worth dating. Men at the church weren't really her type, they didn't love to party. Maybe she could change her image, even go to college to get a better job. Her mother was always telling her she needed to do better for herself. Maybe it was time. Deacon Woods being killed not only scared her, it was an awakening. What did Deacon Woods do to make somebody kill him? Could Gwen be that evil?

Chapter 34

Amos Tucker was eighteen years old. He'd joined the church when he was twelve and had been the drummer for over a year. His grandmother, Grandma Ines, he called her, had been a member for over twenty years. His mother left him with her when he was nine years old and never contacted him again. She was always in and out of rehab. Amos had never met his dad, who was serving a life sentence in San Quentin for murdering his best friend.

No one at church knows about Amos' past. He tried very hard not to be noticed. Now he was sitting on a bench at the police station scared to death. He vowed to keep out of trouble and make his grandmother proud. He's studying to be an architect to get her out of the projects. She's probably going out of her mind not knowing how he is. He thought about getting up and walking out but he was too scared.

Just then, a police officer put a hand on his shoulder and told him he was next. Amos stood up, knees wobbling, and followed the officer. He was led to a small room with a table and three chairs and invited to sit in the chair facing the door. His mouth was dry. He asked for water. The door closed. There was complete silence. He waited.

Entering, Hamilton observed a scared young man. He said, "Amos Tucker—is that right?" Washington followed him in but said nothing. "I'm Detective Hamilton and this is my partner Detective Washington."

Amos tried not to show he was shaking so he hid his hands under the table. "Yes, I'm Amos."

Hamilton held his hand out. Amos brought his hands from under the table and shook hands. The detective felt a soft trembling grip. They sat down. Washington took notes.

"Amos, what do you do in the choir?

"I play drums."

"Well Amos, we're homicide detectives and we're investigating a murder."

"A MURDER!" "Who was murdered?" His voice was shaking.

"Do you know a Kenneth Woods?" They both stared at him with intensity.

"Do you mean Deacon Woods?"

"Well, last night he was murdered. Somebody stuck a knife in the back of his neck." Both detectives waited for a response.

"No! That can't be. Deacon Woods is a nice man. Are you sure it was Deacon Woods?" His eyes filled with tears. His lips were trembling. He looked like a scared little boy.

Both detectives felt compassion, but they kept a stern look on their faces. They both realized this was a young man who from all appearances probably didn't commit this murder. They had a background report and knew his father was in jail.

They passed the box of tissue toward him. Reluctantly and ashamed he took tissue, still not saying a word. He blew his nose and wiped his eyes.

"Deacon Woods was a nice man. I don't know my real dad. Deacon Woods helped me when I had problems. I could count on him to give me advice." He was crying.

"Amos we need to find out who did this. Do you know of anyone in the group that may have a problem with Mr. Woods?"

"Nobody in the choir has a problem with him, not that I know of. We all like him."

"Where were you last night?"

Hearing that question changed Amos' demeanor. He tensed up and his voice became less controlled. "When the van got here nobody had any luggage. It was too early to check in so we went walking on the strip. The other van got here about 7:15 so we took our luggage to the room and went back out. Cory, Jessie, and I walked around the strip. We had dinner and Cory and I went back to the room around 11 o'clock. Jessie said he was going to check out the casino. We saw Gary on the strip around 10 o'clock but he didn't see us. Cory and I went back to the room, looked at TV, and went to bed."

"You say you saw Gary? Who is Gary?"

"Gary is Sarah's fiancé. We saw him walking toward the casino area but I don't think he saw us."

"What's Gary's last name?"

"I don't remember. Wait… I think it was Stevens. Yea, his name is Stevens."

"So you saw him at what time?"

"I think it was 10:00."

"Did this guy know Mr. Woods?"

"Yea, Sarah introduced him after the concert on Wednesday night in Los Angeles. Come to think of it, I didn't know he was coming to Las Vegas. I guess you'll have to ask Sarah." They both started taking notes.

"So is there anyone else you saw that night before going to your room?

"We met Gwen and Diana in the elevator. They said they were going out partying and they were dressed like it."

"Did you say Gwen and Diana?"

"Yea, there're always together."

"Did you see anyone else? Did you see Mr. Woods?"

"No. Cory and I are the youngest in the choir. Everybody else is older so they kind of do their own thing."

"So you didn't leave the room all night?"

"No, I was too tired. I woke up about two and Cory was still snoring. He snores really loud."

Both detectives believed him. They decided to let him go back to the hotel. Like the others, he was told not to talk to anyone on his way out. He agreed. They assured him he was in no danger.

Walking back to the office, they did a background check. It seemed Gary Stevens had a record. He was twenty-five years old, born in East Oakland, and first arrested at age twelve for shoplifting. His parents were killed in an automobile accident when he was sixteen. When he was twenty-one, he was accused of domestic violence. Assault charges were filed in Oakland by Denise Williams, his girlfriend. She changed her mind about pressing charges, so the case was dropped for lack of evidence. Based on his background, Gary was now a person of interest. A call was made to the police officer at the hotel. A picture was sent to officer's cell phone. If found, he was to be detained for questioning. The dispatcher put out an all-points bulletin.

Cory Williams was interviewed after Amos. Cory was twenty and lived with his parents. He appeared younger than his age. He looked scared. His background check came up clean. Cory said he'd been a member of the church since he was born. He was a junior in college studying to be an attorney. He told the same story as Amos. And, as with Amos, he was told not to talk to anyone after his interview. He nodded and left.

Detective Washington had mixed emotions about the whole group. Since Hamilton was familiar with how the Afro-American churches were structured, he understood them a little more. However, Washington's frustration in this case was starting to show.

Chapter 35

Evelyn finished eating and was looking at her notes. There were questions she needed answered. How close were the deacons? When she'd first joined the church, Deacon Jackson and Deacon Woods were assigned as her prayer partners. They called her once a week for prayer. They were both active in the church, but they were different from the other deacons. They were younger and seemed to really enjoy life. The older deacons were stern and pompous. Deacons Jackson and Woods were friendly, especially with the youth and the single ladies. It didn't matter that they were married. Apparently, their wives didn't have a problem with it either.

The phone rang. Cory and Amos had just returned from police headquarters and wanted to talk to her. Even though it was late, she agreed since they were so young. After a few minutes, she heard a knock. When Cory and Amos came inside, she noticed both of them had been crying. They looked like scared little boys.

"Sister Jenkins," Cory said, "we just came back from the police department. Suppose whoever killed Deacon Woods is after us?"

Hugging them, she said, "Boys, I know you're scared, but I really don't believe we're in danger. The police would have kept us if we were."

"I'm afraid to call my parents. I've kept the phone off because I don't know what they're going to do when they hear about Deacon Woods. Can you please call them?"

"Certainly, I'll call them right now."

The phone rang once and immediately Cory's mother answered. "Sister Jenkins, where's Cory? Is he all right? Where is he? I need to speak to him now!" She sounded frantic.

"He's fine. He's standing next to me.

"Let me talk to him NOW!" Evelyn handed the phone to Cory.

"Hi Mom." When he heard his mother crying, he began to cry. It took a few minutes but he finally told her he was OK. He tried to explain everything. When he told her Deacon Woods was dead, Evelyn heard her scream. His mother told him they would be on the next flight there. Later Evelyn found out they hadn't met with Pastor Watson because they had been out of town.

Finally, Cory handed the phone back to Evelyn. She tried to assure his mother he would be safe and asked them to call Pastor Watson, who was aware of the situation. They were shocked that the Pastor knew what happened. But he'd be able to calm their fears and perhaps they could help with the choir when they came to Las Vegas. Both parents agreed and said they were calling Pastor Watson.

Amos was patiently waiting and watching. Afterwards, Evelyn called his grandmother to assure her he was safe. As expected, she was quite upset. She was eighty, and not physically able to travel. Pastor Watson had already come by and told her about the murder. She made Evelyn promise to look after Amos and return him home safe. Evelyn promised.

Cory said, "Thank you, Sister Jenkins. The police searched our room."

"I think they searched all our rooms."

They told her what they had said to the police. She was shocked. Evelyn again tried to assure them they were safe and walked them back to their room.

The fact that Gary might be still around the hotel concerned her. If he was waiting for Sarah, there could be even more trouble. As soon as she returned to her room, looking over her shoulder, she added to her notes. Not knowing the order of the interviews, Evelyn was wondering why Deacon Jackson hadn't called her.

Just as she was thinking about what she learned from Cory and Amos the phone rang, it was Deborah. "Evelyn I tried to wait until you called me but girl; you have got to know this story is all over the place. They had this guy from the police department saying that a body was found in the hotel. He never said the word murder. I guess they're trying to keep this as quiet as they can."

"Lord, this is really bad. Deb, you won't believe what's been happening here. The police are questioning everyone individually. Amos and Cory just left my room; you know they are the youngest in the group. They are freaked out. I had to call their family to try and assure them I would keep them safe. Now I'm a bodyguard. Cory's parents are coming here on the next flight. Apparently, Amos told the police about Gary. It's only a matter of time before they find out about Sarah's black eye."

"Evelyn, I can't imagine what you're going through."

"I've got to find out more about Gary. If he can beat up women, maybe he's a killer as well."

"Girl, listen to me, stay away from that guy. You just met this guy. Hell, Sarah doesn't even know who he is."

"Believe me I'm staying as far away from Gary as humanly possible. I'm still waiting to hear from Deacon Jackson. I can't imagine how he's taking the news."

Chapter 36

Back at the police station, Washington and Hamilton got a message from the Oakland detective. The wife couldn't identify anyone who would want to harm her husband.

They asked the detective if they would follow up with Deacon Woods' co-workers. Couldn't be the guy was a saint. Something didn't match up. He was killed by somebody who knew him well. The Oakland detectives said they would help. Washington also asked them to pull the file on Gary Stevens. They needed to find out about this guy.

Next, Hamilton called the Los Angeles Robbery Division and spoke to a Detective Burns. After telling him about the murdered choir member, he asked for a copy of the police report on Eric Parker. To his surprise, they had arrested two young men who were trying to pawn Eric's cell phone. Both were known drug dealers. When questioned, they told a different story. According to them, Eric approached them asking for drugs. When told the price, he tried to grab it and run without paying. They caught him, took the drugs, his cell phone, and wallet. Then they beat him up.

"Thanks guys," said Hamilton. "We'll talk to this guy again. Listen, would you mind checking out the hotel and see if you can find anything to help with this case?"

The Los Angeles detective agreed to visit the hotel where Evelyn and the deacons had stayed to see if there was any information that could shed some light on the Woods murder. Detective Burns wanted to question Eric again. Hamilton agreed they would question Eric to find out what other information he could provide.

Washington and Hamilton sat back in their chairs. Hamilton sighed, "Man, who the hell are these people?"

"I don't know, but I'm almost ready to throw the whole bunch of them in jail except for those two kids and that Jenkins woman."

As they walked toward the interview room, a police officer stopped them and said a Carol White was looking for them. She was escorted to the interview room.

Chapter 37

Carol was unaware of what took place after she had left the hotel that morning. She turned off her cell phone as asked. Water was offered, which she accepted. She was nervous and her throat was dry.

At twenty-three, Carol White was a light-skinned Afro-American woman who wore her hair in long black braids. Dressed in a dark blue business suit, with a white blouse and a small briefcase, Carol looked like a confident business woman. Her facial expression didn't show her nervousness. She asked why she had been asked to come to the police headquarters.

"Mrs. White, thank you for coming in. I'm Detective Hamilton this is my partner, Detective Washington. We're with the homicide division." They sat down. Washington would take notes. They already knew her husband had died nine months earlier in Afghanistan and she had a three-year-old son. Her record was clean. She lived in Oakland and was unemployed.

"Homicide? What's this all about?"

"Mrs. White, we asked you here because we're investigating an incident at the hotel."

She sat up in the chair. "Is the choir all right?"

Hamilton could see she was becoming agitated so he asked how the job interview had been as was a way to distract her.

The Gospel Choir Murder

"It was good. I think I got the job. Why did you ask me to come here?"

"Mrs. White, we're conducting an investigation and need to know what you did when you arrived in Las Vegas yesterday."

"Well, we got here around 1:30 with no luggage. It was too early to check into the hotel, so we decided to go walking on the strip. I found the Disney store and bought my son a gift. After I left there, I went to some other stores. I ate at one of the hotel restaurants and returned to the desk to check in. I don't gamble, but I walked around the casino just looking. The other van got here around 7:30. I got my luggage and went to my room. I ordered room service and went to bed because I had an interview at 9:00 this morning."

"Were you alone?"

"No, I was with Valarie and Monique. We share a room. But they went back out after we got our luggage."

"So you were alone for the rest of the evening?"

"Yes I was. By the time they got back, I'd taken a shower and was in bed. Why are you asking?"

"So you don't know what time they returned to the room?"

"No. I talked to my son and family, went over the job requirements and my resumé, and went to bed."

"So you have no one to account for your whereabouts between the times your roommates left and when they returned?"

"No, I guess not. Like I said, I called my son and talked to my mother. Why do I need someone to vouch for me? What's going on?"

"Can you give us your mother's phone number just to confirm your whereabouts?

Reluctantly, she gave them the number of her mother. Now she was really upset. "Why don't you answer my questions? What's this all about?"

"Well, Mrs. White, I'm sorry to be the one to tell you, but Mr. Woods was murdered last night."

"What? Murdered? Deacon Woods? Oh my God!" She put her head in her hands and began sobbing.

Both detectives watched and waited. Notifications were always uncomfortable, but they had to do their job. Hamilton pushed the tissue box toward her.

"Who would murder Deacon Woods? Where was he?"

"He was murdered in his room. That's why we are questioning everyone in the choir. Is there anyone in the choir who was angry or had a grudge against him?"

"No, everybody loves him. Nobody in the choir would kill him. None of us have ever been that mad. We are Christians. We are not the kind of people who would harm each other." She looked very sincere and blew her nose. "Please believe me, you have it all wrong. How was he killed?"

"A knife would in the back of the neck."

Carol's eyes widened as she jerked back in the chair. "Ohhhhhhhhh."

"Mrs. White, I know this is a shock, but please try to compose yourself. Are you sure there's nothing you can tell us to help with our investigation? When you left this morning did you see anyone or anything strange?"

"No. Valarie and Monique were still sleeping and I tried not to wake them. When I got to the lobby, I thought I saw Sarah, but I could be wrong. I took a cab to the interview. Deacon Woods must have been mistaken for somebody else. You really should be looking for a stranger. Are we safe? Suppose the killer has targeted the choir?"

Washington responded, "There's no evidence that the choir is in any danger. Here's my card, if you think of anything else that will help with this investigation, please call me. When you're ready, I'll have an officer take you back to the hotel. We need you to remain in town."

"OK." Wiping her eyes and sniffling, she took the card, stood up and walked out the door.

After the door closed, the two detectives sat back and took a deep breath. After a few minutes, Washington used his cell phone to call Carol's mother. The mother verified she'd had a conversation the previous night with her daughter. She was upset and told she could call her daughter within the hour.

During the ride to the hotel, Carol's phone rang. She tried to compose herself and told her mother she would call her back as soon as she was in her room.

Chapter 38

Evelyn stared at her notes trying to understand why Deacon Woods was murdered. Besides her, there were thirteen other people on this tour. Somebody had killed Deacon Woods. While it was hard to believe any of the choir could kill, it was even harder to understand how a stranger got so close to Deacon Woods. What could have triggered such anger within the last four days? But why would a stranger kill him in such a brutal way? Evelyn tried to picture his interaction with each choir member. Nothing stood out. He got along with everyone.

What was she missing? He and Deacon Jackson were friends. Perhaps they were more than friends. In the last four days, they were often together but that's to be expected. Eating, driving the vans, sitting together during church services and working on the same church committee, they seemed like brothers. Nothing she saw indicated they had problems, but who knew?

Cory and Amos were the youngest. They had no reason to get angry with Deacon Woods. What if Deacon Woods had found out what Gary did to Sarah? Maybe they fought, but it still didn't explain why the deacon was naked.

Valarie had just met him, so it wouldn't make sense for her to kill him. Evelyn still needed to find out why she wanted to talk to her, though.

Carol and Randy were older and both had family responsibilities. The only time they interacted with Deacon Woods was while riding in the van. Evelyn hasn't seen anything that would indicate any problems. She just couldn't see either one of them angry enough to put their families in jeopardy.

Evelyn was tired and really needed to rest. She put a chair in front of the door just for safety. Not knowing what tomorrow would bring, she lay down on the bed. It didn't take long before she fell asleep.

Evelyn was running, running down a long hall. A figure was running after her. The hall curved left, then right. The figure was getting closer and closer. Looking down, she saw she was holding a bloody knife. Her nightgown was covered with blood. The person was getting closer. She ran faster but she couldn't run fast enough. Still getting closer. The hall was getting darker. She turned around. No one was there. Evelyn stopped running. As she turned back around a figure was standing in front of her, the face covered in blood. She screamed. That's how she woke up.

It took her several minutes to recover. She sat up in bed. She was drenched in sweat. She kept thinking she was missing a piece of this puzzle. Looking at the clock, she realized she'd only been asleep for a few minutes. She grabbed her notebook. Gary Stevens came back into her mind. What did she know about him? Sarah said he was a successful businessman but never said what type of business. He was an abuser—which she knew. Gary, a tall, good looking young man, was polite in front of the group. He looked like a nice young man. Sarah said he'd accused her of cheating even though there was no reason to feel that way. Was he capable of killing someone? Yes, she thought, he could be the killer.

Chapter 39

Back at police headquarters, detectives were getting ready to interview Randy Sullivan. Randy was terrified. He really wanted to call his wife. Not knowing what was going on was agonizing. Soberly he sat thinking about the first time he was ever in a police station. This was painful. He hated police stations.

He was ten years old. As usual, he had been told to care for his little brother and sister. They both wanted to go outside and play. He gave in. He would let them play outside for just a few minutes. His sister got tired quickly and went back inside. His younger brother had just finished playing with his toy airplane and turned around to run inside. Randy heard a gunshot. He saw a car and the face of the young man in the backseat with a gun. Everything seemed to be in slow motion. His brother's eyes locked on his. His body jerked. Looking down at his brother's small body, Randy saw blood running down the front of his shirt. He was still trying to run to Randy, but his eyes rolled back in his head and his body dropped.

Randy ran to him, picked up his limp body and cradled him in his arms, all the while screaming. That's how the police found him, still screaming. It was obvious the boy was dead. Randy wouldn't let anyone near him until his mother arrived.

Years later, when the family moved to Oakland, Randy got in trouble with the law for shoplifting. Leaving Los Angeles was the best thing that ever happened to him. But watching his brother die from a stray bullet almost destroyed him. Nobody knew he'd undergone psychiatric therapy and didn't speak for six months. He blamed himself for his brother's murder.

With Deacon Woods' help, he changed his ways. He studied hard, got a degree, and married a wonderful woman. With the new job he had just found, he'd be able to support his family, but he was afraid the police would judge him on his past.

An officer escorted him into the small room. He sat in the chair facing the door. Soon both detectives came in and sat down.

Detective Washington spoke first, "Mr. Sullivan, we're sorry you had to wait so long."

"Why are we here?"

"Before we get started, can I offer you some water?"

"Thank you."

"Mr. Sullivan, we have a serious situation. We need your help. What did you do when you arrived in Las Vegas yesterday?"

"In Las Vegas? The detectives stared at him with no expression. "Well, once we got here, I decided to go shopping. We're expecting our first child, so I bought a gift for the baby. Why do you ask?"

"When did you return to the hotel?"

"Well, I stopped and got something to eat and just walked about. I checked in then went to my room. The other van arrived around seven. I took my luggage to my room, called my wife, and watched TV for the night."

"You were in the van with Mr. Woods, is that right?"

"Yes. I was in the van with Deacon Woods. What's going on?"

"What is your relationship with Mr. Woods?"

"What do you mean, relationship? Deacon Woods is a member of my church. He drove the van. He's a nice man. Why, what's wrong?"

"Do you know of anyone who would want to harm him?"

"No, we all like Deacon Woods. He's helped me a lot in the past years. He's almost like a father to me."

"Mr. Sullivan, we know that you've had some trouble with the law in the past. Are you currently involved in any criminal activity?" Washington had his folder open and was reading the background report.

Randy sat back in his chair like he'd been slapped. He knew this would come up. Taking a deep breath, he said, "No! That life is behind me. I was sixteen and stupid. Getting caught stealing from a department store was a wakeup call for me. Pastor Watson and Deacon Woods are the only ones who know about my past. Please, don't tell the choir."

"We have no reason to share that information. Thanks for telling us. So did you and Deacon Woods get along well?"

"Yes, yes we did."

"Is there anyone who didn't get along with him?" Randy looked puzzled.

"No!"

"What did you do when you arrived at the hotel?"

"I told you. I don't gamble. Jessie, Cory, Amos, Alex, and I decided to walk down the strip. We got back around 6 o'clock. We checked in. The other van got here I think it was around 7 or 7:30 last night. We got our luggage, and went to our rooms. Alex and I are sharing a room. I stayed in the room, ordered dinner, and talked to my wife. He had a date with Monique and went back out."

"So you never saw Deacon Woods after that."

"That's right."

"I have some bad news. Mr. Woods was murdered last night."

"What! What did you say? Deacon Woods was murdered?" They watched his face and saw the shock and disbelief. He slumped in the chair. "Who would kill him?" His eyes filled with tears.

The detectives watched and waited. He took several tissues and dragged them across his face, trying not to show the tears.

"Oh my God! Where? Where was he killed?"

"He was murdered in his room."

"MURDERED!"

"I can't believe this. Deacon Woods is such a good man. Why would anyone murder him? I don't believe this. He was so nice." His voice was really cracking. "He was almost like a father to me. My dad left when I was very young. Deacon Woods treated me like a son. He was excited about me getting a new job and starting over. I just can't believe this."

The detectives could feel his pain even though they were still judging his reaction. They waited a few minutes. "Mr. Sullivan, we need to speak with your wife to confirm your alibi. Do you have any objection?"

"Yes, you can call her."

Hamilton stepped outside and made the call. After assuring Randy's wife he was unharmed, she confirmed her conversation with her husband. There was nothing in his record to indicate he'd had any problems since he was a teenager. Based on his reaction and their gut feelings, they didn't feel Randy was a suspect.

"Are you aware of any disagreements Mr. Woods has had with anyone in the choir?"

Randy sighed. "Well, you know how it is when different people get together—there are bound to be disagreements about something or another. Deacon Jackson and Deacon Woods were arguing about something at the concert Wednesday night. I'm sure it wasn't about anything that would cause a murder. I mean, they've been friends for years."

"Do you know what they were arguing about?"

"No, afterward they seemed fine. That's how we are, angry one minute and friends the next. I guess you gentlemen have never been in a church choir."

"No, we haven't."

"Well, for as long as I've been in the choir even when we get angry we quickly resolve it and move on."

"Are there any other members who've had disagreements?"

"Some of the ladies have had some disagreements, but everyone's all right now."

"Are you sure there's nothing else you can tell us about Mr. Woods?"

"No, I'm just so shocked. You can't think one of us murdered him?" The detectives didn't answer. "Was he was robbed?"

"We're looking at everything and everyone. We would prefer you not discuss this with the other members. Here's my card," Hamilton said, handing it to him. "Please call me if you think of anything that might help us in this case. Until this matter is resolved, please don't leave town. I'll have a police officer take you back to the hotel."

"OK. Do we need protection? I mean this could be someone who is targeting the choir."

"Mr. Sullivan, we will have a police officer at the hotel. If you feel afraid, or threatened, call me immediately or let him know. Thank you for your cooperation." Randy stood up, shook hands, and slowly walked out the room.

As soon as he was alone, he called his wife. She was almost hysterical and Randy did his best to calm her down. He was on his way back to the hotel and would call her from there.

While he didn't want to worry his wife, he had to tell her about the murder. And when he did, she demanded he come home immediately. She was afraid he could be next. Randy told her he couldn't leave yet. They talked for over an hour. Only when he had hung up the phone did he realize how scared he was. He decided to have dinner in his room.

Tears were still running down his cheeks, and Randy was exhausted. The gravity of what had happened was sinking in.

After Randy left, a member of the criminal investigative unit came in to discuss their preliminary findings with Hamilton and Washington. Fingerprints were found in the bathroom along with hair follicles on a towel. Once the identity of the person was determined, the detectives would be advised. It would take a week to process the evidence.

Washington was convinced one of these choir members was the murderer. Hamilton wasn't so sure.

Chapter 38

Evelyn was just starting to gather her thoughts when the phone rang.

"Sister Jenkins, how are you? Are you able to talk?"

'Well, Pastor I'm holding up. I haven't talked to Deacon Jackson yet. I suspect he may still be at the police station."

"I just spoke with Cory's parents who naturally are very upset. They're leaving for Las Vegas in a few hours. I told them everything I know. Hopefully they will be able to assist you and Deacon Jackson. Also, Pastor Mason called to offer his help. He's going to assist with the paperwork to get Deacon Woods' body returned to the Bay Area."

"Pastor, you know I don't normally get involved with the church business, but do you know of anyone at the church who might have been angry with Deacon Woods?

"Sister Watson, I've asked myself that question so many times since I heard about this. There's nobody in the church that I know of who would be so angry as to kill him. A few years ago, he did have a falling out with Deacon Jackson."

"Can you tell me what happened?"

"Well, the two work together and for a while they stopped speaking. Neither one of them would give an explanation as to what was wrong. I had to speak with them about it because it was distracting others at church. After that, they resolved the problem and they've been friends since."

"So they never told you why they were mad."

"No. And because they acted friendly again, I never pressed the issue."

"Well, I am concerned that I haven't heard from Deacon Jackson."

"I'm praying he's all right. When you do hear from him, please have him call me."

"I will, Pastor."

Evelyn added the information to her notes. She would ask Deacon Jackson why they'd had a disagreement.

Chapter 40

Sarah hated Gary for what he did to her, but she hadn't told the police about the attack. Sarah came from a good middle-class family. While her dad worked, her mother was a stay-at=home mom who constantly encouraged Sarah and her brother to do their best. Her brother joined the Army. Sarah graduated from community college. She had a passion for writing, so she was thrilled when she got a copywriter job at the *Oakland Tribune* newspaper.

Sarah was totally focused on her career until she met Gary. Her mother said he was a bad boy and was hiding something, but Sarah couldn't see it. She had loved him, but not now. She started crying. That's when the door opened and a police officer called her name. Her legs were weak as she stood up and followed him to the interview room. Standing there in the hall were the detectives she saw at the hotel. They ushered her into the room and she sat in the chair they offered. Taking a deep breath, she tried to calm her nerves.

The detectives observed a very nice looking young woman, neatly dressed in a blouse and skirt with sandals. Both noticed that dark glasses covered her eyes.

Hamilton spoke first, "Thank you for your patience, Ms. Johnson. Can I get you some water or soda?"

Softly she said, "No thank you."

"We're conducting an investigation and need your help. Can I ask where you were yesterday?"

"Is this about why you had Ms. Jenkins in handcuffs?"

"Ms. Jenkins has been released and is back at the hotel. Can you tell me what you did yesterday?"

"Well, I came with the choir to Las Vegas from Los Angeles. We arrived around one or one thirty. My boyfriend Gary followed the van. When we got here, Gary and I decided to go sightseeing. We drove around town and got back just in time to get my luggage from the other van around 7:30 last night."

Both detectives were intrigued and Washington wrote something on his notepad. "So you were with your boyfriend after you got here?"

She adjusted the sunglasses. "Yes."

"What's the name of your boyfriend?"

"Gary Stevens."

"Where is Gary from?"

"He lives in Oakland."

"So Gary was with you all day?"

"No, he followed the van and when we got here I was with him."

"Is Gary with the choir?"

"No, he met us in Los Angeles after our concert."

"So Gary is not a member of the choir, but he came to Las Vegas, why?"

"He said he wanted to be with me. He's on vacation. He enjoyed the concert in Los Angeles and decided to come to the one here in Las Vegas, so he followed us here."

"How long have you known him?"

"Gary is my fiancé. We've been together for almost a year and a half."

"What kind of work does he do?"

"Gary is a businessman."

"What kind of business?"

"Why are you asking questions about Gary? Why are we here anyway?"

He continued, "Ms. Johnson, what did you do after getting your luggage last night?"

"Well I took my luggage to my room that I share with Diana and Gwen. Gary booked a room by himself. He and I went to dinner and a show. We left the hotel about 8:30 and saw the *Blue Man* show."

"So you were with him all night?"

The room was silent. Sarah put her hands over the sunglasses. The detectives looked at each other and waited. Suddenly, Sarah started to cry. They handed her the box of tissues and continued to wait in silence. She took the sunglasses off.

Both detectives looked startled. Then as she spoke, both started taking notes.

"We had a fight on our way back to the hotel. It was bad. He hit me. I ran out of the car at a streetlight. I was afraid to go to my room so I wondered around for hours by myself." She sobbed. "Gary had never hit me before. I was so scared of him. I stayed in the woman's bathroom for a few hours. I know Gary's sorry. He's been calling and texting, but I won't answer my cell phone. Please don't arrest him. I don't think he meant to hurt me."

Washington stood up. "Gary did that to you?" Sarah nodded yes.

"Do you know where Gary is now?"

"No he called me about an hour ago. Is that why we're here? I don't want to cause any trouble."

"What is Gary's phone number?" Sarah fumbled through her purse for her phone and gave them the number. "Is Gary Stevens his whole name?"

"It's Gary P. Stevens. I told you he didn't mean to hit me. Please don't arrest him."

"We'll be right back." They hurried out the room. Washington returned within minutes.

"So you don't know where he was after you left him last night?"

"No, I don't. Why?"

"About what time did you get out of the car?"

"It was around 1:00 a.m."

"So after one o'clock you never saw him again?"

"No I just wanted to get away from him. He hit me." She raised her voice in anger. "Nobody hits me. I don't take that crap."

"Where did you go?"

"I ran to one of the hotels and walked around trying to cool down. I had to get away from him."

"What time did you get back to your hotel?"

"I guess it was around four in the morning. I was afraid to go to my room, so I stayed in the casino area and the women's bathroom."

"Did you ever see Gary after that?"

"No."

"Did you see anybody from the choir?"

"The choir, no."

"So you say you were in the casino. How long did you stay there?"

"For hours. I fell asleep but when I woke up it was like seven this morning."

Hamilton returned. "Well Ms. Johnson, the reason you are here is because Mr. Woods was murdered last night."

Just as he finished the last word, Sarah fainted. Hamilton managed to catch her before she hit the floor. They called for assistance. Luckily, the coroner, a physician on call, was in the building. After a few minutes she regained consciousness. Still a little wobbly she tried to sit up from the stretcher she was lying on, but was encouraged to continue to lie down.

"Did you say Deacon Woods was murdered? Gary didn't kill anybody." Sarah was trying to grasp what they said. Deacon Woods was murdered. "Oh God!"

When Hamilton left the room, he changed the all points bulletin to add a person of interest who might be armed and dangerous, in a murder investigation. They needed to find this guy now. They hurried back to the office.

Gary Stevens was still at large. From their experience, if he could beat up a woman, he could commit murder.

After fifteen minutes, they checked on Sarah. She'd regained her composure. They all returned to the interview room for further questioning. They had pulled a background check on Gary Stevens and it wasn't good.

Hamilton tried to be gentle but he had to find out everything she did that night.

"Ms. Johnson, we need to know if Gary knew Mr. Woods."

"No! Gary met him this week in Los Angeles. He may have seen him at church but he never talked to him. I just introduced everybody to him after the concert. How did Deacon Woods die?"

"He was murdered in his room last night."

"Why would anyone want to kill him?"

"That's what we're here to find out. You say you have been dating Gary for over a year. What else can you tell us about him?"

"I don't know anything else to tell you. We met at a club. He's twenty-five. He works. Up until last night, he was a really nice guy. I've never been at his job. Gary told me he's in import and export business. He's a good man."

"Does he have any family?"

"Yes, he has a brother. I think he lives in Chicago. I've never met him. Gary couldn't have done this. I told you he barely knows Deacon Woods."

"I need to talk to him. Will you call him?"

Sarah turned on her phone and dialed the number. Gary answered. She told him where she was and handed the phone to Hamilton.

"Hello, is this Gary Stevens?"

"Yes."

"My name is Detective Hamilton I'm with the Las Vegas Police Department. We are questioning the choir about an incident that happened at the hotel. I understand you are still in town. Would you come in and help us with our investigation?" There was a long pause on the phone and then it went dead.

"Gary, Gary. Are you still there?" No response.

Hamilton left the room with Sarah's phone still in his hand. She looked shocked. Washington also left the room.

They requested a GPS track on his phone but it had been turned off. They did know he was still in the area. When Washington returned, he asked Sarah if she wanted to file a report for assault and battery. Reluctantly, she agreed to file one. One thing she had hated was that her mother was weak. For years, her dad abused her mother and she took it. Sarah swore it would never happen to her. Now she was in the same situation. She would file the report. It would give the police probable cause to get a search warrant to search Gary's hotel room and car.

With the warrant and a CSI tech, Washington went to the hotel, while Hamilton stayed to file the report. When Sarah had finished, he gave her a business card and told her to call him if she remembered anything.

A uniformed female officer from the Domestic Violence Unit talked with her. Her entire body was photographed. Sarah was exhausted and scared. Another officer drove her back to the hotel and walked her to her room. She immediately locked the door. Everything in the room had been tossed. Sarah sat down and called her mother. When she told her everything that had happened, they both cried. Her mother begged her to come home. They talked for more than an hour before she calmed down. Then Sarah gathered her clothes up and waited for her roommates to come back.

Chapter 41

Gwen had been waiting for a long time. Patience was not her best attribute. She walked toward the dispatcher's desk, announcing in her most insulting voice, "I'm leaving."

Without looking up, he firmly told her, "Sit down."

She tried to keep her belligerent tone. "I don't have to stay here."

He slowly looked her straight in the eye. "If you don't sit your ass down within the next 60 seconds I'm going to put you in jail. When they're ready for you, they'll call your name."

Realizing she was in no position to argue, Gwen walked back and plopped down on the seat without another word.

Meanwhile, Evelyn was starting to develop theories on who could be the killer. She didn't think someone followed the deacon back to the hotel. She was of the mind that he had to have known the killer to open his door. Why was he nude? Sex might be a factor in this case. Maybe whoever did it wanted to disgrace him in death.

Hamilton had Gwen Harrison escorted to the interview room. She sat down in a huff. When offered water or a soda, she asked for both.

Hamilton apologized for keeping Gwen waiting as he read the background check and waited for the beverage. There were two complaints on her record: threatening to commit bodily harm and disturbing the peace. Both had been dropped.

Washington sat impassively. He had just finished reading the report on the dresses they found in her hotel room with security tags from a store in Los Angeles still on them. The detectives were waiting for the store's owner to call back, to tell them if he wanted to press charges.

Gwen demanded, "What's this all about? Why are we here?"

"Well, as you can tell, there was an incident at the hotel and we need to find out if you can help with our investigation. I understand you arrived here yesterday. Is that correct?"

"Is that why you arrested Ms. Jenkins?"

"Ms. Jenkins is not under arrest—in fact she's back at the hotel."

"Really?"

"As I understand it, you arrived in Las Vegas yesterday. Is that correct? What did you do when you arrived?"

"We got here about 1:30 but couldn't get in our rooms. So me and Diana went walking on the strip checking out the sights."

"What time did you come back to the hotel?"

"Well we got back around five and went to our room."

"So it was just you and Diana?

"Yes. Sarah went off with her boyfriend, Gary."

"Did you see or meet any of the other choir members?"

"We saw Deacon Jackson and some of the others walking down the strip."

"Did you ever see Deacon Woods?"

"I don't remember. What's this all about?"

"When did you meet up with the others?"

"We met in the lobby when Sister Jenkins and the rest of the choir got here around 7:30 with the luggage."

"And then?"

"We went back to our room, got dressed, and went out partying."

"Who were you with?"

"Me and Diana."

"Did you see Deacon Woods?"

"No."

"So you never saw Deacon Woods after you got your luggage?"

"No."

"Were you ever in his room?" Gwen's face contorted as she raised her voice and said, "Hell No! Why would I."

"Do you like Mr. Woods?"

"Yeah, he's all right. He's a deacon at our church."

"Have you ever had a disagreement with him?"

"No."

"How long have you known him?"

"Every since I joined the church."

"So you've never gotten angry with him?"

Gwen paused. She had to think. "Well I did get mad with him but it wasn't about anything serious."

Hamilton made a notation, opened the folder and read a report. There was dead silence in the room. He wanted to keep her off guard. "You have a police record for aggravated assault a few years ago. What was that about?"

Gwen was stunned. Her shoulders slumped. She sat back in the chair. That was just where he wanted her to be.

Sounding apologetic she said, "That was dismissed. I was drunk when it happened. This girl was trying to steal my man. I told her to back off but she tried to hit me. She missed and I slapped her in the face. The charges were dropped."

"Sounds like you have a temper. Do you always hit people when you get mad?"

"No."

"Are you the shoplifter?"

Gwen didn't answer.

He raised his voice. "I said are you the shoplifter? You know we searched your room and found clothes with the security tags attached. Are they yours?"

She didn't answer. Her eyes were wandering all over the room. She started fidgeting. They could tell she was trying to think of an answer.

Standing up, Hamilton slammed his hand on the desk, "I said, are they yours?"

Gwen didn't know what to say. She starting thinking maybe Diana told them.

"It was a mistake. I'm going to take them back."

"I was told the choir is not going back to Los Angeles. You're lying. You stole them and unless you can provide me with a receipt I'm going to lock your ass up." He knew she was the kind of person he had to use that tone with.

In a begging tone she mumbled, "I'll pay for them."

"Too late!" "You knew you had them when you walked out that store." Ignoring her, he continued, "what did Mr. Woods do to make you mad?"

"He called me a whore, A WHORE."

"When did this happen?"

"Diana and I were going out last night. We saw him in the lobby. He said we looked like prostitutes. I told him he didn't know what the hell he was talking about."

"What time was this?"

"It was around eleven last night."

"So last night at eleven you saw him in the lobby?"

"Yes."

"Was he with anyone?"

"I don't know. When I saw him he was by himself."

"What time did you get back to the hotel?"

"We got back around two a.m. and went to our room."

"Both of you?"

"Yes."

"Did you leave the room after that?"

"No."

"Listen, if I find that you're lying I'm not going to be the nice guy anymore."

Trying to still be rebellious she said, "I'm not answering any more questions until you tell me why you want to know what I did."

"We're investigating the murder of Mr. Woods."

Hamilton sat back waiting to see Gwen's response.

Her response surprised him. "What! So you think I had something to do with it?" she asked. There were no tears. She didn't look shocked. Gwen sat back in the chair and said, "He's dead! Who killed him?" It was as if she didn't hear the word murder.

"Somebody plunged a knife in him." He wanted to make it as graphic as he could to see how she would react.

Gwen was immune to hearing that people she knew were murdered. Growing up in the projects, it was a normal occurrence. It was horrible to think that Deacon Woods was killed, but she wasn't going to show her emotions.

"He was murdered?" In her mind, she still hadn't processed the word murder. Her voice sounded sympathetic but her body language didn't change. Gwen was thinking of what she did that night. She knew Diana would keep quiet.

"Would you like some water?"

Not saying a word, she took a sip of the water and sat back. "Look I'm really sorry somebody killed Deacon Woods, but I didn't do it."

"I'll give you time to try and remember if there is anything else you need to tell us."

He stood up and asked an officer to escort her back to the empty office. Gwen tried to say something but he cut her off and with an angry voice and said "Because of the possible shoplifting charge you can't leave, at least not now. When I hear from the shop owner, I'll talk to you later."

Gwen immediately stopped talking. Now she was scared really scared. She wanted to go back to the hotel.

"Can I please go back to the hotel?"

"No!" He turned and walked out thinking, this broad has some balls.

Gwen sat shocked. Reality was sinking in. She was in trouble, real trouble. She started crying in silence.

In the hall, Hamilton was greeted by a crime scene technician who told him the other fingerprints were being analyzed. He handed him a glass and asked him to add it to the others.

Chapter 42

As Jessie McDaniel waited for the police, he found himself patting his leg uncontrollably. People around him with guns were ignoring him like he didn't exist. Why was Evelyn in handcuffs? What could they want with the choir? Maybe they weren't the only ones asked to come to the police station.

Jessie was the kind of young man who liked order. You could tell it in the way he dressed. He knew people looking at him often mistakenly labeled him as gay, but he wasn't. He was sensitive.

A policeman placed his hand on Jessie's shoulder and directed him to the interview room and to the chair facing the door. Hamilton walked in with a stern look on his face.

"Mr. McDaniel, thank you for your patience. Can I offer you a glass of water?"

"May I have a soda?"

Hamilton asked the officer outside the door to get the beverage. He sat down opposite Jessie and starting looking in a folder. There was dead silence in the room. It was a copy of the background check on Jessie. Nothing stood out. No criminal record or warrants. Looking up at Jessie, he saw fear in his eyes. "Mr. McDaniel, I'm sure you already know we have a serious incident back at the hotel. I need to ask you some questions to help with our investigation. When did you arrive in Las Vegas?"

"Does this have anything to do with why Ms. Jenkins was in handcuffs?"

"Yes. Ms. Jenkins is back at the hotel. Now when did you arrive in Las Vegas?"

"We got here last night around seven thirty."

'Why were you in separate vans?"

"Eric was mugged in L.A. He had to go to the police station to make a report. The group decided to have members of the choir who did not need to be delayed go to Las Vegas in one van. We had the luggage in our van."

"Who was in the van with you?"

"Ms. Jenkins, Eric, Deacon Jackson and me."

"What happened to Mr. Parker in L.A.?"

"Well, he went to get something from the drugstore and some guys jumped him."

"So after you made the report you drove to Las Vegas?"

"Yes."

"Where were the others when you arrived?"

"They were all here in Las Vegas. Deacon Woods drove the first van. I don't know what they did before we got here. We all met in the lobby. Everybody got their luggage and went to their rooms."

"Where did you go when you got your luggage?"

"Eric and I went to our room."

"Did you stay in your room all night?"

"No, I talked to Sister Jenkins for awhile, and then I went out. Eric said he didn't feel good so he stayed in."

"Were you alone?"

"At first, but I ran into Cory and Amos so we went to dinner together."

"What time was that?"

"I think it was around 9:00 o'clock."

"What did you do after that?"

"Cory and Amos went back to the hotel around 11:00. I stayed on the strip sightseeing."

"You were alone?"

"Yes, Cory and Amos are too young. I played the slot machines. I even had a couple of drinks in the casino. I know as a Christian I'm not supposed to drink liquor but I'm still young and I like to party. I never do it around the choir. After all I have to maintain my image."

'Did you see any of the other choir members while you were out?"

"No. I saw Gary, Sarah's boyfriend, on the strip but he didn't see me."

"What time was that?"

"Sometime before twelve. I tried to avoid him or Sarah."

"What time did you get back to the hotel?"

"It was around midnight. I checked out the casino at our hotel for a while, and then went to my room."

"At anytime did you see Mr. Woods?"

"Deacon Woods? Yeah. I saw him in the lobby when I first got back to the hotel around midnight."

"Was he with anyone?"

"I don't know. I didn't see him with anyone."

"So you didn't talk to him?"

"No he was leaving the hotel, I just saw him from behind."

"How do you know it was him?"

"I go to church with him, I know what he looks like, and how he walks and it was Deacon Woods."

"Did you see anyone else in your group?"

"Deacon Jackson. I saw him later in the casino but I didn't say anything. Like I told you I was trying to avoid anybody from the choir."

"What time was that?"

"I guess it was around 12:30. I didn't want to embarrass him or myself since he's a deacon and all."

"What kind of liquor do you drink?"

"I like scotch on the rocks." Hamilton made a notation.

"Was anyone with him?"

"No."

"Was that the last time you saw Deacon Woods?"

"Yes."

"When did you go to your room?"

"It was around 1 a.m."

"Did you see anyone else from the group?"

"No!"

"You never left the room?"

Washington entered the room and sat down quietly watching Jessie.

"No."

"Have you ever been in Deacon Woods' room?"

"No, why would I be in Deacon Woods' room?"

"It was only you and Eric in your room?"

"Yeah, but he was sleep when I got back."

"So as far as you know, Deacon Jackson was in the casino and Deacon Woods was leaving the hotel. Is that right?"

Raising his voice, he said, "Yes. Why?"

"We're investigating the murder of Mr. Woods." Both detectives watched for Jessie's reaction.

Jessie's body became tense as if he had been hit, then he slumped back in the chair. His face was contorted, with shock, disbelief, and now sadness. "What! Deacon Woods? Our Deacon Woods? He was murdered?" Jessie's voice was trembling. He barely got the words out. "When? Where?"

"That's what we're trying to determine. You may have been the last person to see him alive."

Jessie tried to hide his face. Tears rolled through his fingers and down his cheeks on to the table. There was no sound in the room. He could barely speak. "Are we in danger?"

"No, we don't believe you are in any danger."

"Why would anybody want to kill him?" He grabbed a tissue from the box and started drying his eyes. He was trying to control his emotions.

"How long have you known Deacon Woods?"

"He's been a deacon at our church for years. I just can't believe this. Is that why you wanted to know where I was, you think I killed him? Do you think one of us killed him?"

"That's what we're trying to find out. How was your relationship with Deacon Woods?"

"Well, I didn't kill him, I could never do that. He was a nice man. He and his wife are both nice. We've never even had an argument. Do the others know about this? I can't believe this." He was talking so fast his voice was trembling. His eyes started tearing up again. "I can't believe this. When was he killed?"

"Last night or early this morning someone murdered him in his room. Are you sure you have never been to his room?"

There was a pause and then in a softer voice, he answered, "Yes, I was there."

In a very strong tone, Washington asked, "When?"

Jessie paused and cleared his throat. "I went there around 8 o'clock."

"Why did you go to his room?"

"Deacon Woods let me borrow some money."

"How much money are we talking about?"

"He gave me three hundred dollars."

196

"That's a lot of money. Did he always carry a lot of money?"

"I don't know about always but he said I didn't have to repay him until after the tour. I was running out of money. He gave it to me. I was going to pay him back when we got back to Oakland. Oh God, this is horrible."

The detectives took notes. "What was the relationship between Mr. Jackson and Mr. Woods?"

"They got along well. I've never seen them angry. If you didn't know their names you would think they were brothers 'cause there're always together at church."

"How long were you in his room?"

"About a half hour."

"Was anyone else there?"

"No I didn't want anybody else to know I needed money."

"Why would it take a half hour to get money?"

"We started talking about the concert, tour and other stuff."

"What other stuff?"

"He was talking about going to see a show and asked if I knew which ones were good. I told him about the *Blue Man*. Then he was telling me to make sure everyone behaved themselves."

"What happened next?"

"I took the money and left."

"Did you notice anyone suspicious in the hall?"

"No, I was just glad to get the money."

"What time was this?"

"Like I said it was after I got my luggage about 8:00."

"What did you do after you left him?"

"I went back to my room and called Sister Jenkins."

"So the last time you saw him was late last night?"

"Yes."

"What did he mean to make sure everyone behaved?"

"I just think he wanted us to make sure we acted like Christians. We represent our church. He didn't want anyone else to get hurt like Eric did."

The detectives walked outside the room to discuss his answers.

Jessie was scared. Finally, like the others, he was given a business card and told not to discuss anything with the others. Until further notice, he was to remain in Las Vegas.

He turned to the detectives. "Please, find who every killed Deacon Woods. He was a really nice man."

They both nodded an affirmative. Jessie agreed to call if he thought of anything else. He took the card and followed an officer to a police car. As he sat in the car the horror really hit him. He put his sunglasses on to shield the tears that rolled down his face.

After a while, Jessie turned on his phone and called home. His mother answered frantically. She, like him, talked fast. Within a minute, she'd asked a dozen questions. He told her what had happened up until the time he was released. He told her that despite everything he wanted to stay with the choir. Just as he finished talking, the car drove up to the hotel. Hurriedly, he got out, looked around and headed to his room. He dialed Evelyn.

Chapter 43

When she got back to the hotel, Evelyn had called Deacon Jackson's room. After several rings, he answered.

"Deacon Jackson, you're back. Why didn't you call me? I called you and left a message when I found Deacon Woods. When you didn't call me back, I called Pastor Watson."

With a sad voice he replied, "I'm sorry Sister Jenkins. I'm glad to hear from you. Yes, I just got back. I guess you know about Deacon Woods?"

"Yes," she said hastily. "When I went up to his room, the door was open. It was horrible. He was lying on the bed nude with a knife sticking out of his neck. I almost fainted." She could hear a gasp on the phone. "I have never seen such a gruesome scene in my life. Blood was everywhere. I don't know if he let the person in. It didn't look like there was a fight. There was dried blood on the walls. The bed was soaked in blood. There was a knife stuck in the back of his head." Evelyn realized she was crying. There was silence on the phone.

Then he shouted. "Oh my God! They told me he was murdered but I didn't know you saw him. Is that why they had you in handcuffs?"

"Yes, I didn't know what to do. I called you but you didn't answer. I knew the police were coming so I decided to wait for them. I never imagined they would think I killed him. I have never been so scared in my whole life." Her voice was trembling.

"So you didn't see the maid?"

"What maid?"

"Just as you went up the elevator, a maid came screaming Spanish out the elevator. No one could tell what she was saying except a girl at the register. We couldn't imagine what had happened. The choir was looking for you to come down. When we didn't see you, everybody thought something happened to you. Things got really crazy when someone realized she said 'murder.' Everybody in the lobby started to scatter. We were going outside but the police stopped us and told us to come back in. They had guns drawn. Was there anything in the room that could identify who killed him?"

"No." She didn't tell him she went back in to look for evidence.

Instead she said, "I really didn't know what to look for. I was too shocked. This couple across the room from his let me rest in their room. But I think they thought I was the murderer. After awhile I went back in the hall. That's where the police found me."

"Somebody killed him last night. And the police wouldn't tell me until I was interviewed. They separated us so we couldn't talk to each other. I was asked all kinds of questions before they told me Ken was dead. I can't believe it."

"So none of you knew he was dead until you got to the police station?"

"No, that's what was so crazy. At first, we thought we were potential witnesses to some crime, but when they started asking questions about where I was, I felt like I was a suspect. Have you talked to anyone else?"

Evelyn nodded to the phone. "Yes, Cory and Amos came to my room when they returned to the hotel. They are really scared. Cory's parents are on their way here. Amos' grandmother is too old so she asked me to make sure he is safe. I told Pastor Watson about Deacon Woods. I called you but your phone went to voice mail. Why didn't you answer, Deacon Jackson? Didn't you get my message?"

"I didn't have my phone."

"Pastor said telling Sister Woods was the most heartwrenching thing he has ever had to do. When was the last time you saw Deacon Woods?"

"I saw him last night in the lobby around 11. I didn't talk with him and I didn't see him with anyone. This is unreal. My wife said she's going to visit Vanessa tomorrow and see if she could help with the arrangements." His voice trailed to a whisper and stopped. She imagined he was crying.

She waited a few seconds. "Pastor Watson wants to talk to everybody when they return. I'll call you later."

Deacon Jackson agreed and hung up. Feeling closed in, he decided to go for a walk.

Evelyn sat down and started thinking. Plotting out a timeline when Deacon Woods was seen could give her an idea who the killer was.

Just as she was considering the timeline, Sarah called her. She was upset and wanted to visit Evelyn. Evelyn agreed. She was curious as to what had happened with Sarah at the police station.

Chapter 44

The soft knock on the door startled her. She looked through the peephole, it was Sarah. She quickly moved the chair from the door. As the door opened, Sarah rushed inside.

Crying, Sarah described what happened in the interview and told Evelyn she'd filed a report against Gary for assault. As Evelyn tried to console her, Sarah blurted out, "I didn't tell the police I saw Deacon Woods around 3 a.m."

"WHAT?"

"I didn't want to ruin his reputation. Besides maybe, it wasn't him. I thought I saw him in the elevator with somebody but I could be wrong."

"Did you say three in the morning?"

"Yes. Remember I told you I was just hanging out because I didn't want to go back to my room. I had just gotten back to the hotel. I was on the escalator going to the second floor when I think I saw him. It was weird."

"We have to be prayerful. God's going to help us."

"I'm trying, Sister Jenkins. I think Diana is back so I'm going to my room. Do you think we're safe?"

Evelyn didn't want to tell her how scared she was so she said, "I think we're safe. Besides, there is a police officer in the lobby if we need him. Pastor Watson wants to talk to everybody when they return. I'll call you later."

Sarah left. Evelyn put the chair back at the door then sat down. Her mind was swirling. Soon after, the phone rang again. This time it was Valarie. She just returned to the hotel. Evelyn agreed to let Valarie come to her room even though she was tired.

Chapter 45

Valarie arrived and sat down looking exhausted. She started crying, "Sister Jenkins, What have I gotten myself in? Never in my wildest dream could I imagine being involved in a murder."

Valarie told her she had waited a long time before being interviewed. Since she had no history with the choir, she didn't think she was a suspect. Valarie said she was sitting in the lobby around eleven last night listening to her iPod when she saw Diana and Gwen in the lobby talking to Deacon Woods. She said it looked like they had an angry conversation, then Gwen and Diana turned and rushed away. That's when she saw Deacon Woods talking to Deacon Jackson for about five minutes. Deacon Woods was mad. From where she was sitting, she didn't know what they were saying but it looked as if they agreed about something. Valarie said no one saw her because she was sitting behind some plants. Within five minutes, she saw Gwen return and take the elevator. Monique and Carol were in the room when she returned around 12:30.

This really troubled Evelyn. Deacon Jackson said he didn't talk with Deacon Woods. So he lied. She was contemplating this information when Valarie said that was not why she wanted to talk to her. "How well do you know Sarah's boyfriend?"

"Not well at all, I just met him when Sarah introduced him in Los Angeles. Why?"

"Well this morning around six o'clock while I was at the gym, I ran into Gary. Carol had a job interview and she left early. Monique was still sleeping. I was coming out of the gym when he stopped me and started talking. I thought maybe Sarah was in the gym so I stopped to talk with him. Sister Jenkins, he starting hitting on me. I didn't like it. I would have told him to go to hell but I don't want any trouble with these people."

"What time was this?"

"It was like 6:30. He looked like he'd been up all night."

"I'm sure you'll hear about it but it seems he and Sarah had a falling out. I think that's why he was walking around." Evelyn didn't want to tell her the whole story

"I was going to ask you to talk to him."

"Valarie, I'm so sorry this is happening to you. I thought I knew these people. I'm finding out I don't know them at all. When I see Gary I'll be sure to speak with him about his inappropriate behavior."

"Thanks, I really appreciate it. I'm going to my room and call my parents. They must be worried sick. I don't know how to tell them about this murder. I'm really sorry I agreed to come on this tour."

"I'm so sorry you got involved in all this. Pastor Watson knows what's going on. He wants to talk to everybody when they return. I'll call you later."

"That's fine. Just let me know when."

Valarie left. Evelyn slumped on the bed, then picked up her notepad, and started writing. Deacon Jackson lied about talking to Deacon Woods. Gwen lied and Diana is covering up for her. These people are unbelievable.

Chapter 46

When her phone rang again, she didn't want to answer. Evelyn realized now she was the one everybody depended on. It was a role she didn't relish but reluctantly accepted.

It was Jessie. He began talking a mile a minute. She just listened. When he finally took a breath, she asked if he was back at the hotel.

"Yes, thank God. Eric is still down there. Evelyn, my mother is going crazy. She talked to Pastor but that didn't calm her down at all. How's Deacon Jackson taking it? I know he must be out of his mind. They were the best of friends. God, I'm really scared. I'm not leaving this room. So you saw the body. Girl, how are you holding up? If I'd seen the body, I would be at the hospital under sedation. I never want to see a dead body. Pastor Watson must be going crazy. I know he's sorry he let us go on this tour."

Evelyn had to interrupt him to say, "Pastor Watson wants to have a meeting, so I'll call you. I need your help. I think Deacon Jackson's grieving too much to help. Once everybody gets back to the hotel, I need you to call them and tell them we're going to have a meeting."

"Girl, I'll do anything but leave this room by myself. You just call me and I make it happen."

Chapter 47

Gary Stevens loved Sarah. He'd been in love with her for over a year. It was nice to meet a woman who liked him for himself. But months went by before he asked her out. She was beautiful, friendly, and intelligent. And she was a nice Christian girl. He was a drug dealer and had been for years. He hid it well. Lately he'd been thinking of making a change in his life. Sarah gave him hope. When she asked what kind of work he did, he told her import-export. She never questioned him. That's what intrigued him about her. She was honest, sweet and a gentle soul. He took her to nice restaurants and treated her like a lady because she deserved it. She trusted him and believed whatever he said.

Crazy as it sounded, he wanted to tell her everything about himself but was afraid. The closer they became, the more scared he felt. She made him want to be better. Hitting her was the worst mistake of his life and he knew it. She was the woman he loved. He just snapped. Now he had to find her to apologize. He had to make it better. Sarah didn't know he'd been in the drug business since he was fourteen years old. He was used to dating woman with no ambition. Sarah was different. This was the first time Sarah had bucked his manhood. He wasn't used to anyone going against him. He was wrong. He never should have hit her.

Now he was running around the hotel trying to find her to apologize. Flirting with Valarie was a stupid mistake to try and make Sarah jealous. Deacon Woods had tried to tell him what to do but he couldn't find Sarah to apologize. Now the police wanted to talk to him. They probably already pulled his rap sheet so they know who he is.

He'd glanced out the window when the barrage of cops rushed the hotel. Then he overheard a voice in the hall saying somebody died and he got really worried. He was scared for Sarah but he wasn't staying around to answer any questions. No way he was walking into a police station and talk about a murder. He had to get out of town as soon as possible.

At the very moment he was packing, Washington and the CSI technicians were entering the hotel. They got the entrance key to Room 615 and headed up to the sixth floor.

Meanwhile Gary took the stairs to the garage. As he reached the ground floor, Washington was opening the door to his room.

Gary threw his luggage in the trunk, slamming the lid. When he turned around, he was shocked to see Deacon Jackson. "Deacon Jackson, what are you doing here?"

"I was hoping to find you." Angrily he asked, "Did you kill Deacon Woods?"

His voice shook. "No, Deacon Jackson, I swear I had nothing to do with any murder. Please, believe me. I just want to get out of town. I'm sorry I hit Sarah, that's not who I am. She just kept saying stuff that really made me mad. I love her. Please believe me."

Deacon Jackson stared at him, trying to decide if he believed him. He had to figure out what to do. He could see Gary was scared. And he believed him. Finally he said, "You know the police are probably looking for you."

"I know, sir, but I really don't want to get involved in a murder, I can't. I have a record. Can you please help me?"

Looking in his eyes and remembering how he was when he was that young himself, Deacon Jackson agreed to drive him to the airport.

"Thank you, thank you for believing me. I really didn't kill Deacon Woods. He was a good man."

"He was my best friend."

"Yes, he told me you guys have been together since you were teenagers."

Deacon Jackson insisted on driving the car. Gary lay down on the floor in the backseat covered by a large cardboard box they found lying near the garage dumpster.

Driving out of the hotel's side exit, Deacon Jackson could see police cars parked in front of the hotel. At the airport, he drove Gary to a remote area of the long-term inside parking lot.

Deacon Jackson didn't want to be caught with him so he said goodbye to Gary there in the parking lot. By chance or good luck, as he paused in front of the garage he met a couple who were going to their hotel on the strip. When he identified himself as a deacon, they offered him a ride. He agreed.

Gary prayed the police wouldn't catch him. He had booked a 9:45 flight in the name on the fake ID he'd used to rent the car. There was no way they could trace it back to him.

In the meantime, Washington and the CSI technicians were searching Gary's room and gathering evidence. It was clear he was on the run. The room had been tossed. His clothes and luggage were gone.

Washington called his partner to make sure they put out an all-points bulletin for Gary and the rented car. So far, he hadn't been spotted.

Chapter 48

Evelyn was still pondering over her notes when the phone rang. It was Pastor Watson. He was checking to see if all the choir members had returned to the hotel. Some were still missing, she reported. He asked about Deacon Jackson. Evelyn told him about their conversation and said he wasn't taking it well.

"Sister Jenkins I really would like you to keep an eye on him. I was talking with Sister Woods who said they've been friends since they were teenagers. I know he's going to take his death very hard.

"Pastor, I'll keep an eye on him."

"I was a little surprised too. You just never know who people are sometimes. I won't keep bothering you. When you get the choir together, please call me. I really want to speak with them. I apologize. I didn't ask how you are."

"Under the circumstances, I'm doing as well as can be expected."

"I'm praying for your strength. I asked Pastor Mason to come by and see if he can help in anyway. Since the choir can't sing, he was able to get a local group to take your place."

"That's good."

"I'll be waiting for your call."

She called Deacon Jackson's cell phone but it went to voice mail. She hung up. Now she was concerned that she hadn't heard from all the members of the choir.

Chapter 49

Back at the station, Detective Hamilton was preparing to interview Monique Gilmore. Her criminal background check was clear, no priors, warrants, or criminal record. Monique had been born and raised in Oakland, CA. She was a model with a professional agency. Hamilton was intrigued. As he entered the room, he saw a tall thin beautiful Afro-American young woman. Monique's skin was smooth and her features were stunning. She was dressed in a T-shirt and shorts, with dark glasses, and a large designer purse.

"Please have a seat." He ushered her to the chair facing the door. "Ms. Gilmore, is that correct?"

"Yes, Monique Gilmore." Her voice was soft and polite.

"May I offer you a drink?"

"Just water, please. Can I ask why I am here? Was someone really hurt at the hotel?"

"Ms. Gilmore, where were you yesterday?"

"Yesterday, I was with the choir. We left Los Angeles and arrived here around 1:30. The rooms weren't ready so we walked around town. Later we came back. After getting the key to my room, I waited until the other van arrived around 7:30 and went back to my room."

"Were you in your room all night?"

Monique hesitated. "Well around 9 o'clock I went to dinner."

"Were you alone?"

"No I went with Alex; he's a member of the choir."

Looking at his notes he asked, "Is that Alex Garcia?"

"Yes. We went to a dinner show at the Bellagio. We saw the Cirque du Soleil. After the show, we walked around the strip, and then came back to the hotel and went to our rooms."

"Is Mr. Garcia your boyfriend?"

"No." She didn't tell him it was their first date.

"What time did you return to the hotel?"

"It was around 12:30 last night."

"Did you see anyone from the choir?"

"No. I don't remember seeing anyone. Why are you asking all these questions? Why did you have Evelyn in handcuffs?"

"Are you sure you didn't see anyone from the choir before or after you returned to the hotel?"

"No I really didn't see anyone from the choir. Why won't you tell me what this is about?"

"I'm sorry to tell you, but Mr. Woods was found murdered in his room this morning." He sat back, waited and watched her reaction. There was a long silence.

"Deacon Woods was murdered?" Her voice began trembling and then she started crying. He motioned to the box of tissues and waited. "Why would anybody kill Deacon Woods? He was such a nice man. Where was he killed?"

"He was found in his room. Are you sure you didn't see any of the other choir members when you returned to the hotel?"

"Yes"

"Carol was sleep and Valarie wasn't in the room."

"Did you leave the room after you returned?"

"No, I went to bed. Are we in danger?"

"At this point in time we don't believe you are. A police officer is stationed at the hotel for your protection." After a long pause he added, "I'm sorry for your loss." He wanted to believe she wasn't a suspect but he couldn't rule anyone out.

"I can tell you this, we will solve this crime." He handed her his business card and asked her to call if she thought of anything that might help. An officer drove her back to the hotel.

Chapter 50

Once he had finished with Monique, Detective Hamilton prepared to interview the last choir member, Alex Garcia, an attractive young man with smooth olive skin and long curly black hair worn in a ponytail. He had an Afro-American father and a Mexican-American mother, both middle-class hardworking people. Alex was a schoolteacher and his background check was clean with no criminal record.

Like the others, he was taken to the interview room and offered a beverage. Once he got the drink, Hamilton began questioning him.

Alex told the same story Monique did. Like her, he claimed he didn't see anyone from the choir when they returned to the hotel. After walking Monique to her room, he went to his room and bed. He shared a room with Randy, who was asleep when he returned.

When Hamilton told him about the murder, there was a genuine look of shock on his face.

"Why would anyone kill Deacon Woods? Was it some kind of robbery?"

"At this point we don't know. How well did you know him?"

"Deacon Woods has been a member of the church for a long time. When my mother and I joined he was already there." Alex sank down in the chair, trying to hold back tears. "Man this can't be happening." Now the tears were streaming down his cheeks. It took him a minute to compose himself. Hamilton watched.

"So you never left your room after you returned?"

"No. Once I fall asleep, it's kind of hard for me to wake up. We had a long day. I was tired. Randy was snoring when I got back." Even though he didn't really interact with Deacon Woods, it was hard for him to accept that someone would kill him.

Hamilton gave him a business card and told him to call if he had any additional information. Like the others, he was driven back to the hotel.

Hamilton called Washington, who was still at the hotel and updated him. Washington explained the he just missed finding Gary at the hotel. After they hung up, Hamilton called the coroner to get an update. There were no defensive wounds found on the body. So far, the only blood evidence belonged to the victim but they hadn't finished testing.

Evelyn was reading over her notes when the phone rang. It was Monique. She had just returned and was still crying. She told Evelyn about her interview and confessed she and Alex had been on a first date. "Sister Jenkins, I'm scared. The police say we're not in any danger but I don't know who to trust. I can't believe Deacon Woods is dead."

"Neither can I."

"I called my mother. She said Pastor Watson talked to her and the other parents. She wants me to come home immediately. I just don't know what to do. I don't think the police will let us leave now. What do you think?"

"For now, I think we have to stay here. Pastor Watson wants to talk to us but I don't know how many of the others have returned to the hotel."

"I talked to Valarie and Carol. I don't know where Gwen and Sarah are."

Evelyn suspected they were still being questioned. Perhaps they had kept Sarah to protect her from Gary. Maybe Gwen and Diana hadn't returned because the police found out they lied. She didn't tell Monique.

"I suggest we stay in our rooms until everybody gets back to the hotel."

Chapter 51

Evelyn was trying to absorb all the information she had received from the choir members, but the phone interrupted her thoughts. It was Deborah.

"Evelyn, I just had to call you. The story on the news is saying somebody died at your hotel, but they haven't revealed the name of the victim, pending notification. What's going on?"

"Deborah, you won't believe what I've been through. I think most of the choir is back from the police station. All of them are in shock. The youngest boys, Cory and Amos, came to my room. I had to talk to their family and now Cory's parents are on their way here. Then I found out not only did Gary beat Sarah, he flirted with Valarie trying to make Sarah jealous."

"What the hell? I can't believe this."

"I don't know anything about this boy and I really don't like him. Then Diana tells me she lied to the police. I can't believe these people. Deacon Jackson is like a zombie. I don't expect too much help from him."

"So what are Cory's parents going to do when they get there?"

"I'm going to get them to help with the choir. There will be no more concerts 'cause as soon as we can leave, I'm bringing these people back to Oakland."

"Is there anything you want me to do?"

"Yes, call the pastors in Phoenix and San Diego and tell them there will not be a concert. I hope they can adjust. And cancel the hotels so we won't get charged. If any of the families call, direct them to Pastor Watson. Deborah I don't know how this is going to end but I don't want you involved."

"I'll do whatever you need me to do. Evelyn, you be careful with these people. You already know they lie." They hung up.

Even if all the choir members weren't back, it was time to have the meeting. Evelyn wanted to know how they were. Most of them were probably in shock. Pastor Watson's spiritual guidance was going to be needed.

She called down to the front desk and asked for the use of a small conference room. Under the circumstances, the manager agreed. Evelyn called and updated Pastor Watson. She didn't tell him everything. Jessie contacted the choir members. They were to meet in 30 minutes in Room F. He asked Evelyn if he could speak to her privately after the meeting. She agreed.

Pastor Watson called Pastor Mason in Las Vegas and invited him to attend the meeting. It was comforting to know Rev. Mason would be there to help comfort them during their grieving process. Dressing for the meeting, Evelyn realized she was shaking. If she was scared, the others had to be too. She called Deacon Jackson and explained where the meeting would be.

Just from his voice, she could tell he was really grieving. She grabbed her notebook and went down to the conference room.

No one was there yet, so Evelyn arranged the chairs around the phone and waited. Within a few minutes, everyone showed up except Gwen and Eric. Pastor Mason, a short stocky man, walked in a few minutes later, wearing a suit and tie and carrying a Bible. With him were two deacons from his church. They all stood and held hands while Pastor Mason prayed. He told them how sorry he was that this had happened. Because the church community was gathering for their planned concert, he'd changed it to a prayer service to pray for their strength. He encouraged everyone to keep together, be strong, and know God would bring them through this terrible tragedy.

Minutes later Pastor Watson called. He urged everyone to be prayerful and know that God was their help in time of trouble. He asked them for a moment of silence for Deacon Woods and his family. Then he asked each one how they were doing. Not really wanting to tell the truth, everyone said they were well considering the circumstances. Evelyn told him Gwen and Eric weren't present. He asked to speak to her, Deacon Jackson, and Pastor Mason privately afterward.

His voice was soft and steady. They received comfort knowing he was in charge. Pastor Watson didn't dwell on the murder. He wanted to help them feel they were not alone. He told them everyone at Gabriel was praying for their safe return. He had talked to their families members earlier. If they needed to speak with him in private, he would be available for them to call him anytime.

While he was talking, a stranger, a Caucasian in a very expensive suit, walked in the room and sat in the back. Because everyone was on edge, fear gripped them. Deacon Jackson walked back to talk with him briefly and ushered him up to the group.

He informed Pastor Watson that a Mr. Schuler just arrived.

Over the speakerphone, Pastor Watson introduced Bert Schuler, an attorney who lived in Las Vegas. He'd asked him to meet with them to discuss any legal questions they might have. Mr. Schuler began explaining how the law worked in the State of Nevada and how the police investigation would proceed with this type of crime. He outlined what they should expect.

Choir members started telling him what they experienced. Everyone agreed; the police were polite and they'd been treated with respect. Mr. Schuler assured them that this was just the initial meeting. If they hadn't told the truth, he warned, the next time they were questioned it most likely wouldn't be in the same manner.

"I hope no one told them a lie because they have ways to find out about almost anything you said. From now on, I'll be your contact. If you have any questions or are asked by the police to return for questioning, I need you to call me first. I will be talking with the detectives to determine how long they want you to remain in Las Vegas. I'm going to try and have them release you within the next two days."

"Do any of you want to get an attorney on your own?" he asked. No, they all said and agreed to let him represent them. To help their defense if needed, everyone was asked to write down what they told the police.

He told them not to speak with anyone, not even their family members. They should maintain a low profile. Even though they weren't suspects now, that could change.

Cory said his parents were coming to Las Vegas. Mr. Schuler assured him it would be all right for his parents to visit but they could not insert themselves into the investigation. When Cory's parents arrived, they should call him. He gave each of them his business card.

Deacon Jackson had remained very quiet but now he asked, if they should fly back home or drive.

"I suspect the police have already had the vans checked by the Criminal Investigative Team. I don't believe they expect to keep them for evidence. Driving back is probably still an option but I'll let you know. That's one of the things I will discuss with the police."

The attorney turned to Evelyn and said, "As soon as I find out anything, I'll let you know."

They took a vote and agreed to drive back. Cory was the only exception since he had to confer with his parents.

"If the police contact you, tell them you will have to contact me first. I will be representing you from now on.

Pastor Watson agreed, saying, "I know you are all scared. That's why I asked Mr. Schuler to help. If you follow his instructions, I truly believe you will be home in a few days. Mr. Schuler will be in constant contact with me. From what he's saying, right now the police are just trying to find the killer and they have to eliminate you to do that." Listening to Pastor Watson was putting everyone's mind at ease.

After forty minutes, no one had anything else to say. It was late and Pastor Watson sensed they were exhausted and still probably in shock.

No one wanted to see a doctor. Both ministers had prayer and they dismissed the choir.

Now the only ones left in the room were Pastor Mason, Evelyn, and Deacon Jackson. Mr. Schuler stepped out to make a phone call. Pastor Watson spoke first.

"Deacon Jackson, I can't imagine what you must be going through. I know you and Deacon Woods were very close. I will ask Cory's father to drive one of the vans so you can fly back to Oakland. I know everyone will understand."

"Thank you, Pastor, but I want to remain here. I know that once they release the body someone will have to bring him home. I want to do that."

"Well, if you change your mind let me know. I believe his wife has been in contact with a funeral home and they are in the process of making arrangements."

Pastor Watson then spoke to Pastor Mason. "Pastor, I really appreciate your help. Thank you for meeting with the choir. I know they appreciated seeing a member of the clergy in person. Please call me later. There's something I need to discuss with you"

"Pastor Watson, just let me know if you need anything. I'll call you later." Pastor Mason dismissed himself along with his deacons and left. Mr. Schuler returned.

Pastor Watson continued, "I didn't want to discuss too much of our personal business with Pastor Mason in the room. Sister Jenkins, where are Gwen and Eric? Are they still at the police station?"

Mr. Schuler interrupted. "Pastor Watson, I just spoke with the police. I was told Gwen is being detained on a possible shoplifting charge."

"GOD IN HEAVEN!" shouted Pastor Watson. No one else said a word. "Are you serious?"

"Yes, Pastor I'm afraid I am." The police are waiting to find out if the store in Los Angeles is going to press charges. They will not let her leave until that matter is resolved."

"Sister Jenkins, Brother Jackson, did either of you know about this?"

They both softly replied, "No."

"Pastor, we all agreed to let the police search our rooms. I thought it had something to do with security in the hotel. We didn't know that Deacon Woods was dead until we were interviewed."

Mr. Schuler said, "That's understandable under the circumstances, Ms. Jenkins. Since they didn't know what was going on, I think they asked to search the rooms as a precaution since one of the choir members was murdered. That's why it is so important for me to get everyone to write down what they did or did not tell the police. I'm sure they told you you were not under arrest and that they just wanted some information."

Evelyn replied, "Yes, that's what they said. I didn't know anything about shoplifting. They must have found something in Gwen's room."

Mr. Schuler continued, "Like I told the others, they most likely taped your interviews. If they call you back, and they found that anyone lied, expect them to read you your rights."

"This is exactly why I didn't want Pastor Mason involved in this discussion. I don't like surprises. And I can't explained to you how angry I am especially hearing about this," said Pastor Watson.

There was a chill in the air. It was the first time she had ever heard Pastor Watson angry. Everyone sat quietly waiting.

"Listen, I know none of us are perfect but you must know this is a mind-boggling situation. A murder of all things is just beyond comprehension. Now I find out shoplifting is another component of this bizarre tour."

"Sister Jenkins, I know this an incredible burden to put on you but I'm going to have to depend on you to work with Mr. Schuler. Mr. Schuler, I need you to work closely with Sister Jenkins. Let's talk tomorrow when you get an update on Gwen. I pray she will be released. Deacon Jackson I'm not ignoring you. I just know how difficult it must be for you to function during this time of grieving."

Deacon Jackson interrupted in a meek tone. "Pastor, I can help Sister Jenkins. I'm stronger than you think. Sister Jenkins and I will manage this crisis and get the others back home."

There was a pause. Finally Pastor Watson said, "I'm glad to hear you say that. You can rely on each other for strength."

"Mr. Schuler interrupted, "Pastor, I hate to be the bearer of more bad news, but they are also holding Eric Parker."

"Eric! What did Eric do?"

"The police found the suspects in the mugging in Los Angeles. They claimed he was buying drugs from them and ran before paying, which is why they beat him up."

Evelyn put her hand over her mouth and tried not to make a sound but her shock was apparent on her face. She couldn't believe what Mr. Schuler had just said.

There was complete silence. Nobody knew what to say. Evelyn was mortified and knew Pastor Watson must be livid. Deacon Jackson was shaking his head in disgust.

Finally, Pastor Watson said in the most disgusted tone she had ever heard from him, "Keep in touch with Mr. Schuler. Mr. Schuler, I will expect to hear from you soon as you find out any more about what's going on. Let's have a word of prayer." Sister Jenkins and Deacon Jackson held hands with the attorney. When prayer was over Pastor Watson immediately hung up the phone. It was apparent he was trying to remain in control without cussing.

"Ms. Jenkins, Pastor Watson gave me your number. I'll call as soon as I get the status of the two choir members." The attorney left the room.

Evelyn and Deacon Jackson sat in the room stunned. "This is unreal. I'm going to my room, I'll call you later." Deacon Jackson stood up and left. Evelyn rushed to her room.

Chapter 52

Evelyn sat on the bed and cried. This was the worst day of her life. The phone rang. She reluctantly picked it up, not wanting to hear any more bad news.

It was Gwen. Her voice was uncharacteristically meek and soft. "Sister Jenkins, this is Gwen. I'm back at the hotel. I guess you heard about the shoplifting. The store decided not to press charges since they got their merchandise back. I can never go back to that store again. I'm so sorry."

Evelyn was furious. "For your sake you better have told them the truth about everything, otherwise your ass will be back down there for murder."

There was a pause. "Sister Jenkins, I was sleeping with Deacon Woods."

Evelyn sat up in bed and yelled, "Get your ass over here NOW!" before slamming the phone down. She grabbed a pillow to her mouth and screamed.

Within five minutes, there was a soft knock on the door. She looked through the peephole and opened the door. Not saying a word, she turned her back on Gwen and walked back to sit on the bed. Timidly, Gwen walked in and sat on the chair near the door.

Evelyn still hadn't tried to make eye contact. Trying to keep her composure, she took a deep breath. "Gwen—I'm sorry

231

for my language on the phone but I can't believe you. Tell me about you and Deacon Woods."

"Sister Jenkins, I'm sorry. I don't know what to say. I've been seeing Deacon Woods for a little over a year. I didn't plan it. It started at a church picnic. I'm so ashame. Diana saw us one day so I had to tell her. Sister Jenkins, I'm in real trouble, real bad trouble. I tried not to see Deacon Woods while we were on tour but he called me Monday night and told me to meet him on the corner where you were staying. I'm not a whore, Sister Jenkins. I loved him. He kept telling me he was leaving his wife. I believed him. I know I was wrong. I'm sorry."

"Are you telling me that Monday night you slept with Deacon Woods at the hotel? The same hotel I was staying at? Well, I'll be dammed. Sorry is not going to get you out of this crap. Seems to me the only thing you're sorry about is that you got caught. So that WAS you and Diana I saw in the lobby Tuesday morning."

"Yes, she took a bus to the hotel to get me so we could go shopping."

"What the HELL were you thinking?" Evelyn was livid. She was talking loud, breathing hard, and pacing. Gwen knew not to say a word.

"So Diana knows all about this?"

"Yes, I didn't mean to get her involved."

"Well clearly she is. Were you with him last night?"

Gwen started crying, "Just for a little while but, Sister Jenkins, he was alive when I left him. He was alive. I swear." She started crying.

Evelyn didn't have any pity for her. "What time did you see him?"

"It was around one in the morning in his room."

"So you were shoplifting, with drugs, and having an affair with a deacon of the church. Lord, help me JESUS!"

Gwen was holding her face in her hands sobbing. It took about three minutes before Evelyn could calm herself down enough to formulate words. "What did you tell the police?"

It took a while for her to respond then she said, "I didn't tell them about anything. When they checked the rooms, they found the two dresses and a joint. It was a mistake. It was only a joint so they didn't hold Diana, but they made me stay for shoplifting. They don't know about me and Deacon Woods."

"Are you CRAZY? Were you in his room?"

"Yes," softly.

"Well when they check the fingerprints in the room, guess whose prints they're going to find?"

"I didn't give them my fingerprints."

Evelyn remembered what Mr. Schuler said. "Did they offer you a glass of water?"

Gwen burst out crying.

Evelyn sat down on the bed. These have got to be the dumbest women I have ever known. Now I'm in the midst of this mess. If one of these fools killed Deacon Woods, I am going to find out who it is.

While Gwen sobbed, Evelyn called Attorney Schuler and told him of her discussion with Gwen. He agreed it would be better if she voluntarily told the police about the affair. That way, when they identified her fingerprints in the room they would already have the reason.

Evelyn ignored the crying. She didn't have any compassion for Gwen at all. Mr. Schuler agreed to go with them to the police station the next morning if Gwen wanted him to be her attorney. Gwen agreed. Evelyn asked him not to tell Pastor Watson until they found out what the police said.

Mr. Schuler agreed. He told her Eric had been released pending further word from the Los Angeles police. Evelyn thanked him for his help and hung up. She turned to Gwen and told her what was going to happen. Sadly, Gwen agreed and went back to her room.

Evelyn was exhausted. She was determined to get some sleep now despite this horrifying day. The phone rang. She let it go to voice mail.

Evelyn knew she should call Deacon Jackson but decided not to. He was taking the murder of his friend so hard. She felt he was probably too grief-stricken to go back for more questions. Evelyn wondered if he knew about Gwen. She made a notation to ask. Before she realized it, she said out loud, "Hell he ain't that damn grief-stricken. He knows something." After showering, she went to bed. She would handle this herself.

Chapter 53

Evelyn tossed and turned all night. Sleep was eluding her. Finally, she got out of bed, made a cup of coffee, and prayed. She reviewed her notes and made some more notations. Longing to hear her mother's voice, Evelyn decided it was too early to call her. Instead, she called her brother, Charles. She wanted his advice. Being a police officer himself, he worked all hours but maybe he was still at home.

After two rings, he answered.

"Charles." He immediately recognized her voice and used her nickname, "EV, how are you? Are you all right?"

"Yes I'm all right. You are not going to believe what else has been going on." She told him everything.

"Damn, girl, what the hell kind of people have you gotten involved with? You better watch your back. Since we spoke, I called a friend of mine in LVPD. She gave me an update but if they don't know the stuff you told me, shit's going to change fast. Having an affair means they're going to focus on the wife. Maybe it was a hit. Girl, you better watch your back. Are you sure you don't want me there?"

"Yes. Deacon Jackson is helping even though he's grieving."

"Do you think he knew about the affair?"

"I don't know. I'm telling you to stay out of this."

"EV, you be careful. When the police tell you to leave, leave town immediately. Don't tell anybody you're taking notes, keep that shit to yourself. And, EV girl, when this is over you have got to change churches." They both laughed and hung up.

Evelyn called Deborah and hastily told her all the new news.

"If it wasn't a hit, maybe the guy picked up a hooker and was killed by her pimp. I know you say this Gwen woman was having an affair but if you don't think she killed him than there's another scenario you haven't considered." Evelyn listened intensely.

"I don't want to find a new job so be careful. Call me if you need me."

Evelyn felt confident knowing Deborah had faith in her. "Thanks Deb, pray for me."

"I am girl, I am. Bye."

Evelyn knew this was going to be another miserable day. Deacon Woods was not who he seemed. She remembered the scotch bottle found in his room. Didn't Jessie say he drank scotch? She starting thinking maybe Woods was a closet alcoholic. She had to find out who else was in that room. Gwen didn't talk about drinking but who knows what else she was not saying.

She dressed and went downstairs for breakfast. It was almost eight-thirty, so she decided not to bother Deacon Jackson and ate alone. Afterward, Evelyn walked through the lobby looking around to find the place where Valarie was sitting that night. Finding it, she sat down and looked around. It was true, no one could see her from the lobby. A huge tree was blocking the view.

She noticed the concierge desk near her. Maybe someone there saw Deacon Woods that night. Evelyn asked, and was referred to a young man named Benjamin who worked the late shift. He was just going off duty. She showed him a picture of Deacon Woods and asked if he had seen him.

Benjamin took a good look at the picture and said he was the guy who gave him $20 to buy a bottle of scotch the night before. Since he couldn't leave his desk, the man came down around three in the morning to pick it up. Benjamin said he remembered him because he looked like a minister and he thought it odd that the guy bought liquor. He told Evelyn the police hadn't talked to him yet. She thanked him.

Evelyn was astonished to think she was the only person who knew about this. Deacon Woods was in the lobby at 3 a.m., because he retrieved the scotch. If he didn't drink, then why did he call for liquor? Gwen may have told the truth. He was alive at one o'clock. Still, she could have gone back to his room. Evelyn added the newest info to her notebook.

Mr. Schuler arranged a meeting with Detective Washington for 10 a.m. Evelyn called Deacon Jackson and told him she needed to go to the police station but didn't explain why. He insisted on coming with her and she acquiesced. Mr. Schuler had suggested they meet in the garage. As Evelyn waited with him, Gwen appeared first, and then Deacon Jackson.

As usual, Gwen had on a dress that was two sizes too small. While riding to the police headquarters, Evelyn was trying to decide if she should tell the police about Benjamin. Instead, she decided to tell Mr. Schuler privately when they returned.

During the ride, Mr. Schuler told Deacon Jackson why they were going to police headquarters. His reaction wasn't what Evelyn expected.

He didn't raise his voice. He didn't even look surprised. "Gwen, I don't believe you. How could you? I've know Ken for years and there's no way in hell he would do that. No way in hell."

Gwen interrupted, "I'm sorry Deacon Jackson, but I loved him and he loved me."

"That's ridiculous."

Mr. Schuler interrupted. "Mr. Jackson, I know this must be a shock but Ms. Harrison must tell the police the truth." Deacon Jackson sat with a stone cold look on his face. "They will probably ask you if you knew about the affair. You must tell the truth. Finding out this way is hard, but it's best for all of you if she tells the truth now. Do you think you can maintain your composure or do you want to remain outside the meeting?"

Deacon Jackson, looking like he wanted to punch Gwen in the face, finally answered, "No, I want to be in the meeting. I can handle this."

"I'm glad to hear that, Deacon Jackson. I'm sorry to have to put you through this." The remainder of the ride was in silence.

Evelyn wasn't convinced. She had expected a much stronger reaction than Deacon Jackson displayed. For a man who supposedly knew his friend, he sure didn't act like he was shocked.

Chapter 54

There wasn't a lot of conversation in the car but as they entered the building, Mr. Schuler again told them to let him do the talking. Gwen didn't say a word, just nodded. It was clear she was scared and embarrassed. Deacon Jackson was trying to be cordial. At the station, they were ushered into a conference room

The detectives had worked late the previous night, looking at crime tech videos of the scene and checking Woods' phone records. Gary Stevens still hadn't been found. They hadn't ruled out a robbery gone bad. After a fifteen-minute wait, Washington and Hamilton walked in and sat across from Mr. Schuler and the others.

The video camera in the room was turned on. Attorney Schuler introduced himself as representing the choir and gave them his card. Hamilton said he was confused. If they had all told him the truth, he couldn't understand why an attorney was needed.

Mr. Schuler stated that he wanted to discuss the information or lack of information provided to them by certain members of the choir.

With a stone face Washington asked, "Are you telling me information was withheld? What information?"

"Before I continue, can I ask, what is the status of your investigation?"

The detectives looked at each other. Hamilton responded sternly, "Since you've been retained by the choir you should know that for now they are just interested parties but that can change."

"I understand. Please believe me we don't want to hinder your investigation. That's why I asked for this meeting. Ms. Harrison may have withheld some information pertinent to this case. I told her she must report it to you immediately."

Angrily Washington turned to look at Gwen. "What did she forget to tell us?"

"Ms. Harrison was romantically involved with Mr. Woods."

Washington shouted, "SHE WHAT?"

"Gentlemen, she was afraid to tell you, especially with the shoplifting problem. You most likely will find her fingerprints in his hotel room. I have urged her to tell you everything to avoid any more problems."

Gwen had her head down. Evelyn stared at the detectives thinking this meeting might not have been a good idea after all. She glanced over at Deacon Jackson. He wasn't showing any emotion.

Washington looked at Gwen in disgust. "Well, it's nice of you to finally want to tell the truth."

Hamilton asked, "So, Gwen, how long were you sleeping with the victim?"

She looked at Mr. Schuler who nodded his head for her to talk. Timidly she said, "First, I'm sorry I didn't tell you about Mr. Woods and me. I loved him. He said he was getting a divorce. Ken insisted I see him Monday night, so he picked me up after midnight and brought me to his hotel room."

The detectives looked for Deacon Jackson's reaction. There was none.

"So you two were sneaking around all week?"

"No we didn't see each other until Thursday night. Diana and I were going out. He saw us in the lobby and said we looked like prostitutes, which made me mad. We told him off and left to go party. Ken called to apologize and asked me to come back to his room. Diana went partying. I went to his room. I left around one a.m. He was alive, I swear. I went downstairs to the casino and walked around for a while. I was in my room around two. Diana will tell you. I don't know who killed Ken. He was alive when I left him. You have my word."

Washington jumped from his seat and stood over Gwen.

"Well, I just met you yesterday and as far as I'm concerned your word don't mean shit. You're a shoplifter, a liar, and a mistress. What else haven't you told us?"

Gwen sobbed. "Nothing, I told you everything."

Mr. Schuler interrupted in a soft voice. "Please, gentlemen. You have a right to be angry. That's why I told Ms. Harrison it was better that she tell you now. Her fingerprints are in Mr. Woods' room. I assure you both, Ms. Miller and Ms.

243

Harrison will be available for further questioning, if you need them."

"You can be sure I will question Ms. Miller again. Did his wife know about this affair?"

Gwen jerked, "Oh God, I don't think so." She looked over at Evelyn with a shocked look on her face. "I hope she didn't know about me. He told me they were getting a divorce. I believed him, really I did."

Evelyn decided this was the right time to keep quiet, so she did.

Detective Hamilton asked, "Who else knew about your affair?"

"Just Diana. And she only found out about it on Monday. We really tried to be discreet. We barely spoke at church."

"Is there anything else you need to know from Ms. Harrison?" asked Mr. Schuler. He and the detectives looked at each other for a few seconds.

Washington responded. "No, but don't leave town." He turned to Deacon Jackson and Evelyn, "Did either of you know about this?"

Deacon Jackson spoke first. "I've known Ken for years. I had no idea this was going on. He certainly never talked about getting a divorce. I thought he and Vanessa had a great marriage. I mean our families went on vacation together several months ago. I thought they were happy. I can't believe this."

Evelyn said, "I had no idea they were having an affair until Gwen told me last night."

Detective Hamilton changed the subject. "How well do you know Gary Stevens?"

Evelyn responded, "I don't know him at all. He's Sarah's boyfriend. I just met him Wednesday night. Why?"

"Mr. Jackson, did you ever see Gary and Mr. Woods together?"

"No."

"And you never suspected Mr. Woods was having an affair?"

"No."

"I find that hard to believe. Maybe you weren't as close as you say."

Deacon Jackson looked conflicted. Evelyn felt he was hiding something.

"Ms. Jenkins, did you ever see this Gary and Mr. Woods together?"

"No."

Hamilton growled, "I'm thinking of locking you all up."

Mr. Schuler interrupted, "I really don't believe that will be necessary. I can have Ms. Miller come down and do another interview if you want."

"I want to meet her later on today at the hotel."

"I'll arrange that. Now, may I speak to you in private about Mr. Parker?"

Evelyn, Gwen, and Deacon Jackson went outside to wait for Mr. Schuler. They had a long wait. Gwen continued to cry, Evelyn reluctantly trying to console her. Deacon Jackson sat looking alternately bewildered and angry. He turned his head, trying not to show his face.

When Detective Hamilton told Mr. Schuler that Eric Parker was still under suspicion of buying drugs, he reminded them that the accusers had a police record and would say anything to be released. Eric didn't have a criminal record and was a devout Christian musician. They acknowledged Eric's background and didn't indicate he was a drug user, but it wouldn't be the first time somebody hid drug use. They gave Mr. Schuler the name of the Los Angeles detective assigned to the case. Mr. Schuler thanked them, gathered the others, and left.

When they returned to the hotel, Gwen rushed from the car into the hotel. Deacon Jackson followed her. Still sitting in the car, Evelyn told Mr. Schuler about her conversation with the hotel employee Benjamin about what he had seen in the lobby. Mr. Schuler's eyes widened. He told her he would call her later. He would be with Diana during her interview and would tell the police about Benjamin.

Chapter 55

By the time Evelyn returned to her room, Cory's parents had checked into the hotel, reserving two adjourning rooms and insisting Cory stay with them. They left a message on Evelyn's room phone asking her to call them. Looking at her cell phone, she noticed messages from Jessie, Cory Watson's parents, Deborah, and Pastor Watson.

Evelyn wasn't in a hurry to talk with the Williams, knowing there wasn't much she could tell them. She knew Mr. Schuler was going to call Pastor Watson, so she decided to give him time to digest the new information. She'd call Jessie later. Evelyn started writing notes. She wanted to find out why Deacon Woods ordered scotch. Why make it a point to go down to the lobby to pick it up? She found it strange that Deacon Jackson's didn't know about the affair. Listening to him at the police department, you would think they weren't as close as he kept saying they were. She had to find Gary to see how he fit in.

Just then, there was a knock on the door. She wasn't going to answer, but the knocking was persistent. Looking through the peephole, she saw Jessie. Taking a deep breath, she reluctantly opened the door.

"Hello my sister, I know I should have called but we really need to talk. It's a matter of life and death."

She ushered him into the room. "Jessie I got your message. I am just too busy right now."

He sat on the couch and took a deep breath before talking in his usual fast pace. "I can't imagine what you been through. First, let me say that you have been an inspiration for me. I don't know what would have happened if you hadn't been here. I'm just a bundle of nerves. The others and I were talking because we are scared to death. I know the police say we're safe but honestly, that ain't helping. Brother and Sister Williams called to say they are at the hotel. Now that Cory's staying with his parents, Amos is alone."

"How would you and Eric feel having him stay with you?"

"I wouldn't mind.

"Let me call the front desk and cancel his room. He can stay in your room. Do you need a roll-away bed?"

"Definitely." Evelyn called the hotel manager's office and made the arrangements. Because of the circumstances, the manager agreed to waive the cancellation fee.

"It's incredible. None of us have ever been in a situation like this. I think everyone's in shock. Nobody wants to leave their room. We barely talk to each other."

"Jessie, I hope you don't think me nosy, but have you seen anything between the choir members that could have led to this crime?"

Jessie sat back staring at the floor, before replying. "Sister Jenkins, Evelyn, I have known some of these people for years, Deacon Jackson and Deacon Woods the longest. I have never seen any of these people mad enough to commit murder.

248

You know Gwen and Diana are just crazy stupid but even crazy Gwen wouldn't kill somebody. That's why this is just nuts. A stranger must have killed Deacon Woods."

"So you've known Deacon Woods and Deacon Jackson for a long time?"

"Yes, I mean at church you would swear they were brothers. They did everything together. Not only at church but when we'd go on the Men's Retreat they roomed together. They went on vacation together. Heck they were ordained as deacons the same time. This is just really crazy."

"So in all the years you've know them they've never had an argument?"

"No, not that I've seen."

"What do you know about Sarah?"

"Sarah's been a member for a couple of years. She doesn't talk about her private life. I was surprised she had a boyfriend come to Los Angeles. It was a total surprise to us when she said she was getting married. Randy said he's seen Gary in Oakland hanging with some pretty bad guys. He overheard one of them say Gary was a gang member. You think maybe he killed Deacon Woods?"

"Honestly, I don't know."

"Well I know it wasn't one of us." Evelyn wasn't so sure of that.

"How long do you think we have to stay here? Sister Woods must be out of her mind. There are so many people who loved him. I've been thinking of what songs the choir will sing for the funeral service. Pastor Watson sounded really distraught. I can't imagine what's going on at church. I talked to my mom, she's beside herself. I have to call her every five hours just so she knows I'm alive. Eric's been really quiet since he got back. He won't tell me anything." Evelyn just sat and listened.

"I know I've been talking like a mad man. I'm just really nervous. Well, I'm not going to take up any more of your time." He got up and walked to the door. As he turned he said, "I hope we get out of here before anybody else is murdered."

Ushering him to the door, Evelyn tried to assure him he wasn't in any danger. Finally, the door closed. There was no way she was going to tell him about the affair.

Just as Evelyn sat down to think about all the stuff Jessie said, the room phone rang. "Hello Ms. Jenkins, this is Mr. Schuler."

"Mr. Schuler, I hope you have good news and that I won't be arrested."

"I spoke with the detectives. We discussed your conversation with the concierge. I told them that you were just asking for information and the employee happened to mention to you about the liquor. I said you didn't believe it was important enough to mention. Initially they were angry. I told them you just found out about it. They decided not to charge you for obstructing an investigation."

"Thank you, Mr. Schuler. Oh God, I really don't want to get arrested. Thank you so much."

"You're welcome, that's my job. Pastor Watson was extremely distressed when I told him about Gwen and the affair."

Evelyn was glad she didn't have to be the one to tell him.

"I'll keep in touch. I'm still trying to get the police to release the group. Please ask them not to do anything else to impede the investigation. Will you be driving back or flying?"

"I don't know yet. I don't think many of the others have the funds to fly. Either way, I'll let you know."

Hanging up the room phone, Evelyn called Deborah on her cell phone. By the time Evelyn finished her update and lay back on the bed, both of them were exhausted.

"Evelyn, I swear this sounds like some kind of sick soap opera and it's only been a week. Girl, I wouldn't want to be in your shoes."

"I want to call Sister Woods and offer my condolences, but I better stay out of it. What if she knew about the affair and sent somebody down here to kill her husband?"

"I never thought of that."

"I've been keeping notes to help me put the pieces together."

"You better not let anybody know that."

"I won't. You're the only one I've told."

"Well your secret is safe with me. I passed by the church and saw a news van. Be careful, Evelyn. Let me know if you need anything."

Chapter 56

The members of the choir did not leave their rooms, convinced a murderer was still in the hotel. They didn't believe they were safe.

Detectives Hamilton and Washington were discussing the case. Armed with the new information from Gwen, they now believed Vanessa Woods could be the prime suspect in this case. She could have found out about the affair and hired someone to kill her husband. They decided to have her interviewed again in a controlled environment. This time it would be at the Oakland Police headquarters.

More than twenty-four hours after she was told her husband was dead; Vanessa was still reeling from the news. When the detectives and Pastor Watson left, her sister Janet put her to bed with sedatives prescribed by Vanessa's doctor. She lay in bed trying to comprehend how it could be that her husband wasn't coming home. She needed to make funeral arrangements. Her parents would keep the children with them. Ken's parents were coming in from Texas. Janet was helping her make a to-do list when the phone rang.

Detective Anderson from the Oakland Police Department asked if she would come in to see him. She hoped they had updated news about the murder. Not knowing why the police wanted to talk to her, she dressed and waited for the police car to arrive. Janet was going with her.

When they got to the police station, the uniformed officer asked Janet to wait in the hall and escorted Vanessa into an interview room. The same detectives who came to the house, Anderson and Pierce, entered the room and sat down across from her. "How are you, Mrs. Woods?"

"I'm doing as best as expected from a person who's told their husband is murdered."

They looked at each other. Detective Anderson said, "Mrs. Woods, we brought you here because we need to ask you a few more questions. I know this is difficult but you may know something that to you might be trivial but may help in our investigation.

"I understand. How can I help?"

"We've set up a conference call with the detectives from Las Vegas who are handling the investigation."

On the speakerphone, she heard, "Hello, Mrs. Woods, my name is Detective Washington and I'm here with my partner, Detective Hamilton. First, let me say we are sorry for your loss."

"Thank you. Have you found out who killed my husband?"

"Not yet, ma'am, but it's our number one priority. Would you say you and your husband were close?"

"Yes, he was the love of my life, the best husband a woman could have."

"Are you aware Mr. Woods was having an affair?" Anderson and Pierce watched her response.

"What in the hell are you talking about? Ken wasn't cheating on me. I know my husband. Ken wasn't no cheater."

They waited. Detective Washington stopped talking on the phone.

"Who told you that lie?" Now her voice was getting louder and she was standing up.

Detective Anderson stood. "Mrs. Woods, please have a seat." Slowly she sat down. "Are you saying you didn't know your husband was sleeping with, a Gwen Harrison?"

"GWEN HARRISON! THAT BITCH IN THE CHOIR?"

"So, you weren't aware they were sleeping together?"

"I sure in hell didn't know she was screwing my husband. You're crazy if you think I killed him. Is that why you asked me to come here? I was nowhere near Las Vegas. If I knew he was screwing that bitch, I would have killed his ass here in Oakland. I certainly wouldn't wait until he went on a trip with her. But if I see that bitch Gwen any time soon I may kill her." Vanessa suddenly realized she was talking about killing someone. She'd better shut up before getting arrested.

"I hope you're not serious."

Vanessa lowered her voice. "I ain't goin kill her but I'll probably beat her ass. As for me, knowing Ken was cheating on me. No! I didn't know and I didn't kill my husband. Is that all you needed to know 'cause I need to go?"

From the speakerphone she heard, "Do you know of anyone who wanted your husband dead?"

255

"No!" Vanessa was now walking back and forth. Pierce and Anderson stood up. Pierce reached his arm out in an effort to calm her down, but she jerked back and shouted, "If you touch me I'll scream bloody murder. I'm getting the hell out of here before I get arrested." She walked toward the door, and then turned back, "Did that bitch kill him?"

The voice on the phone responded, "We don't think so."

Vanessa whirled around and walked out the door. Because there was no reason to hold her, the detectives let her go. They closed the door and sat down. Anderson and Pierce had already received permission to help with the investigation. Both agreed Vanessa looked shocked when told of the affair but they were used to wives acting crazy and pretending not to know the truth.

The Oakland detectives would conduct a thorough investigation on the Woods family in Oakland. Washington and Hamilton would be kept in the loop.

In the meantime, Vanessa pushed her way past everyone in the hall. Janet looked bewildered as Vanessa approached her. "Would you believe it, Ken was sleeping with Gwen Harrison, that crazy bitch in the choir." Vanessa pushed open the door to the street.

Until they found out differently, Hamilton and Washington would still consider Vanessa Woods a suspect.

Chapter 57

Evelyn was working on her notebook, confident she could find the killer. Cory and Amos were just too young and it didn't appear they had any reason to harm Deacon Woods. Valarie had just met him so she eliminated her. Carol was focused on getting a job. To Evelyn, her interaction with Deacon Woods appeared minimal.

There were Randy and Alex, both in their twenties. Like Carol, Randy was searching for a job. He didn't seem to have any reason to kill Deacon Woods.

Alex Garcia had been a member of the church for a long time. He hadn't had any interaction with Deacon Woods that she considered suspect. He'd been flirting with Monique and nobody seems to care. Both were single and kept to themselves. She couldn't picture them involved with Deacon Woods' murder.

Then there was Sarah. It was clear she loved Gary despite the way he treated her. Even though Sarah hadn't really accounted for where she was that night, Evelyn believed she was too traumatized over the altercation between her and Gary to hurt Deacon Woods.

That left Gwen, Diana, Jessie, Eric, and Deacon Jackson. Just as she was trying to finish her notes, the phone rang.

"Hello Ms Jenkins, this is Mr. Schuler. The police want the choir to come back down to answer more questions. They didn't say why. A police van will be in the garage in twenty minutes. Can you call the choir members and tell them to be there?"

Evelyn was confused. "Do you think they are letting us go?"

"I really don't know. I'll meet you at police headquarters."

Evelyn's mind was racing. She called Deacon Jackson and told him. Angrily, he started complaining. She couldn't tell him what the police wanted, and in any case she wasn't sure he was as innocent as he claimed. She wanted to believe he was grieving but, that was quickly fading.

Evelyn called Jessie and asked him to help gather the troops to meet in the garage. Within a few minutes, Cory's parents called her and told her they were going with them. She agreed.

Evelyn headed down to the garage. Gradually, the choir members appeared. Their hellos were cordial, but there was a distance between them. Whether it was fear or guilt, it was present and everyone seemed to feel it.

When Deacon Jackson arrived, he suggested they pray before leaving. Afterward, everyone offered their condolences to him, knowing how close he was to Deacon Woods. Finally, the police van pulled into the garage and they drove to police headquarters.

The choir members sat together and waited. Mr. Schuler got there a few minutes later. He took Evelyn and Deacon

Jackson aside to tell them Gary's car had been found. Deacon Jackson was noticeably shaken. "How does finding Gary's car have anything to do with us? We didn't know him."

"I really don't know. Detective Washington didn't elaborate on the phone, but demanded the choir come in. Maybe they think one of you has additional information."

"Well, I'm not answering any more questions. You're my lawyer and that's my position." A few minutes passed before anyone else spoke.

"Ms. Jenkins, do you feel the same way?"

Evelyn was a little stunned. She thought about it. "Yes, I think I do agree with Deacon Jackson."

"If everyone agrees, I'll tell the detectives."

It was unanimous. No one wanted to be interviewed again. Mr. Schuler went to the front desk and asked to speak with Detective Washington.

It was several minutes before he appeared. Mr. Schuler took him aside. He told him that unless they were considered suspects, the choir members would not answer any more questions. "Is there any evidence that makes them suspects?"

"No, but they may know something that can help find the killer." Washington was furious.

"Well, Detective Washington, unless you have some evidence that they are involved, they can't be questioned again. I know you don't like it, but that's how they feel."

Knowing he had no real evidence against any of them, Detective Washington faced them, and gave them a dirty look. "I understand how much of a trauma this must be but I would hope you want to help find the killer. In my experience, people have information they may not realize that is critical to the investigation. That's the only reason we asked you to come back. I'm disappointed to hear you feel you need an attorney but I can assure you if we find one of you has lied, or is withholding information, you will be back, and it won't be a pleasant experience." He spun around and stomped back to his office.

Mr. Schuler assured them that they shouldn't be intimidated by what Detective Washington had just said, and he hoped everyone had told the truth. If not, the police had a right to bring them back. No one said a word; they all stood up and walked out the door in silence.

Chapter 58

Detective Hamilton called the crime lab for an update. Gary's car had been towed to the police garage. They were getting ready to fingerprint it. Suddenly, the technician started yelling. "Come down to the garage immediately. We have a body; we have a body."

Washington and Hamilton rushed down to the garage where they were approached by Tom Chinn, the criminal tech who had just been speaking with them. Talking in short breaths, he pointed them toward the open trunk of a car. In the trunk, they saw a man's body in the fetal position. The victim was a tall Afro-American man. The face resembled that in the picture of Gary Stevens but it was hard to be sure. His eyes were open as if he was looking at the spare tire. A small amount of blood appeared to have dripped from his mouth. There was more blood near the stomach area. He was wearing a blood-soaked white shirt, jeans, and designer tennis shoes. His right arm was folded across his body; his left underneath his body. Across the victim's feet was a briefcase. Since it was well over 100 degrees, some decomposition was evident.

Automatically, the stunned detectives put on rubber gloves and booties and started a closer inspection. Technician Chinn handed them facemasks. No weapon was visible. Without touching the body, they inspected the trunk then stood back.

Chinn told Washington the coroner was on his way, to collect evidence or fingerprints from the body.

As they waited for the coroner, they interviewed the officer who found the car. Officer Reynolds said that after he finished checking the short-term parking lot at the airport he found the car in an isolated area in the long-term lot. Reynolds said the driver's window was open and the car keys were tossed on the driver's seat. He was surprised it hadn't been stolen. There was no one inside the car. Because he didn't have a warrant to search the car, he had it towed to the police garage instead of impounding it.

When the coroner arrived, he removed the briefcase from the victim's feet and began examining the body. The victim had been stabbed with a sharp object, probably a knife. There were no defensive wounds. He estimated time of death at over twelve hours earlier. The coroner's assistant helped him put the body in a body bag. The CSI techs started their process: photographing, fingerprinting, logging in evidence.

Gary Stevens' wallet and airplane ticket were found on the body. And in the wallet, two driver licenses with Gary's picture on them: one in the name of Gary Stevens, the other for an Edward Davis, the name on the airline ticket. In the briefcase they found $10,000. Things were suddenly way more complicated. Now they had two homicides and one choir. The chances that no choir members were responsible had just gotten slimmer.

The detectives looked at evidence as the technicians removed it from the backseat of the car. There were food wrappers, trash, and a half-smoked joint, an unopened letter addressed to Sarah, a pair of sunglasses, a cell phone, a camera, and a hotel room key. When the techs had taken fingerprints and logged them into evidence, they temporarily transferred custody of the cell phone and camera to the detectives.

Chapter 59

Hamilton and Washington went back to their office. Washington took the cell phone and Hamilton took the camera. Most of the pictures in the camera were of Sarah and the choir during a concert. A few were obviously taken in Las Vegas. The call list on the cell phone showed calls to and from Oakland, as well as local calls.

On Hamilton's desk was the CSI fingerprint report from Deacon Woods' hotel room. Among the many prints in the hotel room, there were prints from the victim, the maid, Mr. Jackson, Gwen, and Jessie McDaniel. Other unidentified prints had been found in the bathroom and around the room. Those prints had been run through the AFAS System, but none had been identified. The report further stated that there was no way to determine if the prints were recent or from previous guests. No prints were found on the knife.

Frustrated, they called the hotel and found Benjamin Anderson was on duty. A police car was sent to pick him up.

Hamilton and Washington were still waiting for the autopsy report to determine if the choir should be brought in for further questioning. At least for now, they decided not to tell them Gary had been murdered. They needed to observe their reactions.

Lieutenant Sayers walked in and asked for an update. When told of the second murder, he went ballistic. Once he had calmed down, he asked if they needed help. Washington insisted he and Hamilton could solve both cases on their own. Reluctantly he gave them a week.

Chapter 60

Back at the hotel, Evelyn was in her room on a conference call with Pastor Watson and Attorney Shuler. Not knowing yet about Gary Stevens' murder, Mr. Schuler updated Pastor Watson on the Woods case, while Evelyn listened. Schuler recommended that he officially ask the police to free the choir to return home. There was no evidence any choir members had been involved in the murder. Because it was Saturday, Schuler didn't expect they'd be able to leave until Monday morning when the results of evidence testing might be available from the police. He agreed to call Pastor Watson when he heard from the police, and hung up.

Still on the line, Pastor Watson asked Evelyn to find out if the choir wanted to remain in the hotel on Sunday or attend church services. Evelyn thought that going to church might comfort them after their horrific week.

After they hung up, she called Deacon Jackson to relay the message. His cell phone went to voice mail so she left a message on both his cell and hotel phone. She then called Jessie, who agreed to poll the rest of the choir. Twenty minutes later, he called back and said they wanted to attend church, in honor of Deacon Woods. They also asked if they could participate in the church service.

After Evelyn's call back, Pastor Watson contacted Reverend Mason, who was happy to let the choir sing. He called

Evelyn to make arrangements. They would sing at the morning worship service. Jessie asked if they could get an early start to the church on Sunday morning so they could have a warm-up before service. Rev. Mason and Evelyn made the final arrangements: they would rehearse in the choir room before the 11:00 a.m. Morning Worship.

An hour later, Deacon Jackson called Evelyn, saying he had gone for a walk. He was sure that attending church on Sunday would help him. Evelyn told him she was praying for him in this difficult time.

Evelyn decided it would be a good idea for the choir to have dinner together that evening. She knew they had most likely been eating in their rooms. She and Jessie called the other members and they all agreed, even Deacon Jackson. She made a reservation.

As they ordered and started to eat dinner, choir members were subdued as if being somber was giving reverence to the absent Deacon Wood. Deacon Jackson was cordial but aloof. Tonight, Evelyn had a different image of who these people really were. Now she looked around and saw adulterers, liars, drug users, a thief, and maybe a killer. Her belief that Deacon Woods had been murdered by a stranger was fading fast.

Jessie was trying to cheer everyone up. Eric was in deep thought. And for once, Gwen and Diana were quiet. Valarie and Sarah were focused on their conversation; Randy and Carol told each other about their job interviews. Cory and Amos were competing as to who could eat the most. Alex and Monique paid attention only to each other. When she looked at the silent Deacon Jackson, Evelyn saw a man with a deep secret. The more closely she observed him, the more sinister he looked. She had a gut feeling about him, and it wasn't good. Evelyn and Cory's parents made light conversation throughout the meal. Nobody wanted to talk about what they've been through or what they expected to happen when they got home.

The Williams paid for the meal. It was agreed everyone would meet in the garage to leave for church at 9:00 a.m.

Chapter 61

At the police station, Benjamin was interviewed by Washington and Hamilton. As they had with everyone else in this case, they did a background check. It came up clean. The young man was attending college and working to support himself.

Benjamin told them about the scotch. Deacon Woods came downstairs around 3 a.m. to get it. Benjamin never saw him again. That was the only information he could provide, so they sent him home.

It was late. They now had time to view the video footage from the hotel. The lobby camera did show Deacon Woods in the lobby at 3:00 a.m., which confirmed Benjamin's statement. It also showed Mr. Jackson and Mr. Woods having a heated conversation around 2:30 a.m., near the lobby elevator. This contradicted this statement given by Jackson. He said he didn't talk with Mr. Woods late that night.

They observed another member of the choir speaking with Mr. Woods in the lobby around 3:30 a.m. It was Randy Sullivan. He too had lied. Now they had two more suspects. With this new information, they decided to question both men again. Hamilton called Attorney Schuler and told him to have both of them at the police station at 11:00 Monday morning.

Not anticipating any real problem, Mr. Schuler decided to wait until Monday morning before telling Randy and Deacon Jackson about going back to see the police. The choir had been through so much. He wanted them to have at least one uneventful day.

Chapter 62

Evelyn could really feel the heat on Sunday morning because she didn't like using the air conditioner. Restful sleep eluded her. She was tired. All she could think about was the events of the week. Was it a stranger or Deacon Jackson? Or maybe even Gary? Evelyn knew she didn't have all the pieces to this mystery. How she wished a stranger was the killer, but studying her notes, she had her doubts. This had to be someone who knew him. Her brother called it a crime of passion. That's probably what the detectives decided too. And Randy, who seemed so jittery at the police station the other day, was he a suspect too? Looking at the clock made her stomach cringe. In only a few hours, she'd have to face the choir. As far as she knew, one of them was a murderer.

Evelyn showered and dressed, resisting the urge to call Deborah. She put on a light summer dress, with matching white shoes. Entering the restaurant, she saw Amos, Cory, and his parents eating breakfast. They invited her to sit with them but she politely declined. Looking across the restaurant she spotted Gwen, Sarah, Valarie, Monique, Jessie, Alex, and Randy all sitting together. There was no sign of Deacon Jackson or the others. She sat at a small table. Today she wanted to think alone.

After eating, they all met in the garage to head for church. The women were in their summer dresses; the guys wore white shirts with dark pants. It was hard to be cheerful knowing Deacon Woods was gone. It felt strange driving to church. Everyone was quiet. Deacon Jackson didn't smile or talk to anyone unless they spoke to him first. It was as if he was in a daze. Maybe it was grief, maybe not.

No one knew if church members knew they were involved with a murder. How would they be accepted? When they arrived, Deacon Jackson and Brother Williams parked the vans. They unloaded the garment bags with the robes and were escorted to the choir room. Inside the church Cory's parents, Brother and Sister Williams, took seats in a pew and Deacon Jackson headed up front with the other deacons.

Deacon Jackson sat down and his body language changed. He was grinning and laughing like men do when they greet each other. There was an arrogance about him. When he was escorted to a special seat in one of the comfortable Lazy Suzan chairs in front of the pulpit, he leaned back as if he felt at home.

In the choir room, Jessie gave his instructions as to what songs they would sing. He knew how hard it was for everyone, but he encouraged them to praise the Lord just like at home. He told them to let go and just let God use them. Jessie prayed. Pastor Mason made a special visit to the choir room before morning worship to welcome them and pray with them. He assured them no one knew they were connected to the murder. The church knew someone had passed, which was why the concert had been cancelled. This was the first time the Oakland choir would sing since the murder. Nobody knew what to expect.

All the choirs gathered in the foyer and lined up by voice part. As the visiting choir, they would march into the sanctuary behind the church choir. The organist began playing. The congregation stood. It was hard for Evelyn to look at Deacon Jackson. While waiting in line, she looked back at the tenors, who were lined up behind her. Randy was talking to Alex and Cory, as if he hadn't a care in the world. Suddenly their eyes met. He smiled, she smiled back, but then he turned his head away. Was he uneasy? She turned around as the choir began to march into the sanctuary.

It was a large church, easily able to seat 1,500 members at one time. The décor was dark purple and gold. The church choir robes, the usher uniforms, the pews, and flowers lining the church were all the same colors. As they marched down the aisles, they were greeted with loud shouts of celebration. Evelyn's choir was seated up front on the left side of the church pews. The church choir started singing as soon as the last choir member reached the choir stand. The song was "Stranger in Town." Jessie and his choir sang along with them.

In the Afro-American church, there is an unwritten competition between a visiting choir and the church choir. Just like the ministers, each one wants to impress the other with their best song or sermon. It may occur in other churches, but here they took it seriously. Everyone began praising the Lord. Pastor

Mason, already in the pulpit, began speaking the dialogue of the song, which excited the congregation. The music was loud. Everyone clapped their hands and shouted for joy. It was the same atmosphere they had at their own church. Evelyn was really enjoying the service.

When it was time for their choir to sing, the ushers had them all exchange places. Jessie took his place in front of the choir stand but kept the choir seated. He pointed to Eric and Amos and they started playing. While everyone was focused on them, Gwen stood up on the opposite end of the choir stand where the altos were seated. She stood alone with mike in hand. After the introduction was played, she started singing. Even though Gwen had the worst personality ever known, the girl could sing. Her strong melodious voice filled the church. It was dramatic. Listening to her, you'd never believe she was an adulterous and maybe a murderer. The audience was captured with her first words. "Near the Cross" had been made famous by a Mississippi choir. As she neared the verse containing those words, Jessie had the rest of the choir stand. The audience went wild. By the time they sang the chorus twice, there was pandemonium in the church. When they finished, Gwen sat down and began crying, as did the rest of the choir. Jessie couldn't contain himself. He sat down weeping. It was overwhelming. For over five minutes, people were rejoicing and crying. Rev. Mason recognized that there was no way the choir could sing another song. He knew a Pentecostal experience was taking place and didn't want to interrupt.

It was a few minutes before everyone calmed down and he began preaching. His text was, "God will protect you, no matter what," in concert with the song. As Evelyn wiped her eyes she looked down to see how Deacon Jackson was reacting. It was as if he wasn't affected at all, how odd. He looked comfortable and secure. The last time she saw him like that was at church the previous Sunday. Clearly he wasn't that grief-stricken. She moved her eyes to the right to see how Randy was reacting, but he wasn't there. Randy had left the choir stand.

Evelyn didn't want to attract attention so she stayed seated, wondering was this affecting him at all. About fifteen minutes later, Randy returned to the choir stand. He appeared to have been crying, but she had her doubts.

When Rev. Mason finished his sermon, he asked the congregation to stand and pray for their guests. There was a special offering taken to help with their expenses. Jessie stood up on behalf of the choir and thanked everyone for the love they'd shown and asked them to continue praying for them. After the benediction, members gathered around the choir telling them how much they enjoyed having them at the morning worship. No one said anything about the death or Deacon Woods.

Deacon Jackson was asked to go to the trustee's office. He was given over $700 that had been collected for the choir. Rev. Mason invited the choir to the fellowship hall for food.

Evelyn and the others disrobed, and then gathered in the hall. A special table was set up for them, including Sister and Brother Williams. He and his wife both were in black and white. She wore a stunning black and white hat with matching suit and white shoes. She made it a point to shake everyone's hand and tell them she was praying for them. It was comforting. After an hour and a half, everyone was given a plate of food to take back to the hotel. By then, Deacon Jackson, Randy and Amos had the robes in the vans. It was obvious they didn't want to sit and chat.

Chapter 63

Soon everyone was in the vans riding back to the hotel. The atmosphere in the Evelyn's van was relaxed. While they exited the vans in the hotel garage, however, a stranger approached asking if they were a choir. He had to be a reporter. Just as Mr. Schuler instructed them, no one said a word. They walked past him and into the hotel. Walking together would cause too much attention, so once inside the lobby they all scattered. Luckily, there was no church logo on the van. The man gave up the chase once everyone dispersed.

Outwardly Evelyn, like the others, kept her cool. Oh God, she thought, please don't let this man put us on the news. She sped toward the elevator. It seemed the man was gone. But looking back, she saw Deacon Jackson following her.

Once he got close, he asked, "Are you all right?"

"Yes, he just scared me."

"Let me walk you to your room."

Evelyn wanted to say No thanks, but by then he was standing too close for her to protest. "Thank you Deacon Jackson, how are you? I know we haven't had time to talk."

"I'm coping Sister Jenkins, I'm coping. Church service was wonderful. Gwen really sang that song. Deacon Woods would have loved it."

Evelyn couldn't believe her ears. "Yes I think he would have. You know I felt his presence. He was there in spirit."

They rode the elevator in silence.

"Sister Jenkins I have the money that was collected. Can I give it to you now?"

Evelyn looked past him to see if anyone else was in the hall. There were people approaching. If anything happened, they could identify him as the last person to see her. Reluctantly she said, "Certainly come on in." As she opened the door, fear engulfed her. This was the first time she'd been alone with him since the murder. She walked in and swiftly turned to face him. He pulled the money out of his suit pocket and handed it to her. She took it and, as usual, counted it in front of him so there would be no dispute as to how much she received.

He stood waiting for her to finish. They agreed the total was $756. "Sister Jenkins, we need to refuel the vans."

"Would $150 be enough?"

"Sure, that's more than enough I'll give you the receipts as usual. I still have about $15, so I'll add that to this total. I don't have Deacon Woods' receipt." They both paused. "Maybe the police will give us his personal property before we leave." He turned to go.

"Have you talked to Sister Woods? How is she?"

Turning around he said, "My wife went by to see her yesterday. The children are staying at our house."

He didn't tell her how upset Vanessa had been when someone told her about the affair with Gwen. She was threatening to put him in a pine box too and bury him in potter's field. "Sister Jenkins, I feel so tore apart. I really want to remain here to help get Deacon Woods back home. I also know I need to be with my family, so it's just difficult for me now. Has Mr. Schuler said when we could go home?"

"No. I'll give him a call in the morning and find out if he has any new information."

"Well, I'll see you tomorrow." He turned and left.

There were three messages on her phone, her mother, Deborah, and Pastor Watson. She called her mother first. Hearing her mother's voice made her feel safe, like she was a teenager again. She put on her bathrobe, flicked off her shoes, flopped on the bed, and smiled.

"Hi baby, how are you?

"I'm all right. We just got back from church. They worship the same way we do. It was very emotional. But you know it was strange singing, knowing all that's happened. Everyone broke down and cried. The church members really treated us well. They served dinner and gave us food to bring back to the hotel."

"Do you know when you'll be able to leave?"

"No, I hope we'll find out tomorrow."

"Dad and I want you to be safe. Go home as soon as they let you. It was good to hear your voice. If you need anything, you call us. We love you."

"Love you too; good-bye."

She lay back on the bed looking at the ceiling wondering when this mess would be over. She was about ready to call

Pastor Watson. It was 5:30, so she knew morning worship was over at her church. She dialed. "Hello Pastor, this is Sister Jenkins."

"I just got off the phone with Pastor Mason, who told me how wonderful the service was. They really enjoyed the choir."

"How was service at our church?"

"It was difficult. Deacon Woods was loved and will be missed. I went to see Sister Woods yesterday. She's very upset." Pastor Watson didn't explain why. "And how are the others?"

"There're doing well under the circumstances. It's good to have Sister and Brother Williams here. They help comfort the others. It's been difficult for Deacon Jackson."

"I spoke with his wife. She's having a hard time dealing with Deacon Woods' death as well. I think the wives are very close. Apparently, Deacon Jackson wants to stay and bring the body home, but it's not practical. The mortuary will be retrieving the body. I think it's best if Deacon Jackson returns with the choir."

"I just hope we will be able to leave here soon."

"I can't thank you enough for your help. Mr. Schuler said he's going to try and have the police release the choir. The police want the choir to come back to the police station again tomorrow."

"Did he say why they want us back?"

"No, but Mr. Schuler told me he's representing everybody, so having him there will help. Please call me when you have returned to the hotel from the police station."

It was getting dark. She turned on the light, warmed the food in the microwave, and sat down to eat. Afterward, she took a shower and settled in for the evening. She was startled when the phone rang. It was Mr. Schuler.

"I'm sorry to bother you," he said, "but I received a call from Detective Washington. He wants all the choir members to come to the police station tomorrow morning."

"Are they going to let us go home?"

"He didn't say. I told him we would be there by 9:00 o'clock. That way if they release the choir you'll have time to check out the hotel and get on the road."

"I'll let the choir know and we'll be there at 9. See you tomorrow."

While Evelyn was optimistic that they would be able to leave tomorrow, she didn't want to get her hopes up too high. After calling Deacon Jackson, she called Jessie and asked him to tell the others.

She was now wide awake. She grabbed her notebook and started writing. When she arrived, the room had felt like a nice place to be. Now it felt like she was trapped in a tomb.

She was still perplexed as to why Deacon Woods was killed. Could his wife have known about the affair and had him killed? Or could it actually be Gary or Randy or Deacon

Jackson? One thing she hadn't considered was that it could have been a woman.

Chapter 64

While Evelyn was busy writing in her notebook, Detectives Washington and Hamilton were revisiting the crime scene to make sure they hadn't missed anything. Cutting the seal and crime tape, they entered the dark room. Because the crime techs had processed the room, they didn't have to worry about touching anything.

The room was in shambles. Blood was still on the bed, walls, and floor. They went through different scenarios trying to recreate the crime. They still had questions with no answers. Why did he buy a bottle of scotch that late? Who was the last person to visit him? Why was he nude? Did he hire a hooker for the night? They needed to review the hotel surveillance tapes. They still hadn't ruled out the possibility that a woman killed him but that theory was getting weak.

Finding nothing more in the room that could help move the investigation forward, Washington went to the manager's office. Hamilton went to the concierge's desk with a photo of the victim. No one else had any information that helped. They asked the hotel manager to have the night shift employees schedule a talk with the police on Monday to see if they could provide any new information.

They went back to the office to prepare for more interviews. While reviewing the hotel surveillance tapes, they found footage of Gary meeting with an unidentified tall

Caucasian male. Gary gave the stranger what looked like car keys; in exchange, Gary received a suitcase. It looked like the same one found in the trunk with the $10,000. Was Gary transporting drugs to Las Vegas?

Chapter 65

On Monday morning there was excitement in the air. The choir was anxious to leave and met for breakfast at 7 a.m. For the first time in several days, they were in a hopeful but guarded mood. There was even light laugher. Evelyn was fairly optimistic that the day would end well, as planned. Deacon Jackson and Brother Williams went early to gas the vans. Most of them were packed ready to go.

At 8:15, they climbed into the vans with great anticipation. When they arrived at police headquarters Mr. Schuler met them at the entrance. Walking inside, they were met by two uniformed officers who escorted them to a waiting area and instructed not to converse. One officer remained with them.

Mr. Schuler was taken to the detectives' office. There they told him about the murder of Gary Stevens. As their attorney, he would be present during each of the interviews. Hamilton and Washington wanted to include Cory, but his parents refused to let him be interviewed.

As each choir member was interviewed, it was apparent the nightmare was not over. Evelyn kept looking around to see how the others were doing. They all looked nervous. Every now and then, Randy or Deacon Jackson would stand and pace back and forth. Each member who passed by the waiting area as they came out of the interview room looked upset. Valarie and Carol were crying. Gwen was called next. When she came out, she looked like she was in shock.

Diana was next. When she walked in and sat down she knew this was going to be bad.

Washington spoke first. "Thank you for coming. I have some follow-up questions for you." Her body stiffened. "First, I know you lied." Gwen had already told her what to expect. "When I asked where you were around 1 a.m. Thursday night, you told me you were with Gwen Harrison, who has since admitted she was with Mr. Woods, so—"

Diana interrupted him. "Detective Washington, I'm sorry, I'm sorry. I didn't mean to lie I was trying to protect Gwen. She told me you were probably going to ask me. Please, please. I was in my room alone. Gwen wasn't with me." She started whimpering.

"Were you ever in Mr. Woods' room?"

"NO, NEVER."

"What time did you leave your room?"

"Leave my room? I didn't leave it until the next morning. I went to sleep. I never left the room. Honest."

"What time did Gwen return?"

"I don't know, really. I was asleep."

"How well did you know Gary Steven?"

"I don't know him at all. Sarah introduced him in Los Angeles after the concert."

"When was the last time you saw him?"

"The last time I saw him was when we got our luggage from the van around 7:30 Thursday night."

"Are you sure you haven't seen him since?"

"Yes, I'm sure."

"Gary Stevens was found dead."

Diana gasped. Washington and Hamilton watched her reaction closely. She immediately looked at Schuler. "Dead?" "How did he die?"

"He was murdered."

With her voice raised, "Murdered! Oh Lord. I hope you don't think I killed him. This is crazy. "Diana's hands were shaking.

Mr. Shuler placed his hand over hers in an effort to calm her down. "Diana, if the police felt you were in danger they would have you in protective custody. Isn't that right, Detective?"

"Yes it is. Is there anything you can remember that will help?"

"No but if I do I will call you."

Washington was observing without saying a word. They both stood up and told her she could go back to the hotel. Standing, she realized her legs were weak. She accepted Schuler's help to the door.

Washington and Hamilton weren't completely convinced but they had no evidence to arrest her.

Alex was next. He came out looking upset. He tried to smile at Monique as he walked past Evelyn with his head down. Randy walked over to her.

"Sister Jenkins, what do you think is going on?"

"Randy, I really don't know what's going on. Whatever it is, it's serious."

"Well I can't wait till we get out of Las Vegas. My wife is driving me crazy. Do you know she calls me every two hours just to make sure I'm still alive? My new job starts in two weeks. I need to get back home, pack, and move. I can't believe this is happening. Murder, I tell you Sister Jenkins, I'm scared."

"I can understand how your wife must feel. This is a scary situation. Did you know Deacon Woods or Jackson in Los Angeles?"

"I don't know what you mean."

Mr. Schuler came over, interrupted, and asked Randy to follow him. He didn't stay long. Then it was Jessie, Monique, and Deacon Jackson. It wasn't long before they came out. Now the only ones left were Sarah and Evelyn.

Sarah sat close to Evelyn, shaking. "Sister Jenkins, I'm scared."

"Sarah I know this is frightening. They let everyone else go. I'm sure it's just a formality." Evelyn put her hands over Sarah's, which were cold and clammy.

Mr. Schuler asked Evelyn to follow him. As she walked in and sat down, she noticed that Washington and Hamilton weren't smiling.

"Sister Jenkins, we asked you to come in because there is a new development in this case. Gary Stevens was found murdered Saturday. His body was stuffed in the trunk of the rental car." They sat back to observe Evelyn's reaction.

Evelyn gasped. "Oh, dear Lord! Is that why you called us back here? Do you think one of us killed him?" Before she realized it, tears were falling down her face. "Oh Lord, how is Sarah going to take this?"

"That's what we're trying to find out. We know his girlfriend confided in you. At any time did she say anything that would indicate he was in danger or was doing something dangerous?"

"No, all she told me about was how he abused her. She was angry and scared he would hurt her again. Sarah is in love with him, or was. You can't believe she killed him. She's been with us all the time. When was he killed?"

"He was killed sometime between Friday night, and Saturday morning. When was the last time you saw him?"

"Thursday night."

"So, Sarah never indicated he was in danger?"

"No and I think she would have told me. But who knows?"

Mr. Schuler asked, "Is Ms. Jenkins a suspect?"

"As I said before, for now we're conducting interviews to determine who has information that will help in this new investigation."

"If there's nothing else, can Ms. Jenkins leave?"

The detectives looked at each other, then nodded yes.

Evelyn and Mr. Schuler stood up, followed by the detectives. They walked out leaving the detectives in the room.

Evelyn composed herself as she passed by Sarah. She gave her a slight smile. In a low voice, she asked, "Mr. Schuler, what's going to happen to us? Do the police have any idea who killed Deacon Woods?"

"I know you have a lot of questions, Evelyn. Right now, I have to get back and represent Sarah. When this is over I would like us to sit down and talk about this case."

"I understand. I'll wait in the van."

Sarah was shaking. Even Sister Jenkins had looked upset. Mr. Schuler stood near her and said it was her time to be interviewed. She asked him what it was all about, but he didn't respond. Sarah stood up. Her legs were weak. She shivered on entering the cold room. Washington said their usual "Thank you for coming in."

"We need to find out a little more about Gary. Do you know if he had any enemies?"

"No, not that I know of and what do you mean did?"

"You know Sarah, I think you're lying." His voice was sharp.

Mr. Schuler tried to speak but Detective Hamilton motioned him to be silent.

Ignoring the attorney, Washington continued to stare at Sarah. "Answer the question. Do you know of anyone who wants to harm Gary?"

"No, I don't know of anyone who would harm Gary. I don't know his friends that well, but the ones I met are really nice. Has Gary been hurt? Please tell me."

"When was the last time you saw him?"

"I told you the last time. It was Thursday night when we had a big fight."

"So he hasn't called you?"

"Yes, but I wouldn't answer the phone."

"When was the last time he called you?" Sarah took out her cell phone to look at the phone log. The log indicated the last call from his number was Saturday at 1:00 p.m.

"Have you called him?"

"Only when you asked me to call him on Friday."

"Did he know anyone here in Las Vegas?"

"I don't know. He didn't say he did."

"Sarah, I'm sorry to be the bearer of bad news, but we found Gary's body in the trunk of the rental car."

Sarah fainted. Her body went limp and she started to fall from the chair. Hamilton caught her before she hit the floor. Washington called the medical examiner, while Schuler and

Hamilton moved her into another office and placed her on a couch.

It was several minutes before she came to. By the time the medical examiner appeared, she was conscious. Her vitals were taken and she was all right. She refused medical attention and was getting hysterical. The medical examiner, learning why she fainted, gave her a prescription to help her relax. He suggested the questioning stop.

With the help of Mr. Schuler, she agreed to answer a few more questions. She gave them the names of two friends Gary had introduced her to. Other than that, there was no other information she provided that could help. They ended the questioning and sent her back to the hotel.

Sarah leaned on Mr. Schuler as she walked to the van. Once in, she broke down. She laid her head on Evelyn's shoulder and wept. Mr. Schuler said his good-byes and left. The drive back to the hotel was very emotional. Sarah's crying ignited the emotions of the others. Even Deacon Jackson had tears in his eyes.

When they arrived at the hotel, Sarah bolted from the van and ran inside. Evelyn asked Gwen and Diana to help her. They ran after her. The others hurried out of the van and headed for their rooms. Evelyn was the last one out. Deacon Jackson and Mr. Williams went to park the vans.

Chapter 66

As she walked toward the hotel, Evelyn realized Mr. Schuler had followed them back. He called out to her and asked her to wait for him in the lobby. She did. He suggested they have coffee and ushered her toward the nearest café. After placing their order, Evelyn tried to relax.

"Ms. Jenkins, I don't know what to tell you. The police now have two murders to solve. As far as I know, they don't have any idea who committed these murders. I think they believe someone in the choir killed these men. I'm talking to you as your attorney, which means anything you tell me is attorney-client privilege. Is there anything that you observed that would give you concern?"

"No. I've been with these people longer than a year and I haven't seen anyone angry enough to kill someone. I didn't even know Gary." Evelyn was not going to share her suspicions with him until she had evidence to support her fears.

Schuler said the police had not indicated they could leave yet. He said he would insist on it, since there was no evidence they were involved in these murders. He agreed to call her later after speaking with the detectives again. He left and Evelyn returned to her room.

She decided to stop by Sarah's room to see how she was doing. Gwen answered the door. Sarah was lying on the cot still crying. Gwen and Diana left the room to let Evelyn speak to her alone. Evelyn sat by the bed and tried to comfort her.

"Sister Jenkins, he's dead. Even though he was a jerk, I didn't want him to die. I love him. Why would somebody kill him? My mother's going out of her mind. If we had enough money she would have flown down here by now." Sarah cried harder.

While patting Sarah on the shoulder, Evelyn talked, "I still can't believe Deacon Woods was murdered and now Gary. This is crazy. I think we all need to be very careful while we're here. Mr. Schuler is going to find out when we can leave. I pray it will be soon. I know you loved Gary. Have you talked to his parents?"

"I called his brother. He said his parents are devastated, but they're both coming here."

Evelyn was upset herself but she didn't want to let it show. She stood and prayed for Sarah. Gwen and Diana, who were standing outside the door, entered as she left.

Evelyn went directly to her room, looking around to make sure no one was following her. Once there she immediately locked the door. She returned her mother's call and told her about Gary. Her parents insisted she fly home immediately. Evelyn assured them she was safe.

After hanging up the phone, she picked up her notebook and made notes about today's events. She was trying to put the pieces together. Why would Gary kill Deacon Woods? Maybe he didn't. Maybe he knew who killed Deacon Woods. She started looking at the time frames. If Gary went to see Deacon Woods, then maybe the scotch was ordered for him? She needed to find out if he drank. She also decided to ask Deacon Jackson, as painful as it might be, if Deacon Woods drank liquor.

The phone rang. Mr. Schuler reported that the police reluctantly told him the choir could leave on Tuesday, as long as no evidence turned up implicating any choir members. Evelyn was surprised to realize that she had mixed feelings. She was glad to be going home, but she was convinced that somebody in the choir was a murderer. She would find out who before they headed home. Sitting back on the bed, she formulated a plan.

Chapter 67

Evelyn picked up her phone. "Deborah, you are not going to believe what's happened." After her initial responses of "What? No shit" and "Lord have mercy," she followed with "Why would anybody kill Gary?"

"I don't have a clue unless the guy was mixed up with drugs or something. It just doesn't make sense. Deborah, I don't know if you can help me, but I want to find out when Randy's brother died."

"I'll try. Why?"

"Well, I was talking with him at the station and he mentioned moving back to Los Angeles. I'm just curious why."

Evelyn told Deborah they were leaving for Oakland the next day.

"Hallelujah! Girl, get out of there fast."

Evelyn started making other calls. Mr. and Mrs. Williams were thrilled to be going home.

Jessie was ecstatic. "Girl I can't wait to get out of this town. I don't think I'll ever come back here. Who do you think killed Gary? I'm glad I didn't know the guy. I swear I think he was shady anyway."

She asked Jessie to call the others and have them meet in the garage at 7:00 to go out for dinner. She decided to treat everyone to dinner at another hotel.

At 7:00, she took the elevator down to the garage. The group was already there. Knowing this was the last night in Las Vegas cheered everyone. Monique and Alex were acting like a couple now, holding hands and looking into each other's eyes. Cory and Amos clung to Cory's parents. In spite of the good news, they all seemed a bit wary of each other.

While they were walking to the vans, a limousine stopped in front of them. The driver got out and waved at Deacon Jackson. He gave a half wave and immediately turned away, walking on. The driver looked offended. He got back in the limo and drove away.

Gwen started teasing him, "Wow, Deacon Jackson. Didn't know you knew people in high places." Everyone laughed. Deacon Jackson simply shrugged his shoulders and went on walking. In the van, everyone was quiet. It was as if they all suddenly remembered Deacon Woods was not with them. Jessie asked Deacon Jackson how he knew the limo driver. He said he had met him in the hotel lobby earlier that week. Deacon Jackson seemed embarrassed. Something wasn't right, Evelyn felt.

She had made reservations at the Hollywood Planet restaurant and invited Pastor Mason and his wife to join them. Before giving thanks for the meal, Pastor Mason expressed his sorrow over everything that had happened. He said a special prayer for Deacon Woods' family. He ended by asking God to find the person who had killed Deacon Woods and to give the choir a safe trip home. No one mentioned anything about the second murder.

The meal was good and the conversation was light. During the meal, Evelyn paid close attention to all the choir members. Sarah scarcely said a word and barely ate. The others were reserved. They seemed anxious to leave, but she was apprehensive about riding back with them.

Before they got into the vans to return to the hotel, they agreed they would meet in the hotel lobby at 10:00 a.m. to avoid morning traffic. Arriving back at the hotel, everyone announced they were heading to their rooms and said their good nights. Evelyn decided to find the limo driver.

Taking a seat in the lobby, she waited. It was over an hour before she saw him. He was helping a couple out of the limo when she introduced herself. The driver, Alonso, was very friendly. Pretending she wanted to hire a limo, she told him that Deacon Jackson had referred him to her. Alonso told her that he met the deacon at the airport and gave him a ride to the hotel. A knot formed in her stomach. Alonso told her that a couple who were getting married offered the deacon a ride back to the hotel.

A shock wave of terror went through her body. She smiled at Alonso trying not to show fear in her face. He gave her a business card as they said good-bye. She rushed to sit down. Her knees were weak. Why was Deacon Jackson at the airport? Could he have killed Gary?

Hurrying to her room, she looked around to see if Deacon Jackson was anywhere near. She locked the door and felt a rush of relief. She was trying to remember the time frame to determine when Deacon Jackson could have gone to the airport. She remembered the many times she called him and his cell phone went to voice mail.

Pastor Watson could have asked him to run an errand that required him to go to the airport. Sure, that had to be it, that's what deacons do. Perhaps if he told the police they would accuse him of killing Gary. Yes, that had to be it.

Evelyn tried to make sense of this new revelation. As much as she tried to put things in perspective, it still didn't make sense. She dared not call Pastor Watson and ask him because he had enough on his mind. She decided to wait. It was too serious a matter, to accuse Deacon Jackson of being a murderer. All she had was speculation.

Discouraged, she started doubting her ability to find the killer. It was getting late. She needed to pack for the morning.

Meanwhile, at police headquarters Washington and Hamilton were frustrated. Two murders which they believed were connected had turned up no evidence to help them identify the killer. They decided it was time to contact Crime Stoppers and made a plea to the public. They needed to find out who the unidentified man was in the casino. Somebody must have seen something. The first report would air on the 11 o'clock news that night.

Evelyn showered and went to bed. She turned on the television just in time to hear the start of the Crime Stopper announcement about two murders. Evelyn sat up in the bed in shock. The choir was not mentioned. The hotel was identified, as well as the airport, along with the suspected times of death. While they didn't say the murders were connected she knew they were. They showed a picture of a Caucasian man and asked for help in identifying him. "Oh my God!"

She needed to call Pastor Watson now. "I really hate to call you so late, but I just saw on the news that the police are requesting the public's help in finding a Caucasian man. He must be the killer." After a long pause, she added, "The good thing is they didn't mention the choir, but they are looking for help with both Deacon Woods' murder and Gary's."

"Sister Jenkins, I pray they find the killer, but I don't want the church name dragged through the mud. Mr. Schuler told me you are heading home tomorrow. I know Deacon Jackson wants to stay, but I need him here."

"Pastor I do understand. He hasn't said he wants to stay for awhile, so I think he's resolved to leave too."

"I pray nothing else stops you from leaving tomorrow but if it does, call me immediately. Mr. Schuler doesn't believe there will be a problem. With God's help, I will see you late tomorrow night. Let's have a word of prayer."

After hanging up and sitting back on the bed, Evelyn realized Pastor Watson never mentioned sending Deacon

Jackson on an errand. She decided to ask him about that when they met.

Chapter 68

Waking up to the sound of people talking outside her door, Evelyn saw it was just six in the morning. She was afraid they were reporters and rushed to look out the peephole. No one was there. Evelyn called the front desk to ask that the final night for the choir members be put on her bill. She ordered breakfast, showered, and dressed. By the time she ate, it was past 9 o'clock.

She headed for the lobby with her luggage to settle the bill. When the doors of the elevator opened, the lobby was crowded. The line at the front desk was long. Was everyone in the hotel leaving? It took over twenty minutes for her to reach the desk clerk. Per instructions from Pastor Watson, she paid the previous night's stay for herself and all the other choir members.

Elbowing her way to the elevator, she saw Gwen, Sarah, and Diana exiting the elevator. She explained to them that she had paid for one night. They got in line to check out.

She wheeled her luggage into the elevator down to the garage where the vans were located. Most of the other choir members were already there with their luggage. Jessie, Randy, Valarie, Monique, Cory, and his parents had all checked out. Deacon Jackson and Brother Williams were supervising the loading of the vans. They thanked Evelyn for paying for the final night.

Just then Gwen and the other two women appeared. In a few minutes, the final people arrived and it was time to leave. As they were loaded into the van, Evelyn saw Mr. Schuler walking toward them. She got out to greet him. The others began to panic, hoping he wasn't going to tell them they couldn't leave.

"Hello Ms. Jenkins, I was hoping not to miss you. I just wanted to wish you well and say good-bye."

"Thank you, but I must admit seeing you scared me. I was afraid you came to say we had to stay."

He chuckled. "No, I haven't heard from the police, but I hope the Crime Stopper show last night will help them get the evidence they need to find who committed these crimes. Please give the choir members my card." He handed a stack of business cards to her. "Remind them that if they decide to get another attorney, I need to know, Otherwise, I will still consider them my clients."

"I'll be sure to tell them. Please keep me informed as to how the investigation is going."

"I spoke with Pastor Watson this morning. I'll contact you as soon as I hear anything." Evelyn got back in the van that Deacon Jackson was driving. The trip home began.

Traffic out of town was slow until they hit the highway toward Oakland. Brother Williams and the others were following close behind.

After about four hours, Evelyn asked Deacon Jackson to find a rest stop so everyone could stretch their legs. Christian music was playing the entire time yet no one sang or said a word.

Evelyn was lost in thought. She watched Deacon Jackson as he drove the van. There were times when she thought she could see his stress. He was trying to hide his emotions but there was a faint hint of anger and sorrow on his face.

When they stopped for rest and gas, there was small talk but nothing significant. Then she saw a news flash on the television. There had been a great response from the Crime Stoppers request the night before. Back in her van, they started talking about who could have information that would solve the crime. "I'm sure whoever did it covered their tracks," Randy commented. Others agreed.

Evelyn was still trying to put the pieces together. What drives a person to kill? Greed, passion, jealousy—or hatred. She'd been focusing on passion but she hadn't thought about hatred. If you hate someone, then you might take time to plan a murder.

Months before this tour, choir members were asked to participate. Most said no, but everyone on this tour had volunteered. That gave the killer time to plan when and where to kill Deacon Woods. Everybody going on tour knew the deacons would be given separate rooms as a reward for driving.

In Los Angeles, the members were assigned a place to stay, so it would be more difficult to sneak away to kill Deacon

Woods and get back unnoticed to wherever they were assigned. In Las Vegas, everyone knew the deacons had separate rooms on different floors. A golden opportunity. Was Gary killed because he knew who the killer was? He wouldn't have gone to the police. They were looking for him.

Evelyn started mentally checking off choir members. Valarie just joined, so she couldn't be the killer. Cory and Amos were too young and these murders took planning. Sarah still loved Gary too much and would have no reason to kill Deacon Woods. Since the tour began, Alex and Monique had been almost inseparable. Carol was an unmarried mom focused on getting a job in Las Vegas. Jessie and Eric were most likely lovers. She had seen them exchanging glances. They had no reason she could see to kill Deacon Woods and they didn't have the nerve. Neither did Gwen or Diana. Bullies are cowards. That left Deacon Jackson and Randy. Deacon Jackson was Deacon Woods' good friend and Randy had never shown any animosity towards him. There must be something she had missed.

Chapter 69

Back in Las Vegas, Washington and Hamilton studied the report on all those fingerprints found in Deacon Woods' hotel room. One print was from a member of the choir who claimed not to have been in the room.

Hamilton called the Cold Case unit of the Homicide Division in Los Angeles Police Department and asked them to pull a file. An hour later, they received a call back from an L.A. detective ready to discuss the case. On August 9, 1996, there was a drive-by shooting in Inglewood. Witnesses said there were four occupants in an SUV, all black and all wearing the colors of a local gang. A rival gang member walking down the street was believed to have been the target. As he passed 16070 Alameda Street, bullets rained out. Two bullets struck the target. Another struck Melvin Sullivan, a five-year-old who was playing in his yard. His older brother, Randy, was sitting on the steps keeping watch on his brother. The older boy was unharmed. The report said he ran to his younger brother and tried to stop the bleeding but the child was already dead.

When the police arrived, Randy was waving a butcher knife. He wouldn't allow anyone near him. Not until his mother got home were the EMT's able to get close enough to sedate him. He was hospitalized in the psychiatric ward for several weeks and released into his mother's care. The family moved to

Oakland, California not long afterward. Psychiatric outpatient treatment was recommended for Randy, but not verified.

A car matching the description had been stopped several miles from the murder scene. Four gang members were detained. There was a line-up but Randy didn't identify any of the occupants, so they were released. No other suspects were found. No arrests were ever made in the case.

Hamilton obtained the names of the suspects who had been detained and released. As he hung up the phone, he shouted to Washington, "You are not going to believe this."

Washington walked over and stood behind Hamilton as he did a background check on the four names that had been given to him. In 2008, one of the suspects was killed by a hit and run driver. There were no witnesses and the car was never found. The case went to the cold case file. In 2009, another suspect was found dead in his apartment. He had been shot and then stabbed several times. He was left with the knife still stuck in his chest. According to the coroner, the victim had been dead for several days before the body was found. Notes from the detectives on the case had noted the overkill.

Chapter 70

It was 5:30. Two more hours, and they should be back home in Oakland. She called Pastor Watson to let him know when they should arrive. Then she asked Deacon Jackson if he would make a final stop.

Evelyn went inside briefly to pay for the gas, and then stretched her legs outside while the others bought snacks and visited the rest rooms. She overheard a conversation between Deacon Jackson and Brother Williams as they put gas in the vans.

"Deacon, how are you holding up?"

"It's hard, Brother Williams. Ken and I have been friends for so many years. It's like I'm in a horrible dream. I keep thinking I'll turn around and see him. We left Los Angeles when we were teens. We were trying to be tough guys, you know, and wanted to be in a gang. There was a shooting and a young child was killed. One of the gang did the shooting. The police detained Deacon Woods and me. When they realized we didn't do it, they let us go. That day, both our mothers vowed to get us out of that environment. Moving to Oakland turned our lives around. We were going to grow old together. Now I feel such a void in my life."

"Not everyone experiences the joy of having a friend as close as you and Deacon Woods. To be friends for so long was a blessing. I'll keep praying for you. If you want to talk, call me any time."

"Thanks Brother Williams, that means a lot."

Evelyn climbed back into the van. That was the second time she had heard about a shooting in Los Angeles. On the way to Los Angeles, Randy said his little brother was the victim of a drive-by shooting when he lived in Los Angeles. Maybe she could find more of the story using her smart phone.

Choir members had started getting back into in the vans. Evelyn called up the internet. Within a few minutes, she had found a link and used her credit card to pay for an archived newspaper article. There it was: a five-year-old boy had been gunned down in a drive-by shooting. Nine-year-old Randy Sullivan witnessed his brother's murder He was traumatized by the event and was hospitalized. The identity of the shooter or shooters was unknown. The community was in shock.

At that instant Evelyn knew. Randy must have started planning revenge as soon as he suspected that Deacon Woods and Deacon Jackson were in the gang responsible for killing his brother. And Alex was so infatuated with Monique; he probably never noticed Randy left their room.

"Isn't that right, Sister Jenkins?"

'What did you say?"

It was Gwen in the backseat. "I said, I can't wait to get home, can you?"

Evelyn composed herself, turned off her cell phone, and said, "I can't either."

Randy was in the other van. Now she had to decide what to do next. She had no real evidence, only supposition. Looking up, she saw the Tracy, California sign. In an hour they would be in Oakland. Her hands were sweating. No more stops now. Soon they would be driving into the church parking lot.

As they continued down 580 out of Pleasanton, she watched the fog crawling over the hills of San Francisco toward Oakland. Choir members started shifting in their seats, anticipating their arrival. The reality of what happened tempered their relief at almost being home. Gwen was sniffling quietly, with Diana trying to comfort her. Alex placed his arm around Monique as she, too, started tearing up. It was a sad and somber return. Deacon Woods was alive when they left and now he was no longer with them.

The vans exited the freeway. Approaching the church, they could see that the lights were on. Evelyn knew Pastor Watson would be waiting at the church. Apparently, the whole church was waiting for their arrival, judging by the crowded parking lot. Deacon Jackson drove over to the back entrance where they would unload the luggage. Brother Williams pulled the other van up next to them.

Pastor Watson and Mr. Schuler stood outside with the other deacons of the church.

Evelyn and the others climbed out of the van. Pastor Watson walked over and gave her a Christian hug. He gave everyone a hug. When he hugged Deacon Jackson, it was the first time she had seen the deacon cry. Evelyn was shocked to see Mr. Schuler but kept her composure. The other deacons approached her and hugged her, as they did everyone who got out of the vans. By now, Gwen was almost hysterical. Pastor Watson comforted her. Brother and Sister Williams and the others left their van and received hugs too. Sarah broke down and the others helped her.

Pastor Watson ushered them into the sanctuary of the packed church. As they walked down the aisle, everyone in the church stood and clapped. Family members ran to their returning loved ones. Randy's wife threw her arms around him.

Looking back, Evelyn saw men in suits who stood at each exit. Mr. Schuler walked with Evelyn toward the front of the church. Evelyn assumed the men in black suits were there to protect them.

Pastor Watson walked to the pulpit and said, "Thank God. Let us thank God for the return of our church family members."

In unison, every one shouted, "Thank God."

"Now let us all kneel and pray."

By the time Pastor Watson was in the middle of prayer, everyone was crying and praising the Lord. He asked the

311

congregation to stand and encouraged them to continue to keep the choir and Deacon Woods' family in their prayers. He then gave the benediction. The congregation was asked to quietly exit the building and go home. They were told to check the website for the date and time of the funeral services for Deacon Woods.

Evelyn, the other choir members, and their families were asked to remain seated in the front rows. When the others were gone, Pastor Watson left the pulpit to stand in front of them.

He began, "I can't tell you how glad I am that you made it home. I know this has been a horrific trip but I want to thank you for standing strong as Christians. Because you have all carried yourselves in a Christian manner, the church's name was not plastered all over the news. Sister Jenkins and Deacon Jackson, words can't express how much I, as your pastor, am grateful to you. Deacon Jackson we all know you and Deacon Woods were close so I know nothing can convey how painful this must be." Sister Jackson was sitting next to him squeezing his hand and softly crying.

"I know you're tired and I don't want to hold you any longer than necessary, but I need each of you to meet with Mr. Schuler in my office before you leave." No one knew what was going on but they all agreed.

Looking around they all noticed the men in dark suits standing at the doors. Mr. Schuler came into the sanctuary and escorted the choir members, one by one, into Pastor Watson's office. Brother and Sister Williams accompanied Cory and went in first. While waiting, family members spoke softly with their loved ones.

Pastor Watson pulled Evelyn aside to meet with two deacons in the choir room. She gave them the rental paperwork and they left to return the vans. She also gave them the extra money left over from the trip.

Pastor Watson went back to the sanctuary, leaving Evelyn alone. She noticed a Caucasian man in a dark suit standing near the door. When she tried to pass him to go to the ladies room, he showed her an Oakland Police badge and told her to go back inside the sanctuary. Suddenly she felt a wave of terror over her body. Slowly she walked back inside, not telling anyone else that the police were there.

One by one, as choir members left the sanctuary with Mr. Schuler and did not return, their families moved outside to meet up with them. Pastor Watson left as well.

Chapter 71

Detectives Washington and Hamilton got off their flight in Oakland and went directly to the Pastor's office. Attorney Schuler was present for each brief interview. Afterward, the choir member was taken to the choir room to retrieve waiting luggage before leaving the church.

Now the only ones left in the sanctuary were Deacon Jackson, his wife, Randy, his wife, and Evelyn. Deacon Jackson stood and started pacing. "Sister Jenkins, what do you think is going on?"

"I don't know." Evelyn knew there were police officers outside the exits but she kept her mouth closed.

Deacon Jackson and his wife were called to the Pastor's office. Randy wandered toward the choir room. His wife remained with Evelyn, who sat and held her hand in silence.

"I can't believe this is really happening. Randy has tried so hard not to be involved with any police. This is the second murder he's been around. To this day, he has nightmares about his brother's murder. I hope getting a new job and moving back to Los Angeles near his family will help."

Evelyn couldn't think of anything to add so she sat in silence. A uniformed officer entered the sanctuary and asked Mrs. Sullivan to follow him. Reluctantly, she let go of Evelyn's hand and followed him outside the sanctuary.

Evelyn was now alone. Finally, Pastor Watson and Mr. Schuler entered and sat next to her. It took a few seconds before Mr. Schuler spoke. Softly he said, "Randy has confessed to killing Deacon Woods and Gary."

"I knew it!" Evelyn shouted.

He explained, "Detectives Washington and Hamilton are here questioning everyone. I think Randy suspected something and that's why he confessed. It seems Deacon Jackson and Woods were involved in the murder of his brother. Deacon Jackson has confessed to being the shooter and he's being arrested for that crime. For years, Randy has been obsessed with finding who killed his brother. A few years ago, he started remembering the faces.

"Over the last two years, it appears he killed two of the other men in Los Angeles. The deacons were the last ones. I guess being back in Los Angeles really triggered something in him. Gary saw him leave the room after he'd murdered Deacon Woods. Unfortunately for him, Randy started following Gary. After Deacon Jackson left him in the parking lot at the airport, Randy killed him and stuck his body in the trunk of the car. At first, the police thought Deacon Jackson was the killer. This morning the police report identified Randy's fingerprints inside the trunk of the car. They were also on the bottle of scotch in Deacon Woods' room. I think Randy is mentally ill. Something happened to him when his brother was killed. I'm going to have him evaluated by a psychiatrist. For now, he's been arrested on

315

two counts of first degree murder. It seems he was right—Deacon Jackson just confessed to being the shooter in his brother's murder.

Evelyn listened in shock. She really had solved the crime.

"This is so tragic," said Pastor Watson.

While they were speaking, Randy and Deacon Jackson, handcuffed, were placed in the back of a black and white police car headed toward the Oakland Police Station.

"Pastor Watson," said Mr. Shuler, "I have to leave. I need to be with my clients at the police station. I'll be in touch as soon as I can." He turned and walked away.

Pastor Watson escorted her to the choir room. Deacon Barnes and Morgan were waiting to assist her. They loaded her luggage in Deacon Barnes' car.

"Sister Jenkins, you were remarkable under the circumstances. Without your help I truly don't know what would have happened. If you need anything, please call me." He walked back inside the church. As the car left the parking lot, Evelyn saw the lights being turned off in the church.

To herself she said, "I'll never ever come back to this church again."

316

Do YOU have a character that I can use in my next book, "Murder by Prayer?"

Email me at **mariettaharris@yahoo.com**

If you win, I'll email you and include your name in my next book.

I NEED YOUR HELP

I really appreciate your feedback and would love to hear from you.

Your input will help with my next book. Do you like Evelyn?

Please leave me a helpful review on Amazon

The Gospel Choir Murder

CPSIA information can be obtained
at www.ICGtesting.com
Printed in the USA
FSOW04n2005101115
13116FS